DARK LEGACY

BOOK TWO
OF THE
HIDDEN HERITAGE SERIES

TARA WINTERS

PUBLISHED BY WINTERMOON PUBLISHING

Copyright © Tara Winters, 2014

Visit Tara Winters' official website at www.tarawinters.com
for the latest news, book details, and other information

Date of first printing: December 2014

Editing by: Sue Ducharme of Textworks
Cover Design: www.coveryourdreams.net
eBook formatting: Guido Henkel, www.guidohenkel.com

Printed in U.S.A.

For Mom and Dad

Lies, Secrets, Truth- I see no difference. Deception is only the truth slightly altered

—Lucifer

CHAPTER ONE

PREGNANT?

 Alone?

 Frightened?

 The flyer seemed to be speaking to her. Katie Hennessey stood and walked over to the board. The microphone overhead screeched a list of destination names and their corresponding track numbers. She tugged the flyer from the board and backed onto the hard wooden bench behind her.

 Yup, that described her. Pregnant. Alone. Afraid.

 The Boston Center for Teen Pregnancy? Advertising in Edison, South Carolina?

 Katie tossed the flyer onto the bench and cast an eye toward the other empty benches. A forgotten sweater or even a discarded newspaper would help ease the chill in the train station. She rubbed her still-flat stomach as yet another rumble tore through her empty belly. She tried to remember when her last meal had been. Was it over at Tito's? Or maybe that half-eaten burger she had found in the parking lot of the pub?

 She had to admit, being pregnant really made hunger pains excruciating. Even a few hours without a meal sent shards of pain racing through her head. Well, she would figure it out. Plenty of people got jobs and had babies and were able to make a life for themselves, right? Tomorrow, she would figure out a plan. She just needed some rest and something to eat. Once the windows shut down for the night, she would check the trashcans. That idea was gross, but plenty of food was wrapped tightly in packages when it was thrown out.

She could call Mama.

Or not.

Mama had made it clear, very clear, that she was no longer welcome in her house. The two-hour rant that Katie had endured before she was thrown from her mother's trailer had been torturous. *My fifteen-year-old daughter, pregnant? Didn't I raise you better than that?* Cigarette after cigarette had been stubbed out in the overflowing cereal bowl as her mother screamed at her, hissed her disappointment, called her a whore and a slut.

She had no other relatives, only Mama. Her mother's reputation in the Carson Springs Mobile Home Park was a little too tenuous to allow her to admit that her fifteen-year-old daughter had gotten knocked up. What would the ladies down at the community center think?

Katie had almost been glad to slink away from the house. Her backpack held a few changes of clothes and the meager couple of dollars she'd had hidden in her room. She had forgotten to pack a hairbrush, but thankfully she had enough toothpaste to get through another couple of days. The past month had been a nightmare: sleeping on friends' couches and curling up on friends' basement floors during the day while their parents were at work. The novelty had worn off as the days stretched into weeks. A night or two was all well and good, but none of them could hide her forever, and there was a limit to how much food anyone could sneak out before parents started to notice. None of her friends were rich, after all. And of course, none were pregnant.

Katie had struck out looking for work, but she was only fifteen, after all and jobs were scarce.

Katie glanced down at the flyer clutched in her fingers. Her hands shook, and a few tears threatened to slip out. She wiped her nose, hoping against hope that she had not just smeared her face even worse than she was sure it already was.

Boston Center for Teen Pregnancy.

Would they help her here in South Carolina?

The slam of the wooden windows in the train station closing one at a time made her jump. Eight o'clock. And eight o'clock in Boston. Too late to call?

Katie pressed her sleeve to her nose again when snot threatened to spill onto her lip. She lifted the flyer again and reread it, hoping to find something there to prompt her to either make the call or abandon the idea. She could wait until tomorrow. If she just got some rest, she could think about it.

She huddled in the oversized woolen coat and tugged it closer around her shoulders. She was so glad she had grabbed it on her way out the door. Her mother wouldn't even miss it. It was not like it was hers; it had belonged to one of the last boyfriends. Bill? Bob? Whatever his name was didn't matter—he was just another of the temporary men passing through the house.

The 800 number along the bottom of the page teased her. *No charge.*

Things will look better in the morning, after some rest, she assured herself. She hadn't slept in days. If she could find a safe place here in the train station, she would at least be warm, and she could think in the morning.

She glanced up at the clock. 8:10 p.m. It was still early. She would have to wait until after the last window closed to find a place to sleep. They didn't let you sleep in the train station. After hours, though, people slipped in and found dark corners to sleep in or do whatever. The groans and the occasional scream scared her half to death. Last night she had finally fallen into a deep sleep, but a rough and dirty hand had shaken her awake, searching her clothes for God knows what. She had leaped up and run from the place before she discovered what the dirt-encrusted old bum wanted.

The phone booth beckoned. Katie ran a hand along her belly one more time. This baby was the reason for all of her problems, but she could not bring herself to harm it. That just wasn't her.

She continued the argument, back and forth, rising slowly from the bench. The world around her swam for a moment. She put a hand on the bench to steady herself. She caught the ticket seller watching her, a look of half dread and half disgust on her young, pretty face. When Katie glanced her way, she turned away and quickly began attending to some important task.

Katie clenched the flyer in her hands and realized that her stomach was rocking with fear. *What if someone answers? What if they want money?*

She made it to the phone booth and closed the wooden door behind her, placing the flyer on the small shelf beside the phone.

What if no one answers?

She bit her lip as she lifted the receiver and reached for the keypad. The dirt around her fingernails disgusted her. Even after the sponge baths she tried to take in public rest rooms, they would not come clean.

1-8-0-0-9-7-3…

Deep breath. Deep breath, she urged herself. She would probably only get a recording. She wiped her eyes and once again lifted the flyer into the light to see the remainder of the numbers. *Is that a three or an eight?*

Ring.

A breath exploded out of her lungs.

Ring.

Recording, right? She would get a recording, and she would listen, and then she would decide if she wanted to—

"Hello, Boston Center for Teen Pregnancy. May I help you?" The woman's voice was warm and kind.

"Uhm."

"Hello?"

"Hi, this is Katie."

"Hi, Katie. How are you tonight?"

"I…uhm…" Katie began to shake. "I am okay."

"Katie? I am sorry, but I am having trouble hearing you."

Katie felt a sob escape. She tried once again to speak. "I'm scared."

"Katie, we are here for you. I know you are frightened, but we can help."

"But I am in South Carolina." Katie wailed into the phone, all pretense of self-control slipping as a bubble escaped her lips, her face now awash with fresh tears.

"Well, that is quite all right. We can help you there too." The woman's voice was so nice that Katie cried even harder. "Katie, I am going to have to get some information from you, and then we can arrange to get you some help, all right?"

Katie nodded. It didn't even register that the woman could not see her. "'Kay."

The woman's questions began, and Katie answered them all, her breath coming in short gasps. As they spoke, her sobs began to abate, and her words were clearer.

Yes, she was pregnant. She was fifteen and in South Carolina. No, she had not run away; she had been thrown out of the house by her mother. She had no siblings. She had no father. No other family that even knew she was alive.

Katie felt her tears drying. She used her sleeve to clean her face the best she could as the questions began to wind down. The woman had put her on hold, said she was checking to see how they could get her to Boston as quickly as possible.

"Katie?" Another woman's voice came on the line. This voice was not as kind and warm, more clipped and professional. Katie froze, senses on full alert.

"Yes?"

"Katie, my name is Victoria Ristucci. I am an attorney here in Boston. I run the Boston Center for Teen Pregnancy."

"Hi."

"You have done a wonderful thing by calling us, do you know that?"

"Uhm, okay." Tension coursed through her. *Who is this woman? Is she in charge? Am I in trouble?*

"Katie, the first step in caring for your baby is to put your own needs aside and make sure that you are doing everything you can to ensure that baby is as healthy as possible."

"Uh huh."

"When you get to our home, you will have your own room, plenty of food, and medical care. I promise you that you will be well cared for."

"How much does it cost?" Katie croaked out.

The woman laughed softly. "Cost? Nothing. We are a nonprofit center designed to take care of those who cannot take care of themselves. You are fifteen and homeless, am I right?"

"Well—"

"At fifteen, you cannot get a job yet."

"Uhm…"

"Katie, when was the last time you ate something?"

Tears began to tickle her eyes again, and she looked down at her dirty sneakers. "I dunno."

"I am here to help you."

Katie wished the other woman would get back on the line.

"Jean tells me you are at the train station outside of Edison, South Carolina?"

"Yes," Katie mumbled.

"All right. Katie, we have a ticket for you on the train heading out of Edison tonight. It will take you to New York. I will have someone meet you in New York."

Katie felt fear grip her belly again. "Tonight?"

The woman laughed. "Did you have other plans?"

"No."

"Katie, get on the train. They have warm seats. You can get some rest. When we meet you in New York, we will get you a hot meal and take you to our center. I promise you, Katie, you won't regret it."

"Okay."

"Katie, I will stay on the phone. Go over to the ticket window and get your ticket. Jean has made the arrangements. Go get your ticket and come back and tell me you have it."

Katie let the receiver hang from its cord and opened the phone booth door. The last window was still open. She watched the flash of the woman's hands as she stacked and sorted ticket stubs. Katie approached the window and glanced in at the woman.

"May I help you?"

"Uhm, yes. Do you have a ticket here for Katie Hennessey?"

The woman nodded and handed it to her. "They just called in. This is your ticket. It includes a meal from the food car. The train leaves at 10:40 from track eleven. The food car closes at midnight, so if you plan on eating, grab something before they close."

"Thanks."

Katie grabbed the ticket and the card and ran back to the phone booth. Her heart was racing, and she was slightly breathless when she picked up the receiver.

"Hello?"

"Yes, Katie, I am here like I promised you I would be." Victoria's voice no longer sounded cold and professional; now she was familiar. A friend. "Did you get the ticket?"

"I have it."

"Will you be all right getting on the train? Katie, do you have a pen?"

"No."

"Run over and get one. I will give you my direct phone number. Please call me if anything happens. Otherwise, I will have someone meet you when you get off the train in New York. I promise."

"Okay."

"Katie, everything is going to be all right. We are going to take care of you and your baby."

Katie's eyes stung with tears. "Thanks." She hung up the receiver and slowly opened the door.

Nine o'clock.

In two hours, she would have a meal and be on her way to New York.

For the first time in two months, Katie began to feel like everything would be all right.

CHAPTER TWO

TABITHA DEVINS BLEW OUT A FRUSTRATED BREATH AND ignored Jules's piercing glare. He nodded, his look of disdain barely hidden. She inhaled deeply and once again lifted a shield to hide her thoughts.

"Many people keep these shields up all the time," he stated in a conversational tone. "They live with them to keep their emotions masked."

"All the time? How do they function?" Tabitha's question came out in a strangled croak as she struggled to maintain her concentration on keeping the walls around her mind lifted.

Jules shrugged and indicated that she should release. "We learn young to maintain control and lift and release them at will. You, on the other hand, are childlike, your emotions like a waterfall, letting everything around you be engulfed by your emotions."

She bristled but bit her tongue at yet another insult from the small man. They sat across from one another, leaning against large stones, their lunch forgotten on the ground next to them. He was teaching her to lift and lower shields and about the constant vigilance required to conceal her emotions and guard what she chose to reveal to those around her.

They had been traveling together for several days. Tabitha had long since grown tired of the man's arrogant and condescending attitude. They had stopped at several villages along the way, further delaying their trip to Tabitha's father's home.

She still could not believe that after eighteen years of silence about her father, she was finally going to meet him. When her mother had disappeared from Porta Negra Island four years before Tabitha was born, the islanders had believed that she had been abducted. Then, as suddenly as she had disappeared, she had returned with an infant daughter.

Tabitha had grown up as the island enigma. She had learned at a young age to ignore the stares and the whispers of the islanders. She had no more information than the islanders about her mother's disappearance.

During the summer of Tabitha's eighteenth birthday, her mother had disappeared again. This time, she left a note telling Tabitha not to worry and that she would be back. She was going to offer condolences to Tabitha's father's family.

Eighteen years without even a single word about her father, and then that note. Tabitha ground her teeth, remembering what she could only perceive as her mother's inconsiderate and selfish actions.

"Are you going to stare off into space or listen to me?" Jules Moyer demanded.

Why, oh why, did her father have to have such an insufferable administrator? Why was he the one who had to discover her?

"What?" Tabitha snapped.

"Time to go. We have finished the last of my rounds and visited the areas I was assigned. I would like to get back to your father's estate in a reasonable amount of time," Jules informed her.

He had insisted they travel by journeying: a term the Caskan used to describe their ability to explore distances ahead with their minds and then arrive at that point. The initial lesson had been to simply move herself by holding Jules' arm and following him. She had mastered that quickly. By the end of their first day, she was able to cover a few miles with every leap. It had, however, worn her out. When they'd stopped their first evening, she had collapsed into the bed at the inn without dinner, only wanting to sleep away her raging headache.

And now here they sat, barely a day from their destination, once again working on her shields. Jules had been none too tactful in telling her that her shields needed work. He, as well as any Caskan with the even slightest amount of interest, he said, would be able to easily sense her moods and her sentiments. He had made little secret of the easily detectable feelings she had for Luc.

Tabitha's temper had flared, and the spat that ensued had caused a ripple of laughter through the group traveling with them. Tabitha had quickly relented to his insistence that she become trained to use her shields as she hid her burning face and cursed Jules for his insensitivity.

The days of travel that followed had taken their toll on her, and her nerves were raw. She had spent her life avoiding feeling exposed; now every feeling and emotion was on display for all to see. The exposure was made worse by the minimal interaction she had with the members of the group in which she traveled. Jules had kept her from the others, not introducing her or giving her the opportunity to speak with or get to know anyone else. They treated her with a kind of reverent awe, remaining polite and compliant but rarely approaching her with more than a passing word. Jules always seemed to be there, his beady eyes watching, always ready with a comment.

Tabitha shook her head, letting the fatigue wash over her. "I need some rest. I cannot concentrate so hard on all of this. I just want to get there and meet my father."

Jules pursed his lips, a sure sign of irritation. "We will be there tomorrow. Tonight, we'll stay in a local inn, and you can practice your shielding. Tomorrow morning, well rested, you can prepare yourself to meet your father."

"Well, if we are that close, why not just go there tonight? Why stay at an inn and rest? I mean, I have waited eighteen years to meet him. It is not like I need to prepare my-self—what more can I do? He is my father, after all." Tabitha groaned, wiping off her pants as she rose.

Jules rose as well, his short and slight stature bringing him to just below her chin. He shook his head and glanced around them. The rest of the party with which they traveled were reclining, leisurely chatting in the sun after lunch. There were six of them, all dark-haired Caskan men, quiet and reserved but with an air of tension. Tabitha had not yet decided if these were an entourage or simply protection. The men deferred to the little man in all decisions, but none seemed to have any real purpose except accompanying them. She often wondered if the area that they were head-ing was dangerous enough to warrant such a guard.

"We will dine together, you and I, and we will discuss tomorrow."

Tabitha snorted at the man's arrogance, but she could not discount that she was curious about what he would tell her. What was it they would need to discuss over dinner that he would not tell her now?

Before she could ask him, Jules had collected their untouched lunches and roused their escort to gather their things for departure.

Tabitha swirled the hot wax, watching as it coated the sides of the battered bronze holder. The tiny holes in the sides sent golden sparkles of light across the rough wood of the heavy table at the inn. She let the candleholder drop onto its base and leaned back in her chair with a huff of impatience.

Where the hell is Jules, Mr. Prompt?

She was contemplating ordering dinner and trying to slink off to her room before Jules graced her with his caustic personality when a young man slid into the seat across from her, startling her out of her musings.

"Mind if I join you?"

Tabitha frowned. "I am waiting for someone."

He grinned. "He has been detained for just a moment."

"And you are joining me because…?" Tabitha prompted. He was young, about her age, with shaggy blond hair and light eyes. He seemed tall, but his legs sprawling in the seat as he slumped back belied his actual height.

"I was hoping to get a minute to say hello and introduce myself. I am Cole." He lifted his brows in anticipation.

"Cole? Nice to meet you. I am Tabitha." She responded automatically, unsure why he would think she would recognize him.

When he smiled again, she detected dimples along his cheeks. He was an attractive man and easygoing, from what she observed during their moments together. What surprised her most was his complete lack of any Caskan-like characteristics. Having spent a week with Luc and his family, followed by extended travel with Jules and the other Caskan men, this man seemed much more...human.

"I take it you have not heard of me?"

"No—should I have?"

"Not necessarily. Listen, I only have a few minutes before either the elf comes back or one of your thugs comes over to kick me out." He leaned forward on his elbows and grabbed the candle in the middle of the table. He blew out the flame.

She snatched the candle back from him. "Only a few minutes for what?"

"You are going to meet your father, right? Antoine Montfort?"

Tabitha clutched the candleholder to her chest and stared at him. She felt herself freeze up; she could not recall the lessons Jules had drilled into her about maintaining her shields. Her mouth opened and then closed without issuing a sound.

He leaned back. A slow smirk crept across his face as he watched her struggle. "You seem surprised. This is a small village, after all. Word has spread that Antoine Montfort's daughter is back to visit."

"Ah. Well, yes. I am going to visit my father," Tabitha murmured, pulling the candle away from her chest and looking down to study the solidifying wax.

He reached forward and caught the candle in her hands. When she did not immediately release it, he let his hold loosen. With the slightest whisper of power, the flame sputtered back to life. He glanced up and his voice dropped. "Yes, but how many know you have never met him before?"

Tabitha did not lift her eyes from the flame as she tugged her fingers free of the candle and away from his long fingers. "I am sorry, but what is it that you wanted to speak to me about? I am expecting someone to join me."

"Your shields are back—nice job." He stood and dug something from his pocket. He let a small gold ring drop from his fingers as he turned to leave. "Ask your father about black elves when you see him. I would be curious about his response."

She glanced down at the ring as it spun on its side across the table. Her hand shot out to stop its course toward the edge. She lifted it and almost dropped it in surprise. A gasp escaped her lips.

PNHS was engraved on the side, and she recognized the brilliant blue stone as her mother's birthstone. Porta Negra High School. The year was emblazoned on the side: twenty-two years ago.

She glanced up and found herself alone.

Within half an hour, she and Jules sat quietly eating their dinner. Tabitha pierced a vegetable in annoyance, wondering what had become of her mysterious visitor. How had he obtained her mother's high school ring? Why had he just dropped it and left?

"Jules?"

He glanced up.

"What are black elves?"

"Where did you hear such a thing?"

Tabitha shrugged. "I have been wandering with you for days. I hear things."

Clearly irritated, Jules took a bite of food and chewed rapidly. "Black elves are nothing more than an old legend. Just a ghost story told at gatherings to scare children."

"So are they real elves but…black?"

"They are no more elf than the beef I am eating. It is only a label assigned to them." Jules sighed heavily and put down his fork. "The black elves, it is told, were beings from another world who came over to our world many, many years ago and decimated the land. It was said that only the Faye survived. When they were able to eradicate the black elves, they opened the portals to your world to repopulate this one. It is said that the Faye mated with the humans that they absorbed, and that was how the Caskan race began."

"But if the Faye were the only survivors, what about the elves and sprites?" Tabitha asked.

"They didn't survive. The elves and the sprites are no more from this world than the humans."

"So where did they come from?"

Jules looked surprised. "Well, your world. Didn't you know that? Aren't there tales of elves and sprites in your world?"

"Well, yeah..." Tabitha paused, amazed. "But those are just old legends."

Jules looked triumphant. "As are the legends of the black elves and the ruin of our world. No one truly knows how the humans were absorbed or if the Faye actually did begin the Caskan race. They are all pretty tales that make for fascinating storytelling. "

Tabitha stopped eating and stared at him. "And the tales of the healers? Were they ghost stories as well?"

Jules shook his head sadly. "No, the tales about the healers and their eradication are a very true and terrible part of our history. It has been our undoing."

They ate quietly for a few moments. Tabitha was startled to realize that it was the first discussion they had shared when Jules had been pleasant. She smiled to herself as she realized her disdain for the little man had slipped a notch.

Jules continued eating.

Tabitha felt her stomach begin to knot with the looming realization of the impending meeting with her father. She would finally meet the man who might hold the answers about her mother's disappearance.

A thousand what-ifs haunted her thoughts. Her mother had left this land eighteen years ago with a tiny baby, apparently leaving a second one behind. She had spent the rest of her life in seclusion; battling God only knew what kinds of demons. Was it her father who had driven her mother to madness or had the madness driven her from her father?

Tabitha had no idea what she was walking into, where she was or how to get home from here. Now that the day approached, dread began to set in. Jules had promised her that her father would bring her back to a portal should she wish, but she was putting all of her trust in a man she didn't know.

Tabitha played with her food, her eyes downcast as she practiced Jules's technique for hiding her emotions. She wanted nothing more than to reach out to Luc. She wanted to hear his voice, to feel that warm, rich resonance wash over her and cast out her concerns. But fear held her back. She was a great distance away, and Jules's comments about her feelings for Luc and the brimming over of her emotions had rankled her.

Besides, Luc had given her little more than a perfunctory kiss when she left, and her feelings were still sore over it. She had hoped for more. But to be honest, she had been the one who had suggested they keep their communication to a minimum while she went with Jules.

Jules interrupted her thoughts. "Tabitha, it is time we spoke about tomorrow." He placed his fork down and slowly pushed his plate away from him.

Tabitha pushed at her half-eaten plate. Her curiosity was stirred. The fact that he had called her by her given name for the first time grabbed her attention.

"I know you have been working hard on your shielding and the journeying. I must confess that you have done well under the circumstances," Jules admitted. Tabitha could almost feel the effort it took for that compliment. "However—"

And here we go. There had to be a but...

"I feel you must know that my pushing was all for your own good. You have excellent shields."

She raised an eyebrow. He had just spent four days belittling her talent.

"If you could just let me complete a thought without your theatrics…"

"I didn't say anything!" she exclaimed, but a smug smile played around her lips. It was difficult to hide her awareness that she had irritated him.

He sighed. With a side glance, he continued. "You have excellent shielding capabilities, *but*…you lack self-control and discipline. With some practice, you will undoubtedly be able to maintain them and control what is leaked through and what you wish to contain." He exhaled deeply. She noticed that his eyes seemed to lose their usual hard edge. His expression seemed wary, even haunted, in the candlelight flickering between them. "You have been among friends guarding you closely. Now, as you go to meet your father, I think it imperative that you maintain your wits."

Tabitha felt herself stiffen, and jocularity drained from her expression. She listened intently as he continued.

"You will be meeting your father for the first time, as well as his household. There will be those around him who remember your mother and those who vie for his attention and his ear. Not everyone will be happy to see a long-lost daughter suddenly appear. And your father and mother had a volatile relationship at best. I would recommend very strongly that you listen and pay close attention to your instincts. Trust no one. Not even me. This is not a household like the one your man comes from. People within your father's walls often have a plan and a self-serving intent." Jules glanced up. When their eyes met, Tabitha felt a chill at the intensity of that gaze.

"What are you telling me?"

"I am telling you that you must guard yourself and your thoughts carefully until such time that you feel you can trust and rely on those around you." He leaned back in his seat, an aloof expression returning to his eyes along with the hard set of his narrow jaw. Apparently he felt that she had whatever message he had so struggled to deliver. Whether or not she understood it was another story.

"Did you know my mother?" Tabitha asked softly, picking up the tiny candle flickering and sputtering on the table before them.

"I did."

She sighed softly, not sure where to even begin with the questions she had. "Can you tell me what happened here so many years ago?"

It was his turn to become silent. His lips pursed in indecision, and Tabitha held her breath. After a moment, his eyes met hers. Their direct and intent gaze held none of his earlier disdain. "I can tell you what I saw and what I observed those may years ago, but I would rather not."

"Why? Why would you want to—" she demanded.

He held up a hand to quiet her.

"I have just told you not to trust anyone. What I ask for is your patience. Meet your father and take some time to make your own evaluations and assessments. When you have done that and have made some judgments, we will talk again. You and I can talk about what it was like so many years ago. But I wish to let you make your own conclusions first."

Tabitha groaned but nodded. She put down the candle. "I am so tired of everyone not telling me what happened during my mother's disappearance."

He nodded. "No one wants to offer up their perceptions. Two people need to speak of those years—no one else should share their thoughts until your parents have spoken theirs. One of those people you will meet tomorrow, and the other is hiding from you somewhere within this land. I suggest you start with them."

"Do you have any clue about my mother's whereabouts?"

Jules shrugged. "I have heard rumors. As have you, I am told."

His comment left her thunderstruck. Luc's cousin Tristyn was married to a human who had a talent for finding information. Alena had told her what she had been able to find out about a woman matching her mother's description in the vicinity of Windrift. She was sure Alena would have told Luc and his father, Bertòn. Would they have shared this information with Jules?

"How did you know what I had heard?" she blurted.

He did not respond right away, and she held her breath. "Things are not always what they seem," he answered slowly. "I am not trying to be deliberately difficult. I am just trying to give you time to learn what the stakes are. You may not realize this yet, but there are a multitude of tenuous predicaments in this world. There are factions working against one another and there are people out to maximize their own worth at the expense of others."

He hesitated. He seemed to want to say more, and Tabitha waited for him to continue. She was wary of his change in demeanor. Since meeting him, he had been sarcastic, confident, and completely patronizing. But now she saw a struggle in his face; the mask had dropped, and she could detect the strain as he tried to put into words concepts that he was obviously not ready to share with her.

"Factions working against each other seems a strange way to describe the onset of a civil war," Tabitha quietly commented.

Jules nodded. "There is more afoot than civil unrest. This is a deadly time to be about in our land, and the worst is yet to come."

Tabitha nodded, fatigue at the endless riddles washed over her. She stood, "I will keep you to that promise to talk more once I have spent some time with my father. I guess tomorrow I will finally get some answers."

She started to leave, and his voice drifted after her. "Here is hoping they will be ones you want to hear."

CHAPTER THREE

THE NEXT DAY, TABITHA ROSE EARLY. THE SUN WAS SHINING, and a gentle warm breeze ruffled the leaves on the trees. She ate a quiet breakfast alone in the empty common area and then stepped outside for a few minutes alone. Jules was entering when she slipped out. She was kidding herself if she thought he did not know where she was. She was certain that he was well aware of her whereabouts at any given moment. As much as he irritated her, and she knew that feeling was mutual, he had no intention of arriving at her father's home without her.

She climbed onto a small hill and stared at the scenery surrounding her. The land was springing to life in a grand abundance of shades. The dell spread below her offered a cacophony of colors and smells. Orchards of budding fruit trees were spread out through the valley, and a ribbon of golden-turfed road slipped between the variously colored clusters. The air was alive with the calls of many spring birds as they dipped and darted around her.

Tabitha wrestled with what Jules had told her last night. Her father was the Lord Regent of Windrift, the peace negotiator between the Eastern clans and the Western tribes. He was instrumental in the development of peace. He had asked for a representative of every province to speak on behalf of their people. In the days leading to their arrival, she had discovered that her father had a large spread of land under his control, and he had built small communities of homes for people who struggled to afford a place to live. He worked tirelessly on a cure for the disease that impacted the women of their race, causing them to lose children and many to perish in the first year after childbirth. He led a small organization that placed orphaned children with families unable to have their own children.

From every account, people sang his praises. On the rare occasion when people were told of Tabitha's relationship to the man, people fell over themselves to praise her father. They would send him blessings and tell her of people affected by his generosity. They never realized she had not met the man, and for that she was grateful to Jules.

"He seems a great man," Tabitha had said to Jules one night after a particularly stirring story of her father's intersession on behalf of a family about to lose their home.

Jules had nodded. "It does seem that way."

Tabitha had struggled with the strange comment. She could not figure out what to make of his cagey comments, and she understood that she would never know until she met her father and found out for herself.

She inhaled deeply of the early morning air, trying to calm her nerves. She had tossed and turned all night; so many of the things she had already learned in the past weeks haunted her. She had more questions than answers, and meeting her father was only the beginning.

She still had to find her mother. She hoped that once she had the opportunity to get to know her father, she would be able to follow up on the information that Alena had given her. She had the woman's name and village secreted away. At the first available opportunity, she had every intention of pursuing that lead. She was not sure she wanted her father involved when she found her mother. She was desperate to find her mother on her own and to be able to ask her the questions that haunted her. And judging from the fact that her father was looking for her as well, Tabitha knew that the "sick grandfather" had been another lie on top of every other one her mother had ever told her.

How many lies had there been? Was her mother, the elusive and secretive creature, the real Doni Devins? Doni Devins had stormed away from her boyfriend twenty-two years ago and disappeared into the night. For four years, the islanders had been tortured and terrified as they searched and prayed for one of their own, the beautiful missing cheerleader.

How does one disappear off an island? Well, as Tabitha had found, if they had a way to slip away without ever leaving the island itself, one does not. But if Doni Devins had come here, to Caska, then whose body had they recently discovered back on Porta Negra? As the questions mounted, Tabitha knew she would need some answers before she could return home. Greg had warned her that the police were looking for her and her mother.

And, of course, what of Luc? She had promised to be here when he arrived. She was miserable and desperate to contact him, but it had been her idea to limit their contact. He had several weeks of hard work ahead of him, and she had to be careful to not reveal the fact that she was linked to him. In this, Jules and Bertòn were right; as someone unfamiliar with the land, she had to tread carefully. She could not jeopardize Luc in any way by letting people know they were linked. The circumstances behind them being linked since childhood were too strange. She was not ready for others to know.

She had not yet come to grips with the horror of the scar she had left imprinted on his throat. She could not yet face the guilt and the anguish that accompanied that thought. It was not the physical pain she had caused him but the truth that the Faye had enlightened them about. She had thus marked Luc as her mate. Anyone who knew what those marks meant would hound him relentlessly for the identity of the healer who made them. Any woman he might have a relationship with would walk away before committing herself to him if she found out he was marked as another woman's mate.

And, of course, the fact that his family would now have to cover for her with the Faye haunted her. They had told Bertòn that by not coming forward, he was breaking their treaty. Marcus, Bertòn, and Luc would be called on to explain Luc's scars. They had told her not to worry, that they would find a way, but Tabitha had left with deep pangs of guilt because others were left to try and cover the mess she had made.

She hated to think that she should not have tried to heal Cyra, but Bertòn had been right; she should have used the power sparingly, tried to heal small portions at a time instead of ridding the child of the entire illness at once. How would they explain that? What would happen to Luc? What would the Faye do to try and find his elusive healer? His mate.

She heard Jules come up behind her. She knew he was waiting, and she sighed once again before turning to face him.

"You are ready?" Jules asked.

Tabitha nodded as her heart fluttered in her chest. "Let's go."

They stepped into the clearing before a grand and stately home. It was built partially below ground. Wood and stone pillars with connecting arched walkways and high glass enclosure at the tops were visible, much like the dwellings she had seen in Calais, Luc's hometown. Majestic, arched doorways were set into the hill, circular porches before them. Large windows rose from the stone and earth structure. Tabitha drew in her breath at the size of the place, which stood atop a gently sloping hill. The grounds were carefully manicured, dotted with flowering bushes and trimmed trees. The land that sprawled below the home was dotted with small communities, spread out for miles among deep green forests and carefully tended farms.

Jules nodded to the men escorting them and led Tabitha up to the house. He let himself in, and Tabitha followed.

"How big is this place?" she whispered.

Jules glanced around. "Very. Your father does most of his work within the house as opposed to having a separate governing office. He meets with his guests within the walls of the estate. When the representatives meet here for the peace negotiations, they will be given rooms to maximize the time they spend here."

She nodded and followed him through a large sunlit entryway and up a set of circular stairs leading to yet another large vestibule. An older heavyset woman waited at the top of the stairs. She had dark eyes; her dark hair was spun with silver and held back in a dark bun. "Jules, we did not expect you back so soon."

He nodded and gave a slight bow to the woman. "I found an unexpected reason to return. Polan, may I introduce Antoine's daughter, Tabitha?" he turned to Tabitha, "This is our ambassador of the Southern clans, Polan Tefers of Chandolyn."

Tabitha held out her hands in greeting, as she had learned to do with Luc's family, and the older woman took them with a graceful nod. "I welcome you, Tabitha. Antoine has only recently shared with me that his daughter has returned to the area. He is quite excited to see you. I understand it has been many years."

Tabitha nodded, surprised at the woman's inference that she had only been away. "Yes, it has been awhile."

"Where is he? Do you know?" Jules interrupted.

Polan nodded, releasing Tabitha's hands. "He is down in the appropriations meeting. If you would like to wait in the office, I will tell him you have arrived."

"Please send him to the parlor in his private wing. I think he would rather greet his daughter in his personal space." Jules began to herd Tabitha toward the back of the house, but Polan stopped him.

"Jules, a moment, please?"

Jules nodded, and the two stepped aside to speak quietly. Tabitha was left to wander the large foyer, taking in the grand stairway leading up and the two on each side that wound down to lower levels. As she poked around and explored, she suddenly became aware of a small group of men standing by the tall windows, watching her quietly.

Caution sent her back toward the main staircase and Jules. She heard a deep voice behind her.

"M'oiselle?"

Tabitha turned slowly and found the eldest of the three striding toward her. He was a tall man. His once-dark hair was peppered with gray and tied at the nape of his neck. His clothes were a strange cut, a style she had not seen yet in her travels in this world. His top was a soft but rugged-looking jacket worn over pants that ended in comfortable-looking shoes. With a start, she realized he was wearing soft suede animal skin—something the Eastern Caskans avoided.

"A moment?"

Tabitha glanced up and saw Jules craning his neck, looking for her. "I am sorry, I am expected—"

"Tabitha?" Jules came trotting toward her.

The elder nodded to Jules in respect. "Marquis Moyer, I understood you to be away."

"Lord Regent Viho, I welcome you to Windrift." Jules bowed stiffly, his eyes wary.

"Welcome is not expected, as I have been here for some time. It seems your lord regent has been quite busy, his schedule too compressed to accommodate our promised meetings," the elder man stated.

Jules glanced up the stairs. "I apologize, but as you are well aware, I have only just returned myself. Perhaps when I have settled, I can work you into his lord regent's schedule."

The older man crossed his arms and nodded slowly. "I had expected better treatment in return for the distance I have traveled. Your employer promised me his assistance, but I have gotten little more than a word with him."

"Well, you realize Chandolyn is a large governance. I know his plate is quite full—"

The elder lifted a hand and stopped him. "I have heard the rhetoric. I wait for him, but my patience grows thin. Perhaps my time would be better spent speaking to Lord Regent DesChamps. Marcus has always made time for us."

Jules nodded. "As you wish, but I promise you Lord Regent Montfort has been hard at work addressing this issue. Why, my recent trip will net some assistance. I have left word requesting each of the Northern clans to send representation. The lord regent has also sent a similar request to the Southern clans. If you will bear with us with patience, we will be able to gather the support your people need. I am sure of it."

The elder nodded his head in stately respect and stepped back. "I await word from you then."

Jules nodded, took Tabitha's arm, and began to lead her upstairs.

The elder's voice rang out one more time. "I wonder, Marquis, what issue your lord regent wishes to resolve."

Jules glanced back but did not respond.

Tabitha stood alone, her nerves quaking and her hands sweaty. Jules had left her in a luxurious parlor with large glass windows that looked over the sprawling lawn. Fear gripped her belly, and she barely took note of the exquisite furnishings around her.

My father. Incredible. After eighteen years without a clue as to his identity—or his existence—she now waited for him to arrive. Imagine: the man who had been with her mother during those long mysterious years. Tabitha could not even speculate about what had occurred. But the dark truth remained: her mother had returned home and spent the next eighteen years in quiet seclusion, not mentioning a word about what had happened.

Her musings were interrupted when the large double door swung open. He entered the room. Her breath caught. They stood, both frozen, staring across the room at each other. He was tall, a classic Caskan with deep ebony hair and brows, his face handsome and his physique muscular, with a barrel chest and long strong legs.

He watched her intently for a few moments, taking her in from across the room. Tabitha held her breath.

"Well, Tabitha…Imagine. We finally meet." His voice was deep and pleasant, rich with the smooth articulation of an orator. He stepped into the room, closing the door behind him. She could barely squeak out a greeting. He smiled at her mumbled salutation and walked slowly across the room, extending his hands to her in greeting. "This meeting is long overdue."

Tabitha nodded before he clasped her chilled hands in his large, strong ones. She could do little more than stare at him.

He gestured toward the couch. She slowly sank into it, all thoughts fleeing her mind. After all the years of questioning her parentage, all the years without information, here he sat, across from her, his eyes taking in her features, and she could do little more than tremble.

"What a beautiful woman you have become! If I may be so bold, you are truly more beautiful than your mother at your age, and that is no small accomplishment." His tone was warm and pleasant. Tabitha felt her eyes sting. "My name is Antoine Montfort, and I am your father."

Her tears began to flow unchecked. Tabitha could only gulp in air as she sobbed, trying to stem the flow of emotion that rocked her. He handed her a soft cloth, which she used to wipe her eyes as she tried desperately to get her emotions under control.

He chuckled softly as he handed her yet another kerchief. He sat back, allowing her a few moments to get a grip on her raging nerves.

"I'm sorry. I'm sorry. I have tried to mentally prepare myself for this but...I just can't." Her head was bowed. With a gulp of air, she raised glistening silver eyes to him. "I cannot believe I am finally meeting you."

He smiled and gently stroked her cheek; more tears threatened to cascade with his simple gesture.

"Please take your time. I feel the same, but we are a much less demonstrative people. I have known of your existence, just not how to get to you. I understand from my cousin that you had no knowledge of me at all."

Tabitha nodded. "Your cousin?"

"Yes, Victoria. I believe you met her in your world?"

"She is your cousin?"

"Yes, she is. She tried to contact me to get my permission to speak frankly to you. I fear there was not enough time before your visit. She did tell me of your meeting. I was shocked to hear that you had no knowledge of me. I would have thought that, at the very least, your mother would have told you something about me." His eyes were troubled as he shook his head.

"She never told me anything. Do you know where she is?"

His expression turned sad. "I wish I did. I have known she has returned several times but have been unable to find her or speak to her. I assume she is looking for or visiting our other child. Were you aware you had a brother?"

She shook her head. "No, your cousin mentioned a brother, and that was the first I had ever heard of it before Jules mentioned that I was a twin. She never told me. What happened to him?"

Antoine stood and walked to a sideboard and poured clear fluid into two glasses. He walked back to her, handing her a tall glass. "I wish I knew. For a long time I thought she had left with the both of you, but I found out some years after she'd abandoned me, leaving with our two children, that she had only returned home with one of you. I am saddened to say that I have no knowledge or information about your brother. One night she snuck off with you both, and I have not heard anything since that time. I have searched for him and wondered what she could have done with him, but to no avail. I do not even know if he lives."

Tabitha slowly nodded. He was referring to her mother abandoning him. She almost could not ask the next question, but it was what she had wanted to know all along. She had always begged for the truth, and Antoine seemed to be willing to speak to her. After having wondered about her mother's strange disappearance her whole life, to have come all this way and now not have the courage to ask the one person who could fill in the holes. As frightened as she was, she had to know. To not ask was unthinkable.

"Will you tell me of the night my mother disappeared and what happened over the next four years?

He nodded and took a long swallow from the glass. "I will, if you will tell me about the past eighteen years and what you know of her most recent disappearance."

"Fair enough."

"By the One God, it was…what, twenty-two years ago now? How time does escape us." He leaned back on the couch, his arm extended along the back as his eyes stared off into space, going back those many years. "I was a young man, perhaps twenty years. One night, as I walked home from visiting a friend, I felt a mind reach out to me, to contact me. I do not know what you know of our kind, but people just do not reach out to contact someone at random. It is a great breach of etiquette. The touch was childish and untrained, and I found myself responding, interested despite my annoyance. It was an older woman in the company of a young girl."

"An older woman? Contacting you mentally?" Tabitha leaned forward, her tears dry and her interest piqued as the tale began to slowly unfold.

"An older woman—she considered herself a psychic. Trude was her name."

Tabitha snorted in disbelief. "Are you kidding? Trude? She is my aunt! She swore she had no idea whatever happened to my mother those years when she disappeared, yet now you tell me that it was Trude who contacted you?"

"Well, in a form. It seems that they were having a... hmm, what was that word? A scenic? A seeming? Something where they were trying to contact the dead..."

"A séance? They were having a séance, and they contacted you?" Tabitha was amazed. "But why you? Of all the people here? And Trude contacted you? She believes herself a great psychic and medium, but how did she ever get a hold of you?"

He smiled. "The explanation is not so complex. You see, I have a little trinket I once found on a beach up north during a summer trip." From his pocket, he tugged a small chain with a shiny black rock dangling from it. Tabitha gasped, recognizing the identical rock on the key chain in her pocket. "Ah, so you recognize it? Yes, your mother had the other one. It seems that your Trude had found this fascinating stone on the beach and had kept it as a special token for her abilities. A focal point, if you will. That night, she had given it to your mother to hold as a way to focus her energy for contacting Trude's mother, I believe, who had recently passed away. Coincidently, I had the other half of that stone. Do you know how a portal opens between our worlds?"

Tabitha nodded. "Well, I understand that when they open, the ground burns so hot that they form these little rocks, almost like glass."

He nodded. "Exactly. Well, as I said, coincidently I had a rock from that same portal on my person at the time. Your mother was holding its twin as a means to focus her energy to contact the dead. As your mother and aunt reached out, my stone burned hot, and I heard them. It was fairly difficult to understand them and they were so very distant, but contact was made. It was a strange time for me. I was promised to another woman. But suddenly I could feel your mother's touch as though she were reaching out to physically caress me. I had never seen her and I could not hear her well, but the sheer presence I felt from her contact just took my breath from me.'

'The contact was broken quickly, no doubt from our mutual shock, but it had been made nonetheless. I was shaken by the experience, as was she. You see, it was not your aunt who had been the catalyst for us to speak but your mother. She has great psychic abilities. Her abilities allowed them to contact someone in this world."

"My mother? Psychic abilities?"

He nodded. "Yes. She told me later that your aunt made a living from her psychic talents, but she was not the one I felt that night. I was aware of another presence but only because they were holding hands. It was your mother's presence I felt. Her mind touched mine, and her fleeting touch had struck me deep in my soul. Several days later, alone and feeling much the same as I, she tried again. Alone, focusing on that stone, she was able to contact me again. That began our conversations. We were able to reach out to one another, and we started forming a friendship. I was the one she reached out to when she was upset, the confidante she would speak to about her fears and hopes and dreams. I was the nonjudgmental and impartial friend she could confess her anger over her family and her upbringing to and talk to about her school problems and—" he chuckled, "I was a friend to help her try and understand her current boyfriend.'

'We spoke often that spring. We became closer than friends. I could understand her struggles; she had powers in a world where she would be cast out and abused if her abilities became public. Her abilities frightened and fascinated her at the same time."

Tabitha stood, struggling with what he was telling her. Emotions cascaded through her as she tried to digest the information. She walked to the large windows and stared out at the brilliant blue sky while tears once again threatened to spill.

Antoine walked up behind her and placed his hands on her shoulders. "Are you all right? Shall I continue?"

She nodded, inhaling deeply. So many things were beginning to fall into place. Her mother not only had talents and had experienced the same struggles that Tabitha had fought, but she had also confided them to a friend she'd found in another world. Fear at the similarities in their lives gripped her. Tabitha realized that she had done the same thing her mother had done so many years ago. She had found someone who would listen to her, who understood. She had poured her energy, emotion, and love toward a man who had reached out and been her savior. She had left her world and her family to find him, and she had put herself at risk, without the slightest concern over the pain she left behind.

The lies! Her mother and Aunt Trude had lied all those years about what they knew and what had happened.

"Why didn't she ever tell me any of this?" Tabitha's voice was a hoarse whisper.

He stood silently behind her. She finally shook her head, tired of trying to wrestle with the confusion and pain that seemed to erupt over every aspect of dealing with her mother. "So how did she come to this world? What happened?"

He sighed and walked over to stand to Tabitha's right. The afternoon light illuminated his features as he leaned back against a long desk. Tabitha noticed the lines around his eyes and wondered if these revelations caused him as much pain as they caused her. She had not considered that this might not be easy for him either; her heart grew heavy, knowing that the conversation was difficult for the two of them. For once, she was meeting someone who shared the same pain as she had. Someone else who had loved and lost Doni Devins.

"We grew close those next months. I felt as though I was falling in love with a figment of my imagination. People around me grew concerned that I was growing distant and secretive. No one knew of our relationship. I had no intention of opening myself up to that kind of ridicule. Imagine telling people you had been in touch with someone from another world?" He chuckled.

Tabitha groaned inwardly. "Crazy."

He nodded. "By this time I had broken off my promise. I was fixated on your mother. We had no intention of meeting and did not know if it was even possible, but I could not possibly tie the knot with another when I was enamored with Doni."

"Had you even seen her? I mean physically? Did you have any idea what she looked like?" Tabitha asked.

Antoine shook his head. "Can you imagine? I was falling in love with a beautiful, sparkling voice. She had an effervescence that I had never felt. Everything that she felt was vibrant and just humming with life and emotion. Her anger, her laughter, her very lust for life captured me. I wanted nothing more than to be with her mentally, to experience life as she did."

It was not improbable to Tabitha. Luc's voice had been the lifeline she had reached out for, and had they spent the summer only talking, she was sure she would have felt the same about him—before she knew that physically he would exceed anything she could have imagined.

He continued, his eyes once again lost in his memories. "And then one night, she reached out to me, angry and hurt. Her boyfriend had been cheating on her with a friend. A very close friend, and she was hurt and betrayed. I tried to calm her down. She told me that he had accused her of being distant and of trying to compare him to some idealistic fantasy man." Antoine shrugged with a small self-conscious smile. "Those were not her exact words. But when she told me that, I knew that she felt the same way as I did.'

'She was furious. Her aunt had apparently caught them but had not told your mother. So she was angry with her as well. She begged me to come get her and take her to my world. She wanted to teach them a lesson, and she needed to escape. She had always considered herself to be the most popular, the most beautiful, and she could not conceive how anyone could possibly ever want to be with anyone else. I knew the truth, though. I had perceived his conflict in the words that he had told her. I knew she had driven him away by comparing him to me.'

'So that night I agreed to help her. I knew by then that the rock I had found was from a portal, and I knew approximately where I had found it. I was in St. Mikel at the time. We agreed we would try to get her over to my world. I knew that if she had the stone, she could come across; I would just have to try and pinpoint her. I am no portal tracker, but I felt that I should be able to get her close. So that night we tried. It took several hours. I could not sense her, but I knew that she was close. And then suddenly she appeared, just stepping out into the moonlight like an angel. I was stunned. I knew from her own words she was beautiful, but I had never expected her to be so breathtaking. She just appeared, her hair so light—I had never seen anyone with hair so light before…" He shook his head.

Tabitha realized she had been holding her breath. It was the same portal, and one night she too had met the one she had been talking to. The similarities shook her. Tabitha slowly shut her mouth and tried to remember to breathe.

Antoine stared out the window. "She was the most beautiful woman I had ever seen. She was perfect. I could understand why she was so vain. People had been telling her all her life that she was perfection. Her features were stunning. That long, almost-white hair almost to her waist seemed to float around her. Her eyes carried such life in them, and they were the warmest shade of golden brown. I had never seen anyone like her. She stole my heart that very first night. I had expected that she would come over and we would meet. I would calm her down and send her home. She'd thought the same. She'd considered staying a day or two and then returning. We never expected that she would stay four years.'

'We went back to my home in St. Mikel. I lived not far from Marcus at the time. I understand you know Marcus?"

Tabitha nodded. A pang of guilt stabbed at her. Her father had opened up and told her all she had asked, but she still had to come to grips with the reality that whatever happened here had sent her mother into a dark, reclusive world once she'd returned home.

"You will have to share with me how it was you came to be with Marcus's family, but let me tell you more of our time together first. I promised to answer all of your questions. So, where was I? Ah, yes, we returned to my home and well...suffice it to say, we consummated our friendship."

Tabitha felt a blush sting her cheeks, but she kept her expression impassive. Her father stared off over her head, a pleasant smile playing on his mouth, lost in thought. As the seconds ticked by, Tabitha felt the strain of waiting for him to reel his mind back from wherever he was. She could only guess where this little trek down memory lane was taking him. She cleared her throat uncomfortably.

He seemed to shake himself back to the present. The grin he gave her confirmed that he had gone places she really did not want to think about. "I am sorry. Where was I?"

"Apparently in a place I do not need to go with you," she commented dryly.

He chuckled. "Some things are best left unsaid, but I think you get the gist."

"Gist? Let's hope you are not more blunt next time you want to give me a general idea."

He laughed. "Well, you have got a quick and witty mind. I must confess, your mother did not have much of a sense of humor. She always took herself a bit too seriously. Anyway, we enjoyed the physical relationship as well as our more connected relationship."

Tabitha winced. "Eww. I did not need to know that."

"Ah, I apologize. I must remember to whom I am speaking. But it is important for you to know that initially she stayed because we had fallen in love. She knew her family would worry but thought that having told her aunt that she was coming to meet me, all would be well. Apparently, though, the police became suspicious of your aunt, because she would not come forward to discuss where your mother had gone. Your aunt finally told the police that she feared your mother had eloped and that was why she had not been forthcoming in reporting her absence. It was only the absence of a body, if I am not mistaken, that kept your aunt from being charged in connection with your mother's disappearance. She begged your mother to come home when she visited but ultimately, it was her constant nagging that kept your mother from returning to visit more often."

"Wait. Wait!" Tabitha lifted a hand to halt him. "Are you telling me that she actually returned home to see my aunt? And that Trude knew where she was and never told anyone?"

"It is what I understand. You will have to bear with me— my understanding of how your world works is a bit of a mystery to me. Had she lived in my world and went to live with a lover, everyone would have understood. I think, though, that in your world there was some concern on the part of your authorities. They were not so quick to believe your aunt. I understand there was some misunderstanding about the death of Trude's husband and some people thought that perhaps your mother's disappearance was sinister."

Tabitha sank back onto the chair behind her, her head spinning. "Sinister would be an understatement. I spent my life believing that my mother had been kidnapped by some psycho and then suddenly just reappeared, with me. I had no idea what could have happened to her, but the island people thought that she had been taken and raped and abused."

He gave a wry smile, "Well, I hope that I can convince you that I am not some sinister monster who raped your mother. She came to me very willingly. In fact—"

Tabitha held up her hand again. "Wait. Please do not elaborate."

He smiled. "Of course. I apologize, but it seems that you have seen me in a very unsavory light for many years. I wish to try and convince you that your mother was here willingly, of her own choice."

"Then why did she suddenly leave here one night and take her children? Why did she run away from you if you were so in love? And why stay for four years?"

He nodded slowly. "Well, that was the beginning. We thought she would stay for a few days, but that time extended to weeks. She was not aware that her family did not know where she was. She did not know about the large search or the vigils. She had become a great mystery in your world, but she was happy with me here. It was not long before, understandably, she became pregnant. We talked it over. She was still young—too young according to your societal rules to be having a child and marrying, so we opted —"

"Wait...she became pregnant? She was gone for four years? That could not have been..." A cold fear gripped her. A child was born two years before her? Two years older? "Do I have another sibling?" Her voice was a harsh whisper.

He nodded. "A brother. You were a twin, but you also have an older brother."

"Oh God...Oh God, what happened to him?" Her eyes were closed tightly shut. She felt the color drain from her face.

Please God, please God, tell me this is not why Luc and I are connected.

CHAPTER FOUR

"TABITHA, WHAT IS WRONG?"

"What happened to him?" she repeated. Her heart felt as though it would burst.

"We gave him to a family to adopt. Children here are so very precious. So many people are unable to conceive, so it was not difficult to find a family willing to take the child," he commented, watching her closely and noticing her face blanch. "Are you all right? Would you like water?"

She nodded and tried to swallow the lump in her throat. Bertòn had said that Luc was his child, but Antoine was saying that an older boy, two years older, was given to another family. Was it possible that Luc was her brother and that Bertòn had never told him he was adopted? Was that the reason they were linked?

He handed her a glass of water in and continued. "Your mother stayed to give birth, intending to leave when her child was with his new family. But leaving him was harder than she had expected. She became attached to the infant while she carried him, and she had begun to enjoy her life here. I tried many times to convince her to stay and marry me, but she wanted to return to her own life. She wanted to live in her own world. I was even willing to come to your world with her. But she refused. She had just completed high school and was not ready to settle down with a family. And, of course, she was concerned that the child would have my abilities as well as her own. Your world is no place for a child with such talents to grow up."

"Tell me about it," Tabitha mumbled, still in shock and heartsick over her suspicion.

"So she stayed for a time, visiting our son and getting to know him as a friend of the family. She wanted to make sure he was well cared for. As time went on, she could not seem to tear herself from him. I was happy. I thought that perhaps she would ultimately remain in our world. Watching her son from afar depressed her and the thought of leaving him behind tore at her, but she had had her own dreams and wishes to follow. She withdrew from me and into herself. I tried everything to bring her out of it, but she remained in her shell.'

'It was a difficult time for us all, but I would not give up on her. I wanted her to stay here but she refused and sank deeper into depression. She stopped eating and began to drop weight, as well as so much of the life in her. She would not speak for days on end. It was only at night, in the dark of our bedroom, that she showed any sign of life. She was still passionate when it came to our physical—"

"Will you stop? You keep doing that to me. Just gloss over it," Tabitha snapped, partially disgusted and partially amused that he kept coming back to the same line of thought.

"I apologize. I forget that it is not the way of your people to speak about physical relationships. It is something I have never understood about your people. It is such a natural part of life, yet you act as though it is something unhealthy or disgusting." He seemed genuinely perplexed.

"It is not that we find it disgusting. I would just rather not have the details!" Tabitha exclaimed, the blush returning to her face.

He shrugged. "She became pregnant again, and that seemed to further depress her. I thought for sure that she would be delighted at the opportunity to keep this child, but she had grown restless and wanted to return home. I was hurt. I could not understand. She pulled further from me, accusing me of holding her too tightly and being too possessive. I was crushed. I still felt the same for her, but it seemed her feelings had changed. She wanted to return pregnant and just face the consequences, but I convinced her to stay and then return after she had the child. Little did we know it would be twins.'

'The pregnancy was inordinately difficult for her, and she spent the better part of the latter months lying down. She continued to withdraw, and I was at a loss as to how to get her back. I tried everything I could think of to win back her affection, but the harder I tried, the more she shut me out. She had also closed herself off from close friends she had made, and they were as confused as I was. As the pregnancy progressed, she had little to do with our first son because she rarely left her room any longer. We were barely speaking."

His eyes were once again distant while he relived the torment of losing the woman he had loved. Tabitha saw the pain around his eyes as he recalled the difficult months of Doni's withdrawal. She waited as he pulled his thoughts together, trying to digest this information and comprehend the years her mother had spent here with this man.

Antoine seemed to recall her presence, and he tugged his gaze back from the shadows creeping across the lawn sprawled before them. The afternoon had slowly slipped away while they spoke. "So one night, a moonless spring night, you and your brother were born. He was first, and then, within an hour, you were born as well. You were born in Calais, not far from where Marcus and his family live now. So your place of birth is Calais, St. Mikel. I'll bet that is information you have never heard before. You were born in the house I was living at the time and were attended by a very dear friend of ours, Gwyn."

Tabitha's eyes flew open, "Gwyn? Yes, that is the one thing my mother told me about my past! She mentioned Gwyn!"

Pain splashed across his face, but he hid it behind a sad smile. "Imagine that she mentioned Gwyn but never told you of me."

Tabitha's gaze dropped into her lap, "I am sorry. I did not come here to cause you more pain. I just wanted to know the truth."

He lifted a hand and swept away her apology. "No need for apologies. We are family after all, and you are due the truth. I am happy to give it to you. You deserve to know about your past, though I am not sure that knowing the details of our relationship will ever help you come to grips with who you are."

"But it will!" she insisted. "Don't you see? It is not the details of your relationship that matter but the knowledge of what happened to my mother in those four years. It is not like I was an orphan and fixated on my parents. I was a child born during the four years my mother disappeared from our island. I had no past, and my father was a complete mystery to everyone. People on the island were terrified. For four years, people did not know if one of their own had kidnapped and murdered the island cheerleader or if she had been abducted and snuck off the island. There are many who still will not speak to her. They are so angry about the fear that they had to live with while she was missing. They were afraid for their children and themselves. And then she showed up with a child and refused to tell anyone what had happened. Some people have never forgiven her for that. They feel they have the right to know after the years they spent worrying about what could have happened to her."

Tabitha stood. "And I was that child. I had no past. I didn't even have a birth certificate. We had to go through so many legal channels to try and get one for me because no one had a record of my birth. And of course, as I got older, I realized that I had powers that no one else did. I needed to know what had happened and where I came from. And my mother told me nothing except my birthday was March 1 and that a woman named Gwyn had been with her while I was born."

He nodded. "It must have been very difficult growing up with those questions."

Her laugh was short and brittle. "It was. I was a freak, pointed at and whispered about. And my abilities frightened me. I had no idea what was happening to me, and I could not speak to her about it. She would freak out if I mentioned anything. Once, she caught me playing with my power as a child, just using it with my toys, and she went off the deep end. She had to be institutionalized. Or so I thought. Maybe she didn't—maybe she came back here. Who knows?"

"I wish I had all the answers, but I can only tell you what I know. I have not seen her since she left me that night when you were still a small baby. That was about a month, maybe six weeks, after you were born. Sometime during the night, she left with you both, and I never saw her again. Or your brother, for that matter."

"And the older child, the one who was adopted—do you see him?"

"Yes. I had not made an effort like your mother did to watch him grow. Once we decided to give him away, I made very little effort to see him until he had grown. It was too painful, and he would have reminded me of what could have been. I moved away and began a new life for myself. I followed in my father's footsteps as a land governor and tried to help those in need. I always wondered whatever had happened to Doni, but the truth is, I thought she had returned home with our children and made a new life for herself. I was not able to follow her, so I tried to get on with my life." His tone was once again melancholy, but something about what he was telling her bothered her. She could not put her finger on it; she was still processing everything he had told her.

"Come," he said as he rose and reached for her hand. "It has been a long day for you. I will show you to your room and then we will share some dinner. You will have all the time you need to ask me more questions, and I am sure you have many. I will be at your disposal as we get to know one another and try to answer those last questions that we both have about your mother."

Tabitha nodded, realizing that she was starving. Her head pounded under the sheer emotional load of the day.

The light teased her, gently stroking her cheeks and eyelids as it slipped through the lacy curtains. Tabitha's eyes slowly fluttered open and tried to focus on her surroundings. She recognized the luxurious furnishings of the room in her father's house. The window was open, and a soft breeze fluttered the curtains, tugging them toward the window and then away in a sulky huff. The early morning sunlight danced in a golden hue, sending spinning patterns of shadowy lace along the floor as light cascaded through the curtains. The warm summer breeze smelled of green grass and promised a hot, sultry day at the sun's zenith.

Tabitha stretched under the thin covers, letting the extra pillows on the bed slide onto the floor as she shifted and lifted herself onto one elbow to watch the clouds dance across the azure sky. Two weeks had passed since she had come to her father's house. She felt herself slipping into a warm and cozy life of lazy, pampered days. These two weeks had been a bittersweet vacation from the anxieties of her world back home. Her every need was addressed, usually before she even knew she needed anything. Her father's household treated her like royalty. Many times she would try to imagine what her life would have been like had she grown up here.

She would rise in the morning and slip from the house for a long walk alone. She had come to cherish those quiet moments of peace as she explored the lands around her father's house. Jules had caught her returning once and had cautioned her against wandering alone in such troubled times, but Tabitha ignored the warning. She was accustomed to being active, and she needed that time alone to try and make sense of the past weeks.

When she returned, she would invariably discover a tray of assorted breakfast foods waiting for her. A glass pot of bubbling javé would be waiting for her on a hook in the fireplace, scenting the room with its intoxicating smell. As an addicted coffee drinker, she wondered if she would ever be able to go back to that bitter brew after the smooth and rich flavor of the javé.

On her first day, her father had offered her a selection of new clothes, and the seamstress he sent had measured her to make her a couple of things. Since that day, she would constantly find an assortment of new clothes hanging in the closet, all perfectly tailored to fit her. Her clothes in this world were well made of a soft and comfortable material. Everything she wore was fit to her body and so comfortable that she wondered how she would be able to get them back to her own world with her. She would not be thrilled with having to shop for herself after this treatment.

The house was a beautiful maze of well-decorated and interesting rooms. Her father's private wing on the top floor had a plethora of rooms, and Tabitha was amazed that he lived in so much space alone. The other floors of the enormous chateau housed guest wings and conference rooms, as well appointed and elegant as any of the others in the building. Its warm decor and rich wood accents reminded Tabitha of Luc's parents' house. The top three floors were aboveground, but two additional floors were tucked below the ground. The homes all used earth as insulation, and the windows and doors were built to withstand the elements. Each had an open floor plan with a high glass dome atop to welcome the natural light. But unlike the simple and elegant design that Sybille had infused her home with, Antoine's home was decorated to convey wealth and power. The rich appointments were all well chosen and each decoration art-fully placed. It was obvious that nothing was allowed out of place.

Her suite contained an elegantly furnished bedroom with tall windows overlooking the town below and a glimpse of the river beyond. Outside the bedroom, a small sitting area was carefully arranged with overstuffed chairs and a bevy of throw pillows, each carefully placed to look carelessly tossed but strategic. Each was of a different pattern, giving the illusion of being haphazardly tossed together, but each displayed the same accent colors, some in rich flowers and some in thin pinstripes, but all the exact shades of the same color scheme. A great deal of trouble had gone into making the rooms comfortable and pleasant, though not terribly personal.

Tabitha climbed out of bed, kicking one of the many throw pillows artfully arranged on her bed every day toward the window. She tripped over a half a dozen on her way to shower every morning. After showering and winding her hair into a damp knot, she selected a comfortable blouse and a pair of shorts and slipped her feet into sandals before making her way out of her room through the sitting room toward the main dining room. There she grabbed a cup of javé from the ever-present pot and made her way toward the back of the house, where she had found a private exit.

Once outside, she deeply inhaled the warm scents of the summer morning and then started down the hill to wander through the woods toward the town. She chose the paths carefully, making sure that she could keep her bearings and remember how to get back. It would be all too embarrassing to get lost on her father's property. The sunlight slipped through the greenery above her head and sparkled off the dew that still clung to the bushes along the trail.

Tabitha walked carefully, trying to hold the steaming cup and not burn her fingers. As was her habit, she reviewed the past couple of weeks, trying to piece together the information that had assailed her.

She sipped the hot drink, letting her mind drift as she thought of her father. He had been gracious and pleasant. He had spent time with her every day, introducing her to an indeterminate number of people at the never-ending stream of dinner parties he held. Every night it seemed that he was entertaining a different group of people, whether it was a representative group from the state he governed or a committee or team from one of his many projects. The evenings were always long, exhausting, and tedious. The names and faces all swirled together, and she felt her veneer cracking under the constant deluge of questions about Antoine's mysterious daughter who suddenly appeared.

She also noted that there seemed to be an unnatural number of young men in her age group at many of these meetings. She thanked goodness for Jules's training every time she was in a room with one of her father's many guests. She was able to withstand the constant attack on her senses from the males' interest in her. She knew that her father also had a great deal to do with keeping male interest to a minimum; she had caught him snarling in rage at a couple of men who seemed to be trying their best to get her attention. And yet he continued to provide a constant number of new single young men for her to meet. She was not sure how she felt about his less-than-subtle attempt at introducing eligible men. She wondered, not for the first time, what Jules had told him about Luc, if anything.

The days at her father's estate were a complete change from her upbringing. She had grown up with a less-than-interested mother and an aged and slightly erratic aunt. She had been on her own when it came to her own care. Now, she was getting a sample of what it felt like to have a caring and interested parent, one who seemed proud of her and made every attempt to include her in meeting people within his world. It was a heady feeling for a girl brought up to feel alone.

But she could not ignore the truth about him either. The first day she arrived, he had told her he wanted to hear about her life growing up and about the eighteen years with Doni that he was not a part of. But the truth was that in the past two weeks, he had asked very little about her. He had spent hours daily taking her through the town and showing her his home and village. He had talked about his charitable work and his many projects to help the people in his governance, but he had shown very little interest in her at all. She felt as though he was trying to convince her to stay by selling her on the merits of her father.

She had to admit when she was actually being honest with herself that his constant boasting was wearing on her. The village of humans who lived within his immediate domain spoke to him and about him with awe and reverence, but as she met more and more of the townspeople, she realized that the reverence was tinged with something else. Was it fear?

She also noticed that all the people that he had built the subsidized homes for were human and all the people who worked for him within his chateau were human, but all the people at his dinner parties and the people on his executive staff were Caskan. She could not help but notice that there seemed to be distinct class delineation within her father's world. Luc had told her that in their world, in general, only about ten percent of the population was human and the rest were Caskan, Faye, or elf. It seemed strange to her that the population of her father's village, designed to assist the underprivileged that could not afford a home alone, were all human.

The foliage suddenly opened up and afforded her a beautiful view of the valley below. Tabitha stopped and sat on the large rock outcropping, taking in the beautiful scenery laid out before her. The valley spread out in a glorious expanse of early summer foliage wearing its most vibrant shades of emerald. The woods below were dotted with firs and evergreens, and the deep glades offered a warm carpet of greenery that contrasted with the lighter shades of the farmlands cleared between the lush forests. To her right, she could see the silver stretch of the lower river that joined with the ocean off in the distance. She inhaled deeply, only filling her lungs with the warm scents of the local greenery, not the salty tang of the sea that she craved.

Having grown up on an island, she sorely missed the constant cacophony of the sounds of the sea, the lonely caws of the sea birds, and the endless lull of the waves caressing and withdrawing from the beach. She had always gone to the beach when she needed to think, and these past weeks of landlocked existence had meant a difficult adjustment. She missed the sounds and smells of the ocean and found it difficult to adjust to not hearing the constant hum of the ocean's song. In the absence of that steady crash of the waves, she had learned the sounds of the forests and trees. Those sounds, while not as familiar, had their own sweet and lulling qualities. The soft caress of the wind through the treetops made a gentle whisper that soothed her agitation and allowed her to sort out her feelings and confusion.

So much had happened these weeks. Her thoughts about her mother's disappearance had suddenly taken on a whole new light. She had to come to grips with the details her father had given to her. So many questions still remained. She sorely wished she could find her mother. She wanted desperately to talk to her, to understand what she had gone through. The holes in her father's story still waited to be answered, and the one person who could answer them was still missing.

Frustration welled within her. Tabitha remembered that despite all of her father's promises to assist her, he had yet to offer her any proof that he was, in fact, trying to find Doni. Her questions had gone unanswered, and although he had told her on numerous occasions that he had people out searching for her, he had yet to find her. When she pressed him for details, he would brush off her inquiries, saying it would not mean much to someone unfamiliar with the land. She, he would remind Tabitha, would have to learn to trust him.

Tabitha tilted her head back, letting the warm sun beat on her face as it climbed into the sky. The morning was waning, and it was time for her to head back before she was missed. She wondered if Jules had told her father about her morning wanderings. Her father had not mentioned it. The maid who left breakfast may or may not be aware that she was not in the bedroom because Tabitha was always careful to close the inner door, hoping that the woman would assume she was sleeping late.

She rose, picked up her empty javé cup, and dusted off her shorts. She took one last look at the scenery before her and turned to leave. A startled cry escaped her mouth when she found herself face to face with a young man, leaning carelessly on the rocks and watching her. He was tall and lean; his long blond hair hung in a loose cascade over his shoulders. His light eyes watched her with an amused glint, and his mouth quirked into a grin at her alarm.

Her memory clicked, and she gasped. "You! How did you find me?"

"I didn't find you. I have been watching you, waiting for a good time to find you alone," he replied.

Fear turned into embarrassment at being so startled. "It would have been more polite had you announced yourself instead of sitting there watching me, like some creepy perv."

"Creepy perv?"

"Yes, creepy pervert," Tabitha retorted, stooping to pick up the cup she had dropped.

"Ah. Well, sorry. I didn't mean to startle you. I thought you would have been able to detect my presence. You are in possession of some fairly rudimentary skills, I assume?"

"What is it to you? And who do you think you are, making assumptions like that when you sneak up on someone?" Tabitha snapped.

He shrugged. "Well, I thought you would be aware of me behind you. Had I known you would be so surprised, I would have made my presence known."

"Where did you find my mother's ring?" Tabitha forgot her anger, recalling the night he had dropped the ring on the table and disappeared.

"Where do you think I got it?"

"Did you get it from my mother?"

He shook his head, "No. From her friend."

"Friend? What friend?"

"Dedrel. Do you know the name?" he asked.

She inhaled quickly at the mention of the name. Alena, Tristyn's wife had given her that name back in Calais as a contact to find her mother. Alena had told her that her mother had visited a woman named Dedrel in Windrift. "How do you know that name?"

"I was told to tell you to come meet Dedrel. I can take you to her." He glanced over his shoulder. "Of course, you will need to get away from the house undetected. I would rather not have your seven-foot giant following us."

"Seven-foot giant? What are you talking about?"

"You mean you don't know? Every morning when you head out, one of your father's 'hired help' follows you. No doubt protecting you from being accosted by one of the more unsavory locals or, even worse, the likes of me," he commented, a knowing grin on his face. He seemed to delight in the fact that she seemed to have no idea about her escort.

Tabitha shook her head, "No, I was not aware. So how is it that you found me today, apparently without my shadow?"

"You have a tendency when you are deep in thought to disappear, telepathically speaking. He has trouble following you," he explained.

"Hmm. I had no idea." She was annoyed, knowing now that apparently her walks were not as solo as she had thought, as well as by the fact that she had been unable to detect she was being followed. She had to admit, though, that her training with Jules had centered around keeping herself shielded from others, not so much on being able to detect the presence of others. She would have to correct that if she wanted freedom to move around as she chose. She glanced up to find him watching her.

"So when can I meet her?"

"We can't talk here. The man who follows you will be seeking you. You cannot just wander off. We need to plan so you have some time to meet with us without your father finding out," he explained enigmatically.

Her mind began to wrap around the caution he was expressing. She began to slow herself down and paused. "What is it that you are worried about? My father wants to find my mother too. I can go with you now. I do not have to answer to him. I came here to find my mother. Just because I am here with my father does not mean that I can't come and go as I please."

"It is not that simple," Cole stated. "You have met your father and heard his side of the story. Now meet with me and Dedrel." He smiled. "Pretend to be ill this evening and sneak out of your room at dusk. I'll be waiting for you. We can talk all night and compare notes. I have never had the opportunity to hear a first-hand account from the royalty of the land."

"I assume you mean my father?"

He grinned. "I do. He is like the king around here and trying to make sure that everyone knows it." He started walking and Tabitha fell into step beside him. He had such a casual and relaxed aura about him that she could not help but like him. She realized that after several weeks with predominantly Caskans for company, she had missed the more relaxed demeanor of regular people. As much as she enjoyed the very elegant, stoic, and pleasant Caskan people, she missed people who were comfortable and at ease with themselves.

Cole glanced over at her as they walked. "He is going to try and make you his little princess now. Be cautious. Your father doles out relationships carefully and usually expects a great payment in return."

"What do you mean?" A shiver crept down her spine as she recognized the truth behind the enigmatic words—a truth she could not put her finger on. She realized it was a caution she needed to heed.

"Your father does not do much without expecting a return of some kind. He never does anything without an ultimate goal already in mind."

She glanced up at her tall companion. "You don't think much of him, do you?"

"I think quite a bit about him. We all should think quite a bit about him," Cole commented, the humor evaporating from his eyes. "He is not to be trusted, and we should all be thinking very hard about what it is he is doing."

"I don't understand." Tabitha ticked off her father's many accomplishments as they walked. She was, in truth, not trying to convince Cole of her father's merits so much as trying to determine what was bothering her as well. Perhaps he would be able to shed some light on what was nagging at her.

"Yes, on the surface, he is truly a wonder. But we must all take note of what's below the surface."

As they approached the fork in the trail that would take her back to her father's home, he stopped walking. Cole indicated with his chin that she should go back without him.

"Plead illness tonight and then sneak out here at dusk. If they think you have gone to bed early, we'll have the night to talk. I can have you back here bright and early tomorrow so they will believe you are returning from your morning walk. I will wait here for you. Don't use the same door you always leave from. They watch that now. Come out another way and sneak up here."

She nodded and turned to say good-bye as he disappeared into a shower of sparkles. Tabitha gasped as the tiny lights disappeared and she found herself alone.

CHAPTER FIVE

SHE HAD TO GIVE HERSELF CREDIT FOR A SPECTACULAR performance. She had picked at her breakfast with her father, pleading a lack of appetite. Antoine seemed distant and thoughtful, and he accepted her excuse for her lack of interest in her breakfast. He stabbed at his own meal, chewing with angry determination as he read through a stack of paperwork before him. He seemed to be less than enthused about speaking.

Jules glanced at her with a frown, but Tabitha ignored his veiled attempt to get her attention. After what seemed an acceptable amount of time, she excused herself and rose to slip back toward her bedroom. She thought she had made it out safely when her father's voice sharply halted her.

"Tabitha."

She turned. His scowl had deepened and his piercing glare pinned her to the spot. "Where were you this morning? I understand you were out wandering quite early."

Tabitha had not expected the question. She felt herself flush as she panicked, wondering how much to confess. "I went for a walk. I like to get up early, and I enjoy the morning air."

"You disappeared for a time, I am told."

"Disappeared? Was I being *watched*?" She hoped that a defensive approach would deflect the need to respond.

"Of course. You are, after all, my daughter. Your safety is of my utmost concern. You are in an unfamiliar place. Anytime you wander, you need to be watched and guarded." He was clearly angry. She had not expected him to be so direct. "I would expect that since you are not familiar with our world and its dangers, you will pay more attention to your own safety. Now, answer my question. You disappeared. Where were you? Did you speak to anyone?"

"Just because—" Tabitha began to retort but Antoine cut her off.

"This is my world. You could have been in grave danger. I am responsible for your welfare, and I will not be ignored. Where were you?" He stood abruptly, and Tabitha found herself taking an involuntary step back.

"I went for a walk. I wandered up to the rocky outcropping up on the hill, the one to the right. I didn't disappear. I simply followed the trail."

He stared at her, absently chewing as he watched her, as though he was deciding if what she told him was the truth.

"And you spoke to no one?"

She laughed shortly, not sure why she was hesitant to tell him about meeting Cole. She had no rational reason not to tell him about what seemed to be a totally innocent meeting. But her instincts warned her to keep silent. "Who would be in the woods at that hour?"

He nodded and sat again. "I apologize, but I will be unable to have dinner with you this evening. Some emergencies have come up that require my attention."

He bent his head back to his papers. She seemed to have been dismissed. Tabitha turned and made her way back to her bedroom, wondering what had set off his temper. She shut the door behind her and wandered through her sitting room, settling in a deep, plush settee to ponder the morning's events. She could not help but wonder where Cole planned on taking her and what information he would share about her mother's visit.

Tabitha wandered through the empty apartments later that afternoon, trying to find some way to waste time until the evening. She knew she should be trying to get some sleep, but she was just not tired and the warmth of the day had permeated her bedroom. She stopped in the richly appointed living area and sank into a stuffed settee, wrapping her knees beneath her as she tried to relax and enjoy both the view and the warm breeze slipping in the window.

Despite her certainty that she would be unable to sleep, as she lay back on the comfortable pillows her eyes drooped and her head nodded. She slipped into a light sleep. Her dreams slid through a myriad of images and nonsense until the sound of men's voices slowly intruded on her nap. As her eyes slowly fluttered open, she realized that the voices were not in her dream but there in the room with her. She slowly started to raise her head, realizing that whoever was in the room was unaware of her presence on the settee facing the window. The slam of the door and the sharp tone of her father's voice pushed her farther down into the pillows. She hoped her presence would remain unnoticed.

"Dammit, Dylan, how could this have happened? Don't you have better control over the situation than to let something so sloppy and arrogant happen?"

"Of course. Who would have been able to guess that one would be left?" the other voice retorted before something was slammed into what sounded like the desk.

A sharp growl ensued that Tabitha assumed was her father. She knew she should make her presence known. This would be a good time to stand, but fear and curiosity silenced her tongue as she slipped lower into the couch.

"If there is any way for this to be tracked back, you must leave at once. I cannot risk that all of my work might be unwound by something so careless!"

"It cannot. There is no way for anyone to know that it was anything less than it appeared. Even if he has the courage to speak, who would believe him?" the other voice retorted. As he moved across the room, his voice assumed a more confident tone. Tabitha, her eyes closed tightly, could hear his steps approaching; her heart thudded in her chest. She felt a slight jerk from the couch she was lying on before his voice continued, close by. "You are worrying needlessly. Besides, you and many others can account for my presence here last night."

Tabitha slowly opened her eyes. She saw a man leaning against the back of the couch, his hands resting on either side of him. He was a younger man, probably a few years older than her judging by his voice. She noticed ebony hair, a strong muscular back, and his hands gripping the top of the back of the couch. His voice had a low, confident, almost sneering timbre when he spoke to the older man.

Her father snorted in disgust. "You arrived so late for dinner that many had already left. There would not be many who would be able to attest to your presence here for the night. You'd best be able to find someone else to confirm your whereabouts should your activities be questioned."

Dylan's laugh was low and sardonic. Tabitha felt the settee shake with his mirth. He was so close; she could see the stitching in his well-made shirt. "Plenty can attest to my presence."

Antoine blew out his breath at the other's confidence. "Make sure it is not someone who was with you on this ill-fated trip."

Dylan's head bobbed as he nodded to the man across the room. "You should give me more credit than that." His voice was sarcastic and edgy. "And what of our other deal? Have you been able to finalize that liaison? I understand Katie's time will soon be here. What of the final promise? Will they accept the child in exchange for their fealty?"

"Of course. She will do anything to placate her daughter, who has been unable to have children. She will be more than willing to commit to our cause once we produce her grandchild." Antoine's response was a low growl. Tabitha heard the drawers of his desk slide open and shut.

"You have not secured her promise as of yet? By the one God, you are a fool—"

"Speak not to me of foolishness! You will address me with the respect due my station!" Antoine roared, cutting off the younger man's insult.

Tabitha watched Dylan's head bob and his shoulders slump forward slightly in a bow. "I apologize. I spoke out of turn. But I would have thought this would be signed and delivered before the child's birth. It must be close. I have seen Katie only on occasion in many months. The child should be almost due."

"You should stop in and see her. She still pines for you. We thought her in danger of losing the child once you stopped keeping her company. She cried for weeks over your apparent abandonment. She seemed under the impression that you would wed her. It was careless of you to lead her along with idle promises," Antoine reprimanded. His chair creaked as he sat at his desk.

"I spoke no such words to her. She simply assumed that my lust was love. She was the one with flowery words of marriage and love. I never uttered such drivel. It is her own fault for believing that I would marry her or even that I loved her." He chuckled. "Imagine her believing I would wed a human! Ridiculous."

"Well, had she lost the child in her depression, it would have ruined our chance of drawing in the Southern chancellor. We need her support, and she is desperate for the baby. Had Katie lost it, we would have been forced to find another." The chair creaked again as Antoine rose. "And she is a young woman. Had you kept up your pretense, she could have given us another child."

Dylan scoffed. "She is losing her figure to pregnancy. If I need to spend months in a woman's bed, I would rather enjoy a slimmer shape."

Tabitha's teeth clenched and her fists balled. It was everything she could do to not leap up and attack the younger man who displayed such blatant disregard for the human girl.

"Well, it seems Victoria may have found another likely prospect. Perhaps you will find this one more to your liking. The girl is not yet committed, but once Victoria has her lined up, perhaps I will send you to accompany her here. I worry that Katie may have become a liability. She seems to be too emotional." Tabitha gasped at the detached, cold tone of Antoine's voice.

"You will send her back?"

Antoine's response was a snort. "Be serious. You know as well as I do what would happen if we were to send her back. No, I think that once she bears the child, we may have to take other steps. There is no shortage of young women looking for a home. The promise of monetary compensation seems to be of great allure to these girls."

Dylan stood from the couch. Tabitha saw him stretch his arms over his head. "Speaking of which, have you made any decisions about which man to engage? I understand you have quite a few interested parties."

Antoine walked around his desk, and Tabitha held her breath as his footsteps approached. Dylan had moved away, but as Antoine's steps approached her hiding place, Tabitha slid silently off the settee and quietly rolled beneath it. She held her breath. She could see Antoine's dark boots wander toward the window in front of her. He stopped within a few feet of her new hiding place. Her movements caused her to miss the first few phrases of his response.

"—and has caused quite a ruckus. I believe that first factor to be a true indicator of the potential benefit to the union. One complication will be convincing your sister that this is a viable option, one that would be mutually beneficial. Strangely enough, there is one option that has yet to be considered as a serious contender, but I understand he has a promising future. He is a young man I am very much looking forward to meeting. If I am not mistaken, he is a friend of yours? Marcus DesChamps' nephew, Luc DesChamps?"

"Luc? Truly? Yes, he was a close friend, but I have not seen him for a few months. I had not understood he was a potential suitor in this appointment. He would be a worthy candidate, but I am surprised. How did his name come to be considered within such a prestigious group? Don't get me wrong. I have heard nothing but good things about Marcus, and I think highly of Luc. He will impress you. But he is, after all, half human," Dylan replied.

Tabitha held her breath, wondering what they could be discussing and what connection Luc had to Dylan's sister. As hard as she tried, she could not hold down the intense jealousy that gnawed at her belly.

"That he is, but he has trained under his father. Let's not forget that Bertòn trains only the most talented of the Caskan. From what I have been told, Luc is as adept as he is powerful and he is well able to hold his own against any full Caskan."

Dylan joined Antoine by the window. Tabitha slid farther beneath the couch, praying they would not see her. "I would be happy to have him as a family member. I think of him as a brother. You will be very impressed with him."

"Well, I am considering other more notable names. I have Marcus's allegiance, so I will not need this relationship to win that. There are others I may need to win over with this opportunity. He is but one of several options. He maybe not the most strategic politically, but surely he is one of the easiest to persuade," Antoine replied.

"How so?"

"According to Jules, there is already some existing relationship, so the commitment may not be a long stretch if there is already be a potential connection," Antoine replied.

Dylan laughed. "Leave it to Luc to find the most beautiful woman to woo to his bed. And I thought him interested only in his studies. While I am away, he seduces my sister."

The two pairs of boots headed toward the door. Tabitha clung to the shadows beneath the couch. Tears stung her eyes as the image of Luc in love with Dylan's sister tore at her heart. The door closed behind the two men as Tabitha silently sobbed beneath the couch.

CHAPTER SIX

TABITHA TUGGED HER THICK HAIR INTO A LONG BRAID and slipped into a knit sweater against the chill of the evening air. She had been in bed, pleading illness when the maid came in to offer her dinner. Now, several hours later, with the sun safely tucked beneath the horizon, she prepared to sneak out and meet Cole.

The conversation she overheard still played continuously through her mind as she tried to make sense of what she had heard. She had stayed under the couch for another half hour after they left to avoid running into the men as she left the living suite. Now she wondered what she had stumbled across. The questions seemed to multiply with every reiteration through her memory.

With a long final sigh, she let fatigue wash over her; the emotions that cascaded through her over the day had wreaked havoc on her nerves. She felt tired. She wanted to just stop thinking and let everything in her mind settle.

She slipped down the darkened hallways, avoiding people and looking for a safe exit route. She found it down a back stairway that led through the large kitchen. The room was a bustle of activity; a back door had been left ajar to allow the cool breeze to enter. She waited until no one was nearby and slipped down the stairs and out the door. She treaded softly across the manicured grounds, looking for a quick way off the property and into the woods.

The rising moon cast a silvery blanket on the grass, and she was afraid anyone looking out a back window would see her sneaking across the grounds. As she approached the nearby wooded path, a low moan caused her to freeze. The sound of muffled huffing seemed to emanate from the bushes to her right. Tabitha dared not breathe. A man's whisper carried on the soft breeze, and she held her breath, wondering if someone were following her. A scattering of twigs and leaves on the path eliminated slipping away soundlessly. Paralyzed, she furtively glanced around for a dark place to hide. The seconds ticked by. When she was about to turn and run for it, she heard a woman's furtive whispers, followed by a murmured male plea.

As the bushes rustled gently and another low moan slid from the darkened brush behind Tabitha, slowly understanding dawned on her. She could feel the blush rise on her cheeks, and she laughed quietly to herself, relief and embarrassment vying for the more dominant emotion. She raced up the path toward the place she would meet Cole.

She came to the fork in the path and stopped to catch her breath after her jog uphill. She glanced into the shadowed woods, and fear began to take root as she stood alone in the dark.

In a few seconds she heard a soft call. Cole stood a few feet away on the opposite trail, hailing her quietly. She trotted over to where he stood.

"Any trouble slipping out?" he asked.

"None," she commented, although she could not help but giggle when she told him about almost disturbing a couple wrestling in the woods.

Cole grinned and then led her down the dark path toward the small town nestled at the base of the hill. "There are worse things you could have come across tonight."

She nodded. "I do not seem to have been followed."

They wound through the dark forest. Tabitha stayed close behind him, stumbling and tripping over roots. Exasperated, he stopped to help her up after she stumbled over an uneven patch of the trail.

"You do not seem to understand the concept of stealth. We were hoping to make it to the house without anyone knowing we were coming."

Tabitha cursed. "Well, if you were not going so damn fast in the dark, maybe I could have kept up, but I can't see where I am going!"

He stopped, staring at her. "You're using your eyes?"

"How the hell did you think I was walking through the woods? Using my hands to feel my way?" she shot back, dusting the brush off her pants.

"It did not occur to me that you were trying to see where you were going." He was almost apologetic, but she could see the curve of his cheekbones as he struggled to hide a smile. "If you stop trying to see where you are placing your feet and start to use your other senses to direct you, you can do this with your eyes shut."

She frowned but tentatively extended a thought to the path in front of her. He started walking, slower this time, as he let her adjust to using her senses to guide her over the rough trail. After a few moments of practice, Tabitha found it became easier, and they were able to pick up the pace again. Once she got the hang of it, she could not believe she had never thought of trying it.

The trail began to smooth out. Tabitha realized that the actual walking time had been fairly quick; the edge of the village was probably less than a mile or two. Cole led her along the darkened back paths that ran behind many of the cottages to a larger cottage situated at the end of a long lane. The outside was dark, but the small glass enclosure atop the cottage burned cheerfully above the small dirt mound that had settled on the cottage's roof.

"The cottages in this village are all like a stone cottage, but most of the other houses I have seen have mostly dirt exteriors. Why is that?" Tabitha asked quietly as Cole led her along the path toward a back door.

"The village is relatively new and was built quickly. Many of the older homes with the dirt walls have been there for many years. They are mostly stone under the dirt, but over time, the dirt insulation has been gradually added to form an exterior that blends into the landscape," Cole explained as he walked up to the wood door in the back patio. "These homes were built more recently, so the residents have not yet had time to complete the insulation or bring the dirt needed to finish them."

As he opened the door Tabitha followed him into a warm and inviting kitchen. A bright fire crackled with heat, and a multitude of warm lights bathed the room in a soft glow. An older woman stood as they entered. She walked over to Tabitha without comment, her hands extended in a greeting. She was a short, round woman with gray hair dancing around her plump face. Her mouth curved into a sweet and welcoming smile, and her twinkling blue eyes captured Tabitha immediately.

"Gwyn?" She did not even know where the name came from until she breathed it. Without a doubt, she knew this was the woman her mother had spoken of who was with her when she gave birth.

Gwyn nodded, and tears sparkled in her bright blue orbs, making them even more brilliant. "Tabitha! By the Word, I thought I would not live to see you again! I never thought you would come back here once your mother got you away!"

Tabitha found herself enfolded in a warm hug as the woman wound her arms around her. Gwyn released her and stepped back, grasping Tabitha's hands as she studied the younger woman. "But let me see you! You are a truly beautiful young woman! The very image of your mother at her age, although, if I may, you are even lovelier. Funny that none of you got your mother's white hair."

Tabitha was aghast. "You know my brothers?"

The older woman smiled and nodded. She tugged Tabitha over to a set of chairs in front of the fire. Cole was setting a steaming mug on a wood tray and lifted a bowl of food onto the tray and added a plate of fruit. He gestured with his chin to the stairs. Gwyn smiled warmly at him and nodded. "If you would be so kind."

"Of course, Gwyn. I will be back shortly. You two can catch up, but don't talk about anything new until I get back!" Cole hefted the tray and walked to a set of stairs nestled back along the far wall, ducking his head to enter the narrow stairway.

Tabitha turned back to find Gwyn smiling at her as she handed her a steaming cup of tea. They each took a chair. For just a few moments, Gwyn could only shake her head.

"It still amazes me you have come back. I take it your visit is going well?"

Tabitha nodded as she sipped from the cup. "Do you know Dedrel?"

Gwyn laughed, "I do indeed—she is me."

"You? But I thought…"

"Dedrel is my middle name. It is quite uncommon, so I occasionally use it with people I know well to keep my identity hidden and yet they still know who they are referring to."

Tabitha's brows knit in confusion. "But I was told that a woman named Dedrel was living down here and that my mother had been to visit her. I don't understand. How would anyone have known to use that name?"

"Well, truth be known, I gave the message to another to carry to you. We have a bit of a network, if you will. I knew you had come over searching for your mother, and so I sent the message along in the hopes that someone asking about her would get the message to you." Gwyn explained. "I sent that message to Calais with a contact of mine and knew that if you were asking about your mother, you would be led to me."

Tabitha's heart pounded. "Was my mother here?"

"Well, she *was* here, but she has left," Gwyn said, her eyes filled with sadness.

"Where did she go? Do you know?" Tabitha asked, exasperated. Tears of frustration stung her eyes. "I know she knows I am here...and she keeps avoiding me! I mean, what is it? Does she not want to see me? Am I that much of an embarrassment to her?"

Gwyn leaned over and gripped Tabitha's hands in a warm clasp. Her blue eyes gazed at Tabitha with such warmth and compassion that she understood what her mother had told her so many years ago about Gwyn, the woman assisting her in giving birth. Doni had told Tabitha how the woman's merry blue eyes and warm disposition got her through the pain of childbirth.

"Tell me, Tabitha, what do you know of your mother? Of her time here with us and her background?" Gwyn asked gently. "It might help if I can fill in some of the blanks about her to help you understand that she is not hiding from you. She is eluding you to protect you."

Tabitha felt the warmth dissipate as she tugged her hands from the older woman's grip. She leaped upright. "Stop! Please stop! Don't say another word! I am so sick and tired of people telling me everyone is trying to protect me and saying what is for my own good!" She spun and paced before the fire, raking her hands through her hair in a wild desperate motion.

"For as long as I can remember, everyone has been 'protecting' me. Apparently I am some delicate china doll that needs to be kept from the truth and locked away in a silly old dusty closet. It is like she and Trude wanted me to be ignorant and content enough not to question who or what the hell I am."

Gwyn sat on the edge of her seat, her eyes wide; her mouth pursed to respond, but Tabitha continued, not prepared to acquiesce to one more person asking her for patience. "She is eluding me to protect me? From what, Gwyn? Heartache? Disappointment? From life? From truth? What? What is she protecting me from? I get it, this is a strange world. Okay, I get that! I understand! Does she want me to just return to my own world and go back to a life that is not even mine? I make every decision based upon *her* actions. I'm going away to college because I have to get away from the one family I have to escape *her* legacy. I am working my fingers off on that Godforsaken island to try and get the hell away from her and have a life without any more secrets."

Tabitha stopped pacing and stared into the flames, tears once again pouring down her face. She wiped at them angrily. "Do I look protected? Do I look like I am a happy, well-adjusted girl, waiting to go off to college? I have cried more in the past weeks than I have in my life. I have pushed everyone away from me for my whole life. I cannot tell the truth about my family and my own past because I don't know it. I broke the heart of a great guy back home because he made the mistake of trying to get too close to me, and I would not let him because I did not even know enough truth to offer him so he could understand me. I cannot let anyone close except my cousin Callie because once they get close and start to ask questions that I cannot answer, I feel as though a part of me is missing. I am an incomplete person who no one will finish because they are trying to protect me from the truth."

She sank back into the chair and lifted tortured eyes to the older woman, her energy sapped, the fight gone. Her voice dropped to a whisper. "I have slowly begun to understand some of what happened to her. In the past weeks, I have found out enough to start to understand some of this. I know where she was. I know my father. If everything he tells me is right, I even have a slight clue about why she was so depressed all my life. But I don't understand why I have had to claw my way through all of this to find out what she could have told me from the start." Tabitha leaned forward and once again grasped the other woman's hands. "Don't you see? She is trying to protect me, but had she given me the truth in the first place, I would not have had to come here to find it. She wants me to go home. This world is dangerous. I understand. I will make you a deal. Tell me everything. Tell me it all, and I will leave this place and never return."

Gwyn stared at her, her face unreadable. She slowly lifted a hand to Tabitha's face and stroked her cheek. She nodded. "I will tell you everything I know. And you will promise me that once you have unlocked it all, you will leave?"

Tabitha slowly nodded. "If you can answer all of my questions, I promise to leave and never return."

The image of Luc flashed before her eyes, but she shook it away. She had never meant to stay here anyway. Just maybe finding out about Dylan's sister was a good thing. It explained a lot. She now knew that Luc's feelings for her, as warm as they were, were not the same as she was feeling. She would leave and give him the opportunity to get on with his life.

The image of the twin scars on his throat haunted her; guilt washed through her. Pain lashed through her heart but she ignored it, determined to discover what Gwyn could tell her, to go back and talk to Jules in his long-promised conversation, and then pack up and go.

Cole trotted down the stairs and placed the tray on the kitchen counter before coming over to join them. He snatched an apple off the counter and leaned against the back of a chair.

"Did I miss anything?"

Tabitha's laugh was brittle. "Only a tirade."

"Already? Well, glad I missed that." He grinned. "I've seen a glimpse of your temper."

Gwyn swatted him off the back of the chair, and he slipped into the seat with a pained expression on his face.

Tabitha watched the fond glance between them; it piqued her curiosity. "What is the relationship between the two of you and my mother?"

Cole glanced at Gwyn. The older woman nodded before she spoke. "Well, to start back at the beginning, I first met your mother when I worked for Antoine's father. I was a caretaker for his mother before she passed away. I then stayed on to watch over an elder relative for them. Antoine brought Doni to meet his parents late in the summer after she arrived. They had no idea she was from your world, and, frankly, I didn't either in the beginning. They seemed such an intense couple, very passionate and capricious.'

'His father was less than enthused with her. He was accustomed to subtle and reserved Caskan women. Your mother was alive and so very vibrant that the air around her seemed to hum. Antoine's father was worried, to say the least. They were so intensely in love one moment and then fighting violently the next. Oh, to watch them was both fascinating and painful. They were two very similar people who were just worrisome together. They seemed to adore the attention, good and bad. Parties were always a favorite venue for their antics. They became a bit of a joke. People wondered whether they would face overly loud and outlandish hosts or perhaps a dark and scowling couple fighting."

Gwyn stopped and cocked her head slightly.

"Cole, would you please—" Her words faded off as she gestured toward the upstairs with her chin. He nodded and stood, heading up the stairs.

"When Doni became pregnant, few were particularly surprised. The pair made no secret of their passionate relationship. Truth is, Antoine's father spoke to him on occasion about the more, uhm, *loud* evenings. The household could hear them in their closed room."

"Eww…More than I need to know," Tabitha grumbled, wondering why it seemed that people delighted in bringing up her mother's sex life.

"I apologize, but it was so unusual. The Caskan are a very passionate people but also a very private people. It was very unusual for a couple to be so demonstrative and so public about their more private relationship. It was unusual indeed."

"Were you with her when she delivered my brother, the older one?"

Gwyn nodded. "Oh, yes. By that time she wanted only to go home. But she was a young girl and did not want to return pregnant. She was frightened and unsure. Antoine made arrangements for the adoption of her son. She was devastated."

"She did not agree with it?" Tabitha asked, noting an inconsistency in Antoine's story.

"Well, truth be known, I am sure she probably did at one time, but I do not believe it was what she truly wanted. I think Antoine convinced her to give up the child. No doubt he saw the political advantages of the adoption, and I am sure he convinced her it was for the best. But I don't think she ever truly wanted to give up her child."

Cole rejoined them. Gwyn sighed as she poured them each another cup of the steaming tea brewing on the hook over the fire. "By that time, she was becoming more and more of his prisoner and less of his guest. I am not sure she realized that he had no intention of letting her go. I am sure that she still believed he would let her return home. Once she gave birth, so much of her spirit left her. She became a different person. The attention-seeking and the antics disappeared, and she began to become more and more withdrawn."

Gwyn continued. "Your mother wanted to leave when she gave up the baby. She'd had enough of Antoine and this world. She wanted to go home."

"Obviously she did not, since I and apparently a brother were born some time later," Tabitha commented, trying to prompt the information that Gwyn seemed hesitant to provide.

Cole sat back, shoving his hair behind an ear. Tabitha started when she noticed his ears were pointed. She could hardly help but gasp. "You are an elf?"

He laughed. "Hardly. I am half Faye. But wait..." He leaned forward with a mischievous grin. "The story gets better!"

Gwyn continued. "Your mother gave birth and was preparing to leave when your father discovered something truly amazing about her. This changed everything."

Tabitha frowned. "Well? What could he have possibly found out?"

"Well, as I understand it, your father's cousin had been instrumental in helping to place their child with a new family. You see, the decision to put your brother up for adoption really was politically motivated. You father's father had passed away quite suddenly by that time, and your father was following in his footsteps, going into politics. Suddenly, your parents' overt and wild behavior changed, and he became quite a conservative, upstanding, serious gentleman. Your father selected the family to adopt his child based upon the most advantageous political alliance. It was what started him in his political rise.

"There is no more precious commodity to our people than our children. So many couples can have only one, if any at all. People will pay any price for a child," Cole interjected, his face losing much of its humor.

Gwyn nodded sadly. "Since the loss of our healers, the price of childbirth is too high. So many of our young women die from the fever that tears them apart during the pregnancy or from the birth.

"Your father's cousin Victoria had assisted in placing his child in a good home. When she came to meet with Antoine and discuss options, it seems that she recognized your mother as someone who had—"

"Wait," Tabitha held up a hand. "Did you say Victoria?"

"Yes. Do you know her?" Gwyn seemed puzzled.

Tabitha nodded. "Assuming my father has only one cousin with that name, I did meet her, but that was in my world. She is an attorney in my world, and she sent a letter, from I guess my father, that caused my mother to disappear again."

Gwyn nodded. "She did indeed. Your father sent the message that her father had passed away, and she came quickly. Luckily, she came directly here and was gone before your father was aware of her return. He was quite cross with me that I let her know of his lie before he could intercept her."

"Her father? Wait, she told me it was his father. Her father would be my grandfather, and he died years ago." Tabitha felt her head swim.

Cole grinned again, his pointed ears giving him an even more mischievous look than his twinkling eyes. "Wait, it gets better!"

Gwyn held up a hand. "Yes, he would have been, had your mother actually been related to those people. Tabitha, your mother is not human—she is from this world. When she disappeared, she did not run from your world. She came home."

Tabitha felt the blood leave her face. Her hands began to shake. Questions piled up on her tongue, but numbness stole over her brain. All rational thought seemed to seep out. She felt like she could not grasp what she was being told. Her mouth opened and shut a number of times but no sound emitted. Gwyn was on her feet; she snapped something at Cole as she grabbed the back of Tabitha's neck and pushed her head between her knees, with a gentle admonishment to breathe.

The room stopped spinning, and slowly, as she stared at the wood floor between her feet, reality began to settle. Tabitha's breathing became more even.

"I'm okay," she mumbled. She shoved Gwyn's hand off her neck. She sat back, tossing her hair behind her and allowing air into her lungs, her head tilted back. It took her a moment to realize that Gwyn was sitting beside her, gently rubbing her shoulders, while Cole sat at her feet, concern written across his features.

"Just stop. Leave me be. I am fine, really. Just give me a minute. I think I am going to throw up now."

Cole immediately jumped back, which made the slight hint of a laugh slip from Tabitha's mouth.

Gwyn offered her another cup of tea, but Tabitha stood, pushing the tea and the hand away from her. She had always been a solitary person, not particularly accustomed to being touched or comforted. As Tabitha's world veered sharply away from all of the known facts of her existence, the older woman's gentle administrations were too much for her.

"I have to go outside. I just need some air. Please, just give me a minute to myself," she mumbled and headed for the door.

The warm summer night carried the slightest hint of a dewy chill. Tabitha inhaled the cool air deeply, letting her mind settle. She wanted so badly to cry but she couldn't. She could not break down, letting her mother once again cause her to fall apart. She did not know how to react to what Gwyn had told her, and she could not bring herself to even try to imagine how in the world her mother could not be related to Trude and Ellen. That would mean that she and Callie were not cousins.

The memory of Greg's words came back in a horrible rush: *It seems that a body was found down in the Hollow and has been down there for—oh, I don't know—twenty years, give or take?*

If her mother was from this world, how had she gotten to Porta Negra? How could she possibly be Ellen's sister? And whose body had they recently found in Dark Hollow?

"You all right?" Cole came out behind her.

"Yes, but please leave me alone. Just for a moment. I have to think." Tabitha did not want to be rude to him, but she needed to be alone. She just could not deal with him right now.

"I can't," he said simply as he walked across the small walkway and leaned against a tall post supporting the overhang. "I need to keep you talking. I need you to hear the rest of this."

"I just need a minute to try and figure out what the hell this all means."

He let his gaze drop and then he lifted his eyes to the sky. She could see the corners of his ears peeking through his hair. Even in her stress, the sight still amazed and shocked her for some reason. "You have to at least hear the end of your mother's story, up to her leaving. I can't risk you running from here tonight in shock and going back without at least hearing that much."

She slowly shook her head. "I wanted so much to hear everything, I wanted to understand. But the more I hear, the more confused I am. Antoine, my father, told me a long love story of her falling out of love with him and her coldness and neglect as she withdrew. That story I can live with. I can understand the withdrawal, the solitude—her inner demons haunting her and keeping her in her own little hell. I can understand that, but now Gwyn is telling me a story that is so different. It has too many other twists and…God!" She dragged her hands through her hair and tugged it back from her face as she stared up at the bright stars. "I can't take any more. I cannot try any longer to try and figure this out!"

Cole came up behind her and gently took her shoulders. She tensed at his touch, wondering where he was going with this. She could feel warmth and deep affection emanating from him. She immediately tugged away from him, but his hands tightened.

"Don't," he ordered quietly.

"Cole. Wait. I am not sure what you are looking for here, but I am just not—I mean, I am just—" She tried again to pull away, but his hands tightened on her shoulders and pulled her back against his chest.

"Tabitha." He gently lowered his head to rest his chin on her head. "Please. Just listen. Just think. I need you to understand."

Tabitha spun out of his grasp and stared back at him. "You cannot do this to me now. I am really at the edge here, and I am not prepared for you to start—well, anything."

He laughed softly and reached out, backing her against the pole behind her, his hands gripping her shoulders as he forced her to face him. "I don't want anything from you. Just think. Please."

She stared up at his face and saw the gentle smile playing on his mouth. He was a handsome man. His features were fine: a long straight nose, brows that slashed in a devilish tilt above his eyes, and a small dimple that played on the edge of his smile. His long blond hair hung in casual disarray around his shoulders. As his light eyes stared at her, confusion swelled through her. The feel of his hands brought forth a warmth that seemed to fill her with a tender and gentle emotion.

She tried to turn away, but he held her shoulders and gently shook her until she was once again facing him.

Think, he had said. Something was important for her to understand.

He smiled once again. Something about his expression, his slow, casual smile, seemed very familiar. She had felt comfortable with him from the start.

"I don't understand," she said softly.

"Your mother is of this world, Tabitha. She is part Faye," he said quietly.

"Faye? So when I met the Faye in Calais and they told me she went home, she meant to them?"

He shrugged. "I did not know you had met the Faye. But if that was what they told you, then yes, that is what they meant."

"But I don't understand...she is a Faye? If she is Faye and Antoine is Caskan, then I am not human either," she stammered, following a line of thought that she had no idea where it would go, until—

She glanced up again, thinking through the evening and what she had been told. The moonlight slanted through the trees and illuminated her and Cole, standing close, staring at one another. Suddenly he tilted his head ever so slightly. His hair curved away from one of his ears.

She felt lighter than air as a delighted laugh slipped from her, the first in more years than she could remember. She slowly lifted a questioning hand to his hair and brushed it back from his ear. "You are half Faye?"

He nodded, his smile widening.

"Are you half Caskan?" she asked as the sting of tears burned her eyes.

He nodded again. She saw a slight brightening in his pale eyes as the connections started to make sense to her. She lifted a hand to her mouth and fought back the tears. "Were you born in Calais eighteen years and several months ago?"

He smiled and dropped his head down until their foreheads touched. "A full hour before you were."

Tabitha cried out and flung her arms around him, the connection, the warmth, and the feeling of completeness finally making sense. The loving warmth emanating from him was now just right, not confusing and threatening. He needed her, and she needed him. A connection had been made somewhere in the universe. She could almost hear a *click* as they hugged, tears streaming down their faces. Tabitha sobbed gently against his shoulder, feeling as though she had finally found something she had been looking for. They stood, clinging as if they could make up for eighteen years of separation in a single evening.

Gwyn stepped quietly out onto the patio and as they stepped apart to greet her, tears flowed from her eyes, too, as the three of them hugged.

"Forgive me, Tabitha. Forgive me for the way I told you about your mother. I was trying to break it to you slowly, but once it started to come out, I could not seem to stop," Gwyn said through teary eyes.

Tabitha shook her head and gently released them both; her emotions began to come back under control. She found a railing behind her and gently lowered herself against it, wiping at her eyes and drawing in a ragged breath in wonder.

Cole leaned against a pole nearby, a gentle smile on his face as he crossed his arms over his chest. Gwyn perched on a rough wooden bench across from Tabitha.

"This is a lot to take in in one night," Gwyn said gently.

Tabitha nodded. She glanced at the moon as it slowly sank behind the trees. "Dawn will be upon us shortly. I have so many more questions."

Cole answered, "I suggest we wrap up with a few more questions and then I will take you back. We have a lot more to talk about, but I think you should return soon. If you are missed, it will be that much harder to get out the next time."

Tabitha nodded. "He is right. I do have to get back before they realize I am gone. But before I go, tell me—how did my mother become a part of my family if she is Faye? And why do you have pointed ears, yet I do not?"

Gwyn laughed. "There are very few babies mixed with Faye. The Faye very rarely mate outside of their own kind. But in mixed babies it is not unusual for one sibling to have pointed ears and the other not. I will tell you that you did have pointed ears when you were born. Many babies outgrow them, though. It is possible that your mother had yours fixed in your world, as hers had been."

"Her ears were fixed?" Tabitha gasped. She felt the tops of her own ears in wonder, looking for any clue as to why hers were no longer pointed.

Gwyn nodded. "Yes, from what I understand. I did not know your mother back then, nor did I have anything to do with her going to your world."

Tabitha nodded thoughtfully. Fatigue was tugging at her. She felt as though she could sleep on her feet. "Let's plan our next night together, and then I will head back. I am asleep on my feet. I want to get some rest and take some time to think."

Cole nodded and also stood. "I will take you back. We can decide on our next night on the way."

Tabitha turned and hugged Gwyn and followed Cole down the path toward her father's house. They walked in companionable silence. Tabitha tried to sort through it all as they walked. Questions would occur to her and Cole would answer as he could. He told her that it was Gwyn with whom their mother had left him as a baby. Gwyn had been quick to find a home away from their father to spirit Cole to. That family had become his family, but he had grown up knowing Gwyn, as well as knowing his mother was a friend of Gwyn's. It was not until the death of his adopted parents that he came to live with Gwyn and slowly began to find out the truth.

Although Cole knew of him, Antoine had no idea the blond man living with and assisting Gwyn was his son. He thought him a relation who was simply there to assist the village nurse and midwife.

Cole left her outside their father's grand estate with the cryptic comment that he would be in touch. Tabitha entered quietly through the back kitchen door and treaded softly up the steps to her rooms, not concerned with what means he might have to get a message to her.

She undressed and slid into bed as the first rays of dawn were just beginning to brighten the eastern sky. With everything she had been through and all the turmoil spinning in her head, surprisingly she drifted right off into a dreamless sleep.

CHAPTER SEVEN

"COME IN!"

As Jules opened the door, Tabitha emerged from her bedroom into the sitting area, tugging a light shirt on over a matching camisole.

"Good morning." He nodded gracefully in greeting and took a seat. He nodded as she gestured to the pot of javé hanging on the hook over the fire. "I trust you are feeling better?"

"Much," Tabitha said as she poured herself a cup of javé from the steaming pot. After her long night out with Cole and Gwyn, she had spent the better part of the previous day sleeping.

"Excellent," Jules said, accepting the cup of the hot brew she offered. "Tomorrow night your father will be greeting a number of delegates from other provinces. This will be a formal event. I thought I would assist you by explaining some basics about our customs and a little geographic information. Then when you are introduced to people, you will have some rudimentary information about the lands from where they come."

Tabitha nodded, irritated that she would apparently have to put off another visit to Gwyn and Cole for a night or two. She had tried to gather a list of questions she wanted answered beyond the tumultuous relationship her parents had shared in the time up to her birth. So many questions remained unanswered. Not the least of which was: where was her mother now?

Tabitha took a seat across from the man, studying his impassive face as he settled himself into a chair across from her. He sighed and opened his ever-present portfolio to begin.

"Jules, how is it that my father knew I was here?" Tabitha asked directly before he could start his dissertation.

The small man's lips pursed, and he slowly closed his case. "Well, I should have been expecting such questions to emerge." He inhaled deeply and responded, "I told him you had arrived."

"And how did you know?"

"I was told by an acquaintance who felt your entrance into this world," he said evasively.

Her eyes narrowed. "You know I have no intention of letting such a comment go. Who told you? And don't play coy with me. You promised me some answers, and it is about time you delivered. I have done everything you asked, but I am still stumbling along, still ignorant, trying to determine what to do next."

He seemed to consider how to answer. With a final nod, he admitted, "Your mother told me just before she disappeared."

Tabitha stared blankly at him. "My mother?"

He nodded. "Your mother."

"Does my father know?"

"No, he does not," Jules replied.

"Hmm…So she knew I came over and she told you? Why you?"

"So I could tell your father and encourage him to send me in search of you."

"And why not tell him herself? Why all the intrigue?"

Jules leaned back in his chair. Once again Tabitha noted that his face lost much of its aloofness. "I promised to keep her identity out of it. I presented the information to your father in the form of a report of collected information that I compile daily from a variety of sources. He begins his day with this report and has an update on his desk every morning. As far as your father knows, he simply found out from one of his many 'sources.' He then sent me on a search to find you through Marcus's northern province in the guise of a diplomatic envoy."

Tabitha was intrigued. She slid her legs beneath her on the couch as she studied the little man. "May I ask you why you would not tell my father that you saw my mother?"

"I tell you only because I believe that you will keep that to yourself. You have proven yourself more than adept at keeping secrets, and I trust you to keep this one to yourself. I place that trust in your hands in exchange for answering your questions." His irritated and defensive tone was what she had expected, but she could see that this was not his usual surly attitude. For once, she felt as though he was being himself with her, and she was intrigued.

A small smile played on her lips. "What makes you so certain you can trust me?"

"Because the risk to both of us in this charade we enact is too great. This is not a game. The sooner you get the information you need, the sooner we can get you home." His voice took on an edge.

Tabitha frowned. "I am surprised, Jules. I thought that if my father wanted me to stay, you would not want me to remain here. What if I want to stay?"

Jules snorted. "You are not a stupid girl. You know the stakes. If you have spoken to Gwyn, you understand that you are now treated with deference and respect, but as soon as you indicate that you wish to leave, your father will treat you like a hostage, as he did your mother."

"He kept her here against her will?" Tabitha asked slowly. All teasing evaporated as she stared at him.

Jules nodded. "When she gave birth to your older brother, she wanted to return home, but he kept her hostage. She was not a prisoner in the house, but she was kept here by other means. Chains and ropes are not the only tethers with which one can be restrained."

Tabitha glanced at him in surprise as something he said registered. "You know I met with Gwyn?"

He nodded. "How did you think Cole knew to look for you on those morning walks? Who do you think has been pulling strings?"

Tabitha was dumfounded. "You, Jules? But—I don't understand...you do not even like me..."

Jules raised a finger at her. "Don't make that assumption. I was tough on you because I had to be. You needed to learn the basics of protecting yourself before you arrived here. The sooner you can get your questions answered and get out of here, the safer you will be."

"You went through a lot of trouble to put me in danger. Why not just meet me in Calais to tell me the truth and send me home?"

"Would you have been willing to sit at Bertòn's table and hear all of this? Would that have been enough? You needed to come here, meet the man, and decide for yourself. I know you question his motives, and you should. I told you to trust no one, only your instincts. Now, as the truth behind your mother's story begins to unfold, you must understand the risks. Your father believes you are happy here and is working on encouraging you to stay." Jules leaned forward, his small eyes intent. "Tabitha, your father has every intention of finding you a suitable mate and seeing you promised and wed. In your father's world, your hand in marriage offers a very powerful bargaining chip. It would secure an alliance with any number of provinces that your father must yet solidify. You are a very pivotal piece in his next step. Do not assume that your father will have your best interest in mind. He will introduce you to any number of potential candidates and try to manipulate a match for you."

Tabitha was thunderstruck. "Me? Marry? Are you serious? Arrange a suitable mate? You are kidding me—you have to be. No one arranges marriages or seeks suitable mates, especially not at eighteen. That is just…"

Jules smiled. "That is true in your world. Here, we have an inordinate number of males and few women. Our people struggle with pregnancy and childbirth. Most women cannot conceive after twenty-five years of age. Our people can and will die out if we do not do everything in our power to procreate our next generation. With the annihilation of our healers, our numbers have decreased, making it that much more difficult to continue the race. Tabitha, have you ever heard the statistics? One out of three pregnancies does not carry full term; one out of five live births results in the death of the child in the first year. One out of four women die, either in childbirth or in that first year, from the same illness that claims the infants. Only one of ten women can actually bear more than one child, and even fewer can conceive after the age of twenty-five."

He shrugged at the amazement on her face and continued. "You come from a world where childbirth and pregnancy are common. That is not true here. Once people cannot reliably produce offspring, reproducing becomes a matter of urgency. We are desperate to find out the cause of this illness and why it affects our women and infants. Marriage is simply a mating ritual, an attempt to have a child. Marriages are often broken if the woman cannot conceive. The parties are then free to find another mate, regardless of whether the man believes the woman is unable to conceive or the woman believes the man is unable to impregnate her. Perhaps we have a much lower expectation of our marriages. They are not formed for true love, although a mutual attraction is a requirement. But with the mortality rate so high for both children and women, many men are not necessarily looking to marry a woman they love. If she should indeed conceive, he then runs the risk of losing her.'

'In later life, after the age of conception, a couple is more apt to separate and search for that one mate they wish to spend their life with. That is why we have levels of commitment. We have the promise, when a man and woman exchange tokens and promised to wed. The initial marriage is between young couples hoping to conceive a child. Of course, it is imperative that the couples actually like one another and wishes to be together. If they have a child, they are expected to remain together to both raise and care for the child. And then we have a committed marriage, which many couples seek in their later years once careers are established, when they want to find a mate to share their life with."

Tabitha stared at him in amazement. "You are serious? I have never heard of such a thing. You make it sound so clinical. But arranging marriages…that is just so—"

Jules cut her off with a snap. "It is so practical for a race of people that is dying out. Don't pass judgment on our way of life because it does not fit in with your more romantic beliefs. We cannot understand your lifestyles anymore than you can understand ours. And the arrangement of marriages is as beneficial to the woman as it is to the man. The status each can gain from the power of their mutual or individual families can offer them many opportunities. A woman has the choice of her prospective spouse, and she can be a tough negotiator when determining the benefits that she or her intended spouse bring to the relationship."

He shook his head at her dumfounded expression. "I understand you disagree with our lifestyle. I am not trying to explain this for your approval. I am telling you this because your father is positioning you as a potential bargaining chip in his political strategy." He continued, ticking off her merits on his fingers. "You have great value to him. You are half Faye and half Caskan and a woman of marriageable age who happens to be untouched."

"Oh God, *that* again!" Tabitha moaned, her hands to her face.

"Tabitha, listen to me. You are from the other world." He stared at her intently.

"Why would that be an advantage?"

"Because your mother not only had two successful pregnancies, but one was a set of twins. That is unheard of. Your mother did not lose one child. Women who live in your world are not exposed to whatever it is that threatens our infants and women."

Understanding began to dawn on her. "So he believes that not only would I have a better chance of getting pregnant but that the child would probably live."

Jules nodded. "And probably multiple times."

"Good Lord, a baby factory?"

"With your genes. He is desperate because you carry some very unique genes. Half Faye and half Caskan? You as well as your children would be more powerful than a true Caskan," Jules commented.

"The Faye are more powerful?"

Jules nodded.

"So if that is the case, why didn't my mother just break away from my father?" Tabitha wondered, half aloud.

"Because she had never been trained. She grew up in your world. Her powers were quite substantial but less than focused. She did not know she was more powerful. Once she learned that she had the power to break free and elude him, she did," Jules responded.

Tabitha was again overwhelmed. "This is crazy."

Jules nodded. "You need to be aware. Play the game until you are ready to leave. Should your father have any inkling that you do not wish to remain here, your freedom will be sorely limited."

"Wow." Tabitha rose and went to refill her now-forgotten cup of javé. "What next?"

"You have to prepare for tomorrow night. There will be several gentlemen your father will wish you to meet. You must remain pleasant and attentive. Do not give away any clue that may lead your father to believe that you are not content here. However, I would not suggest that you let him believe that you are willing to stay, because you will find yourself married before the week is through. You must let him continue to charm you into potentially remaining here with us."

Tabitha nodded; chewing absently on a nail as she slowly lowered herself back into her seat. "And what of my mother? Where is she, do you know?"

Jules shook his head. "I believe she may have returned to the Faye. I would suggest you do what you can to learn what you came here to learn. She will come to you if she wishes to be found. And I also think it time that we start planning your departure."

Tabitha nodded. "Okay, so fill me in. Tell me what I need to know to get through tomorrow night so I can re-turn to see Gwyn and Cole. I just need to understand a little more, and I have to make one last effort to find my mother."

Jules nodded and re-opened his inevitable case. "Did I tell you that the seamstress will be here with some more formal clothes for you to try on?"

Tabitha groaned and waved him on with a sigh.

CHAPTER EIGHT

LATER THAT DAY, TABITHA SLIPPED FROM THE ROOM, taking a break from the constant attention and demands on her. Jules had spent hours reviewing the geography and history of the Caskan lands. He had taught her the appropriate responses, titles, and salutations for each level, background, and heritage. She had once considered this world to be a simpler place, and compared to the nuances of her own world, it did seem that way. But upon further exposure, she found the differences in the formalities harder to understand. How one addressed people was as important as the title and body language. Because her father was a lord regent of a province, she was not expected to avert her eyes or extend her bow below another's, but she would be expected to understand the various titles and how they differed whether one was married or under the rule of a man or woman, as well as the status of their families.

Every Caskan was expected to be productive, both professionally and publicly. As this concept was ingrained within the society; it was expected that people be unavailable professionally when they were required to focus on their public work. As with any society, people gave at different levels, but since each family was directly affected by any one member's performance, they seemed to have higher expectations. There was little public support for people who did not actively contribute, so there was little opportunity to be less than industrious. Tabitha was intrigued and tried to get Jules to elaborate on the societal framework, but, pressed for time, he opted to move on to other training.

The next few hours were spent being fitted for a formal dress for the festivities. Having been brought up with few opportunities to dress elaborately, she found it tedious, and the attention to detail made her crazy. The beautiful dress the seamstress had designed for her in soft, elegant, shimmering silver flowed about her ankles. Tabitha appreciated all the work the woman put into her wardrobe, but the standing, pinching, and constant adjusting were more than she could take.

When the seamstress wondered aloud to her assistant how they should accent her breasts and the curve of her waist, Tabitha knew it was time for her to flee.

She tried to slip outside for a quick breath of air, but every doorway and entrance seemed busy, a plethora of people constantly entering and exiting with bundles or flowers or food in preparation for the next night's event. Trying to avoid the constant stream of people, she found herself exploring new hallways and floors of the chateau. Thinking she had found a quiet hallway, she started past a long series of doorways, hoping to find a quiet exit or an unused room for a few minutes to herself.

The silence of the hallway lulled her toward the far end where a large room with a long set of windows faced the southern end of the estate. Large plush sofas clustered around low, heavy wood tables. One end of the room featured a stone fireplace centered between dark wood bookcases filled with an assortment of vases, figurines, and other handcrafted items like those she had seen displayed in the quaint shops in town. The room was empty, and Tabitha gratefully slipped over to the windows, letting the silence of the room ease into her and sooth her edgy nerves.

Once again, she wondered how different her life would have been had she been born and brought up here in her father's house. Despite her misgivings, Tabitha had tasted a life she had never known. People were attentive and took a genuine interest in her. Even her father's concern for her whereabouts was a welcome change from the ambivalence she had grown up with. She wrestled with her instinctive concern over her father's intentions and the knowledge that her life here with him would have been that of a cherished and privileged daughter.

Was that so bad? Was it wrong for her, knowing that he had kept her mother a prisoner, to imagine what she and her life might have been like? She sighed and wondered for the millionth time if what Gwyn had told her was more true than her father's story? How was she to know the truth without the one person who could balance the two sides of the story? And was her mother's perception skewed by some kind of mental illness that had seemed to torture her throughout her life?

How could she know which path was the right one? Or was the truth some mixture of the two versions? Jules had told her not to trust anyone. Well, if that were the case, how could she trust that Gwyn and Cole had rightly assessed her parent's life together? Had her father actually done anything all that bad? What information had he used to keep her mother here that he had found out from his cousin? And, of course, the question remained of how in the world Trude had gotten a young niece from another world?

What the hell did that crazy old woman get herself into? Tabitha wondered as slid her fingers along the panes of window.

The million-dollar question was whose body had the police found down in Dark Hollow? She had yet to find anyone to confide in about that information. Who would she ask? Who would even know? Her father? She had asked him one night about black elves, but much like Jules, he had laughed it off as legend.

So why had Cole told her to ask him? What possible reaction did Cole expect from bringing up an old legend?

The questions kept piling up, and Tabitha was running out of people to ask.

Maybe she should ask her father again?

As if her thoughts had drawn him, she heard the creak of a door and her father's voice as he entered the next room. Tabitha slid closer to the doorway and peeked around the corner.

"Well, looks like the baby should be here any day." Antoine was wiping his hands on a cloth as he entered the room from a doorway set behind a bookcase in the far corner of the room.

Another man nodded as he turned to shut the door. "I had hoped to be able to present the Chancellor with her grandchild tomorrow night."

She recognized his voice as she got her first look at Dylan. He was tall with dark hair and a handsome face with rugged features: dark slashed brows over light eyes and a long straight nose. But his striking features were marred by the cruel and cynical twist of his well-shaped mouth. Tabitha hugged the doorway, hoping to avoid detection.

"Patience. The time will be decided by the child and no other. These things cannot be pressed. It will be born when it is ready and not before," Antoine commented as he walked across the room with the younger man in tow.

"Does not have to be so," Dylan growled. "She has had long enough. Were you to call the midwife, there are surely ways to remove the child, with or without her assistance. I grow tired of her bleating, and I worry that should she find some way to escape, our promise to the Chancellor would be nothing but hollow excuses."

Tabitha froze at his chilling statement. Her fears that she may have misunderstood were confirmed when Antoine quietly said, as they left the room, "We will wait for the child to be born on its own. It will only be a matter of days. No need for violence. She is much too far along to attempt any dramatic escape. If she had a plan, she would have tried to make some kind of break months ago."

Dylan's response was lost when they walked from the room down the hall, but his caustic tone was easily discernable. She watched them depart and her curiosity got the better of her. She tiptoed into the room that they had just left. With a last glance down the now-empty hall, she hurried over to the dark door set in the wall. No doorknob or lever hinted at how to open the door.

But there must be some way to open the door.

She inspected every inch of the door, letting her hands slide over the smooth wood, looking for any clue that might trigger the door to open. She was fearful of inspecting it with her senses in case the door was sealed with power. It could possibly be a trap should she try to open it that way.

She glanced out the window, knowing that they must continue along the side of the house toward the room sealed within the wall. The window slid open noiselessly, and without hesitation, Tabitha swung a leg over the high sill and placed her feet on the narrow ledge that ran beneath the window along the length of the house. She was several floors above the ground. That side of the house faced the grounds, so the bustling activity for the party was focused on the other end of the house. Tabitha slid her feet along the edge, hugging the wall as she made her way slowly along.

Her progress was slow. She carefully slid one foot and then the other along the ledge, sweat beginning to dot her brow as she crept along. She did not look down but glanced around every several steps to see how far she was from the windows of the adjacent room. She had to ease herself around the gentle curve of the house to make sure no one from the ground could see her. It would be a tad difficult to explain what she was doing out on the ledge.

When the window came into view, Tabitha edged her way over to it. She was fairly sure what she would see in there. She gently grasped the edge of the sill and peered around the window frame, risking a quick glance into the room. The room was expansive. A huge bed jutted from the far wall. A small sofa faced the windows, and a young woman stood, her face sad as she stared out a window. Her hands were placed at her waist, as though to support her large belly. Tears gently coursed down her face as she ran one hand along her belly in a gentle caress.

When the girl caught sight of her staring in from the far window, Tabitha wondered what it was she expected herself to do.

The girl's eyes lit with surprise, and she quickly came over to open the window. Tabitha lifted a hand in alarm. The window opened outward and would have knocked her off the ledge. The girl laughed gently, realizing what she had almost done, and shook her head at her own idiocy. She went to the next window and unlatched and opened it.

"What are you doing out there? You will fall to your death! Get in here!" the girl admonished as she helped Tabitha climb over the ledge.

"Thanks. Sorry to sneak up on you," Tabitha said as she slid her feet to the floor. The two of them quickly closed the window behind her.

"Well, yeah! I was a little surprised to see you out there. What *were* you doing out there?" She had a pleasant accent. Tabitha struggled to place the dialect. It seemed familiar. She had light brown hair and soft brown eyes in a pretty, slightly rounded face, obviously slightly swollen in advanced pregnancy. She stood taller than Tabitha, and her pleasant smile and eyes radiated a friendly light. Obviously the girl felt no reason to be concerned about the woman creeping along the ledge outside of her room.

"Well, this may seem odd…"

"Odder than you climbing along the ledge outside my window?" The girl giggled and went to the sofa, slowly lowering herself onto it.

Tabitha smiled. "Well, truth is I was just curious to see what was in this room. I saw Antoine and Dylan come out and could not for the life of me figure out how to open the door. They were talking about a woman about to give birth, and I had to find out if someone like that was in here."

"Well, here I am!" the girl said with a bright smile, her arms held out to either side. "You can see that I am here and so very pregnant! My name is Katie, by the way. Katie Hennessey."

"I am Tabitha Devins. Nice to meet you, Katie. Tell me, how long have you been here?" Something about the girl rang a warning bell in her head, but Tabitha couldn't identify what it was.

"Oh, just shy of two years now. It is a beautiful place, but to be honest with you, I am so bored and sick to death of nothing but the view of the grounds." She huffed, lifting a tall mug and taking a long drink. "I woulda thought that I'd have some opportunity to go into the city at some point, but they keep telling me it's not safe for me to travel. All that pollution, blah blah blah!"

"The city? What city?" Tabitha was taken off guard.

"Well, duh! New York City. Being so close to the Big Apple, what other city would I possibly want to go see?" Katie laughed.

Tabitha was thunderstruck. "New York City? You think you are in New York?"

As Katie stared back at her, a slow dawning seemed to illuminate her face. "Ahhh…And where do *you* think we are?"

Tabitha could not help but laugh. The girl obviously thought she was delusional. Imagine that. "Well, I thought we were actually closer to the Jersey line. So tell me, what brought you here? Two years ago, right? And how did you get pregnant?"

"Oh, the usual way! You know!" Katie laughed. "I am so darn fertile, it is like a boy just has to touch me once and boom, there I am again!"

"Again? So this is not your first pregnancy?"

"I wish. No, I came here pregnant. I mean, it is a home for pregnant mothers, right? So no big surprise there."

Tabitha nodded. "Katie, how old are you?"

"Seventeen. I'll be eighteen come January," she replied.

"And you have been here two years?"

"Yes, do the math. I was pregnant at fifteen. Go figure."

Tabitha nodded. "But how did you come to be here in the first place?"

Katie held up a hand, and her eyes narrowed suspiciously. "You're not a reporter or something, are you? I mean, I'm not so sure I should be talking so much..."

Tabitha sighed and nodded. "Fair enough. I really need to come clean with you before I expect you to give me answers. I am from Porta Negra, Massachusetts. I grew up there. I recently found out that my father lives down here in...New York. So I came to meet him. My mother lived here and gave birth to me here, but she took me back to Porta Negra when I was a baby."

Katie's eyes brightened as she sat forward in her seat. "She left here? With her baby?"

Tabitha nodded. "Yes, eighteen years ago, but she did. Why?"

"Oh, Tabitha, I have been asking to go home. I don't want to give up another baby! It broke my heart to give up my first baby. I just want to go home. I wanted to try to call my mother, but as soon as I went looking for a phone they locked me in this stupid room. Trying to keep me safe, they tell me. You would think a damn house this size would have some phones or a damn TV. Nope. Nothing but fresh air and this damn organic food. I want to break out and get me a burger and fries, that is for sure!"

"So you told them you wanted to go home and not give up your second baby?"

"Yeah, but you know how these people can be…they started telling me my mother would kick me out again. Okay, like, sure, I was living on the streets before, but I can get a job. I know I can. But they are so full of themselves, like only they know what is good for the baby. And then they come back and tell me that I would have to pay them back for my room and board from when I got pregnant if I want to leave, and I can't afford that. I have no money. Well, they locked me up to keep my baby safe." Katie sunk deeper in the couch in a huff. "Trying to keep my baby for the money they'd make from 'adopting.'" She made little quotation marks with her fingers. "We all know that they are selling it to the family that can afford it."

Tabitha nodded. "So you have been here for two years and you came here pregnant?"

Katie nodded, "Yes, my mom threw me out of the house when I got pregnant. I lived on the streets for a while, shacked up with friends when I could or just found people to take me in for a night here and there. I was in the train station, trying to stay warm, and I saw this ad for pregnant women with no place to go. It promised a safe home. They would pay all of your medical bills and assist you with finding a job after the baby was born. So I called.'

'Well, I got the woman who runs this program. They purchased a train ticket and had it waiting for me. All I had to do was go to the window and pick it up. So I hopped on the train and never looked back. I got off in New York, and some guy was waiting for me. He took me out to lunch and got me some food. I was so hungry and tired by that point that I just fell asleep on the way here. Damn fool, too. I woke up here and can not for the life of me tell you where the hell here is."

Katie heaved herself up and stood, placing a hand on her back. Tabitha jumped up to help her but the girl waved her away.

"And you've been here ever since?"

Katie nodded. She walked over to the sidebar and pouring some more of the clear juice into a tall glass. "Yeah, you must think me just something, rattling on and on. I don't see people much, so I get so darn bored. I kinda wish this baby would just be born already so I could get out of here, but then again, every day that I don't give birth I still have him with me." She glanced down at her belly, stroking it with a slow contemplative hand. When she glanced up, her smile had faded. "I am not sure I can give up another baby."

Tabitha leaned back on the couch, the conversation she had overheard between Antoine and Dylan nagging at her. "Katie, is Dylan the father of your baby?"

The girl nodded as she walked back and gingerly lowered herself onto the couch. "Oh, yes he is. I thought things were going to be so different. I thought he loved me..." Her laugh was a short brittle crack that ended in a choked cough. "Ain't that something you never thought you'd hear a pregnant teen admit? I thought he loved me. Damn fool that I am. Just like my mother, always looking for a man to take care of me. I'm looking for love, marriage, and that white picket fence." She glanced at Tabitha, her eyes mirroring her pain. "Does anybody ever get that? Their happily ever after?"

Tabitha shook her head. "Beats me. You are so asking the wrong person."

Katie nodded. "So, yeah, damn fool me. I coulda been out of here, getting my life back together. But nope, I meet this handsome and charming man who just swept me off my feet. We met while I was still pregnant with my ex's baby. We used to take walks outside or just sit and talk. He used to rub my feet. Sometimes I would fall asleep just lying in his arms. He was so sweet and kind. He never made me feel stupid. I actually thought he wanted to be with me. Well, then I had my baby and was recuperating. They give you a couple of months to try and get yourself back together physically. They give you counseling and start trying to get you interested in taking classes and all that." She snorted, "I coulda given a shit. I just wanted to be with Dylan. Well, wasn't long before we were going at it."

Tabitha could feel a blush tinge her face, but Katie didn't seem to notice.

"It was like we could not get enough of each other. Well, wasn't long before I was knocked up again, but I thought, hey, no big deal, right? I mean, he lives here. I'll just move in with him and we can have our baby together. Yeah, right. Well, in the beginning, he was all about us being together, and then it was like suddenly he lost interest. He just stopped coming around much and without so much as an explanation. I tried to find him in this damn huge house but I couldn't, and they kept me from walking around much.'

'Well, finally, he shows up, and—you ready for this? He has a frigging hickey on his neck. It seems he had taken up with a new little love and wanted nothing to do with me. I was so pissed, I threw everything that I could lay my hands on at him. Well, he then takes off again, telling me I am crazy after he just played with me.

"Well, next thing Antoine comes in, and we discuss my options. He lays down the rules for me and basically tells me, hey, either I leave my baby here or I owe them a whole boatload of money for my room and board. I told him I was going to the authorities, but he just laughed and said that I owed them for the months I had stayed. Well, one night, I did get out and I took off, heading any way to get out of here. I finally found a town, but I guess those people all work for this damn baby mill place. They turned me back in. I can tell you, the people in that village are petrified of these people. They wanted nothing to do with helping me. As soon as I said I wanted out, they clammed up and called for someone to come and get me. And you know what? They showed up in a damn horse and buggy, like this was the old friggin' West or something. I had it by that time. I wanted out, and I wanted some civilization.'

'Finally Antoine and I cut a deal. I told him I wanted out with my baby, but he refused. He told me that if I wanted out that bad, leave the baby here. I hate to do it, but I don't have a job and I don't have any money. He said once the baby is born, he will help me get on my feet and get a job."

Tabitha listened to the girl, her heart sinking. Her instincts suggested that the chance of Katie actually getting away once the baby was born was probably pretty slim. "I take it you are due soon?"

Katie nodded. "Yes, probably any day now. The midwife thinks it will be within the week. I just don't know what to do. I mean, he promised me I could go and that they would help me, but Tabitha, I don't want to leave another baby."

Tabitha nodded. "Well, I am not one to give you advice, but if you were to get out of here with your baby, what would you do? Where would you go?"

Katie shrugged. "I could try to go home. I am not sure if my mother would let me back, but I haven't talked to her in so long she probably thinks I am dead." Katie leaned forward, her hands resting on her knees beside her belly. "But I have something on them. They will have to give me what I want or else I tell the police what I know."

Tabitha felt a chill run up her spine as Katie glanced behind her. She was almost afraid to hear what the girl had to say.

"Dylan was telling me some pretty scary stuff that he has been involved with," Katie whispered. "He is a pretty arrogant guy, and he likes to brag when he thinks he's all tough and manly. He thought I was just so into him, he used to tell me all kinds of shit." Katie released a low and throaty chuckle.

Tabitha felt her mouth go dry as the noose around her own freedom began to tighten, "What kind of crimes?"

"Well, he is into some kind of gang thing. He has some kinda gang called the Black Elves...." Katie erupted into laughter and had to grab a cloth to wipe her eyes. "Black Elves? Can you believe a gang would call themselves something so stupid?"

Tabitha frowned. "So what did he do with this 'gang'?"

Katie shook her head. "I am not really sure, but I think some kinda home invasion shit. He brags like has some kind of control over these gang guys. He tells them where to go and who to attack. He was in someplace called Vuelac or something like that and left those people terrified. He comes around every once in a while with a gun and pretends like he is some cowboy or something." Katie shook her head.

Vuelac? Vuelac? Why did that sound so familiar? Tabitha's gut tightened when the story from Luc's council meeting came back to her. Homes were broken into in the dead of night, the occupants dead and children missing.

"A gun?" Tabitha whispered as theories began to formulate. The account about the break-in had reported that the people had been killed without any markings. And children were missing.

A cold chill ran through her as she went to the window, rubbing her arms. The last time she had overheard Antoine and Dylan talking, Dylan had done something and left a clue. Left a survivor.

"Yeah, you know, breaking in, brandishing guns like in an old mobster movie. People cowering...He got off on how scared they were."

But where had they gotten guns? Here?

"Katie, do you remember the name of the people you first called when you found that ad? Who did you speak to?"

Katie stood and joined her at the window. "Some attorney in Boston, I think. Victoria something...it was like some Italian name."

Tabitha inhaled deeply. Pieces were beginning to slip into place. She turned back to Katie. "You know you have to get out of here."

Katie's expression shifted from a defiant stare to uncertainty to a long and sad look. After many moments she slowly nodded. Her voice was barely a whisper. "I know. I know. I want to believe that they mean what they tell me, but I am afraid that once my baby is born, they will kill me."

"I have friends. Let me try to help you get out of here. Let me see if I can find a way to get you and the baby out of here."

Katie's face beamed. "Will you really? Do you promise?"

Tabitha nodded. "I have to get out of here without being seen first, and I promise I will see what I can do to get you out of here."

"Tell me how to help. What can I do to—"

Tabitha laughed. "Nothing. Trust me. Just stay put, and don't do anything stupid." She went over to the door, looking for a handle or something to open it with. "Don't mention that you met me."

Katie nodded eagerly and followed her with a worried and determined look on her face. Tabitha felt guilty for giving her hope. Could she possibly deliver on her promise? Would Gwyn and Cole help her and risk their own safety and possibly their lives? What about Jules? How much did he know? Could she trust him to help get Katie away before Antoine and Dylan took her child and then quite possibly killed her?

The door remained sealed. Tabitha crouched on the floor by the seam in frustration. There had to be some way to get the door open. There had to be some simple trigger.

Maybe it required power. If she used it, would she leave some personal mental print that would give away that she had been here?

She shushed Katie and let her senses extend to the door's inner mechanisms. As she traced the seam and let her thoughts extend into the doorway, she felt along, trying to find the latch to open the door. She had seen it slide soundlessly when Antoine had come through, but how...? And then she found it. A small lever was pressed down to the door latch. She could feel the imprint and the barely detectable shimmer of power that held it in place. She knew if she touched it, she would leave behind her own imprint so she traced along, looking for other options. If she could just manipulate the latch instead of the lever, she might be able to slip the door open without leaving evidence behind.

Suddenly, she could feel another mind on the outside of the door. She realized with horror that someone was coming in. She swallowed the cry in her throat and jumped from the door, throwing herself behind a tiny table holding a lamp.

She was out in the open. Her heart thudded in her throat; whoever was walking in that door would see her if they simply glanced to the left.

Katie's eyes were huge with fear as they jumped from Tabitha's panicked face to the door as it quietly slid open.

CHAPTER NINE

TABITHA HELD HER BREATH, HER HEART THUMPING AS Dylan strode into the room. Katie's face was a mask of undisguised panic. She glanced at Tabitha, who quickly shook her head and signaled for Katie to relax.

"What is wrong?" Dylan demanded.

Katie swallowed visibly, her agitation getting the best of her for a moment. Her mouth opened and snapped shut but nothing came out.

Dylan stood with his hands on his hips. "What is it? You look like…"

He started to glance around the room. Katie cried out and grasped at her middle. "I think I may be going into labor."

"Wait, I will get the midwife." Dylan started to turn just as Tabitha was crawling out from behind the table to slip behind the drapes.

"No!" Katie cried out, as though another pain shot through her. She tugged his arm and he assisted her to the couch. When his back was turned, Tabitha slid behind the drapes and tried to catch her breath.

"Why are you here?" Katie snapped as she shoved his hand away from her and settled herself on the couch.

Dylan stood, his arm hanging before him as though he was unsure what to do with it. "I was worried for you. I knew you were upset—"

"Oh, screw you. You know what? Take your worry and hit the road. I could care less if you thought I *was upset* ..." Katie bracketed the last words in a snide tone, her fingers forming quotation marks.

Dylan knelt before her, his arms held out beseechingly. "Katie, it doesn't have to be like this. I know you were hurt over that other woman, but I am not with her anymore. I missed you. Forgive me. I was just playing around with her. You are the one I want, you and our baby."

Katie slapped his hands away from her as she glared at him. "I am not buying any of your shit today. Get out of here. I don't know why the hell you came back. You could care less about me. Where the hell have you been all these months? It was like your only objective was to get me pregnant and then you took off like your ass was on fire."

Tabitha hid a soft laugh and thought that Katie was probably closer to the truth than she knew.

Dylan continued to cajole and whine in an effort to gather some semblance of forgiveness. Katie ignored him, her rage at his absence still at full throttle. She winced again in pain. Dylan rose to get the midwife, but Katie refused.

"It could be hours," she mumbled as she reached for her glass of juice. As she lifted it toward her mouth, the glass slid from her fingers. The contents splattered across her front.

Dylan leaped out of the way. Katie's eyes watered as she moaned about her soaked clothes. "Goddammit, Dylan, look what you have made me do! You come in here and get me all upset and look what happens! Help me up. Right now! I have to get out of these wet things!"

Dylan seemed at a loss as he stood and helped her off the couch.

"Well, don't just stand there like a lout, help me into the other room. I could use some help peeling these wet things off me."

Katie started to head into the adjacent room, shoving Dylan toward the door. As she entered the other room, she glanced back at Tabitha and with a wink and a slight motion of her head indicated that she should leave.

Tabitha wasted little time and slid over to the door. She gave the latch a mental nudge, sliding it out of the lever, and the door soundlessly opened. She hurried through and locked it, leaving the room in all possible haste.

Tabitha's breath was ragged. She envisioned Dylan racing behind her at every turn of the stairwell. She had to give Katie credit. After just discussing the possibility that her life might be in imminent danger from Antoine and Dylan, she had recovered enough to get Tabitha out of the room.

Tabitha rounded the last curve in the stairwell and headed toward her rooms, her nerves still humming from the near escape, when Antoine's voice cut through the hallway, halting her.

"Tabitha!"

She turned to find him at the door of his private study. "Join me, please. I have something to discuss with you."

She wondered if she had any possible excuse for putting this off, but remembering Katie's composure, she squared her shoulders and entered the room. The door shut behind her with what felt like an ominous click.

Antoine waved her toward a chair and went behind his desk to retrieve a box. He slapped the long narrow box against his thigh as he came around the desk to where she perched on the edge of her seat.

"You look ready to flee. Please, relax!" He chuckled as he sat on the couch across from her. "Jules tells me you have not been feeling well. Are you recovered?"

Tabitha tried to relax and leaned back in her seat. "Yes, thank you."

"Good, good. Jules has told you of the ball I am hosting tomorrow night? I also understand that the seamstress is working on an appropriate ensemble for you?"

"Yes, it is lovely," Tabitha mumbled.

"Excellent. You know, Tabitha, you will be meeting many of the elite of my world tomorrow night. I shall be most proud to present you as my daughter." He leaned back, lifting a hot cup of javé to his lips. "Tell me, are you enjoying your stay here with us?"

Tabitha nodded. "Yes, your home is beautiful."

He laughed softly. "This is your home as well, you know. My door will always be open to you. Truth be known, from what I have been able to discover your own world has little to offer you. You seem to have left at odds with your aunt, and if I am not mistaken, you and your most recent love recently parted company. Greg? Was that his name?"

Tabitha actually felt her mouth drop in shock. Where had he gotten this information about her? How had he found out about her life? She was not prepared at all for this, and no answer escaped her.

He continued. "We have so much to offer you here. You would live like royalty. You would have your choice of mates, your choice of lives and where to live. I can open any door you wish."

She stammered, still struggling with his knowledge about her, but he lifted a finger to delay her response.

"Please. I am not asking that you tell me tonight that you wish to stay." He extended a hand and gently squeezed her fingers. "I only ask that you consider it. I want nothing more than to make up for all the time I lost not knowing you as you grew into such an incredible woman."

He lifted the long box and presented it to her. She took the box and gently lifted the cover. A long silver chain, exquisitely made, sparkled back at her from the deep ebony velvet of the box. On its end hung a silver charm, a crescent moon with a single sparkling diamond at its top.

She gently lifted the chain and let the elegant charm spin before her eyes. She dragged her eyes away from the dangling charm and met his cool and calm gaze.

"I am not sure if you are aware, but in our world, young boys and girls are given a token when they enter adulthood. I wish I had known you back then to give this to you, but alas, I can only do it now. The token is a very special and intimate design; it captures the personality and the soul of its wearer. Parents take years designing their children's tokens. I did not have that option. But I thought of this for you. You are so very like the moon, a single luminescent envoy, so cool and calm but yet so distant. I wonder how many people truly know you or get the opportunity to get beyond your surface sheen. You sparkle and shine, yet you remain so very far away," he observed.

Tabitha did not know what to say. She felt a strange sensation of fear about wearing the charm, as though she would be committing herself to this world. She was not sure she was ready for him to think she could possibly do that.

"So are you aware of the importance of the token?" he asked. She shook her head, and he continued. "Boys are given a gold chain and girls silver. When a couple is promised to commit to each other in marriage, they exchange tokens in the promise ceremony. The man wears the woman's token and she wears his until they actually tie the knot. It is important that upon being presented tomorrow evening you appear with your token." He paused, his gaze intent. "It would not do to have people wonder about your upbringing. We do not wish people to know you are new to our world. That would beg too many questions."

Tabitha nodded and slipped the necklace back into its box. She bid her father good night and left. As she made her way slowly to her rooms, confusion reigned over her emotions.

Was she wrong to think the worst? Where was proof that everything people were telling her about her father was true?

She entered her room, her thoughts still distant before a shadow separated itself from the gloom, startling her. Her fear dissipated as a young girl stepped forward. "I did not mean to frighten you. I apologize."

Tabitha smiled and shrugged. She was tired and heavy from the day, and she just wanted to slip into bed.

The girl stoked the fire and gestured toward a tray of food set before the fireplace. "I thought you might be tired tonight and wish to dine alone," she said quietly.

Tabitha nodded and thanked the girl. To her surprise, the girl did not depart immediately but began to pick up stray pillows and things around the room, setting them in their places. She disappeared into the sleeping area. Tabitha could hear her turning down the bed and setting out a steaming pot of water for tea.

"You have had a busy day?" the girl asked, her soft voice barely above a whisper.

Tabitha nodded. "It has been a long one. You know those days when there is more emotional turmoil than physical? They sometimes are the more exhausting."

The girl nodded and took a seat across from her. "My name is Lena."

Tabitha smiled. "Hi, Lena. You are the first person in my father's house staff to bother to introduce yourself. Most of them try their best to be unobtrusive. It is nice to have someone be friendly."

Lena's smile was shy, and she ducked her head behind a curtain of long brown hair. She glanced back up, her large brown eyes were doe-like, and her face was small and heart-shaped; her tiny mouth puckered into a pleasant smile. She was small and slender, her limbs long and willowy. As she moved around the room, she made hardly a sound.

"I have been waiting for the chance to speak to you. It is not always easy to ensure I am in your personal room. I had to wait until the right opportunity."

Tabitha frowned. "Speak to me about what?"

Lena grinned, a little shy smile that alluded to some intimate secret. "I am here on behalf of Cole."

"Cole? He sent you?"

She nodded. "I not only have a message but I wanted to meet you myself."

"Really? Okay, so what is the message?"

"Cole is fearful that with the upcoming ball you will find it difficult to sneak out. Of course, with the visiting dignitaries you will be hard-pressed to leave unobserved. He will communicate the best nights for you to meet with him and Gwyn through me."

Tabitha nodded. "Okay, great. Thanks. So will I be able to get messages to him through you as well?"

Lena nodded and smiled. "Yes, but do not write them down, only tell me when we can meet. I will get the message to him." She cocked her head and looked at Tabitha with interest. "It is so funny to think of you as brother and sister. You do not look much alike, although I can see your smile and his are the same."

Tabitha lifted a brow in surprise. "You know we are brother and sister?"

Lena laughed as she rose. "Cole and I do not have secrets."

Tabitha stood also and then caught on. "Oh! So that is why you wanted to meet me?"

Lena nodded as she went to the door. "He was so very happy to finally find you. He had spoken often of feeling as though he was missing something. Even though you did not grow up together, he always knew he had a sister out there and wanted so very badly to know you."

Tabitha felt tears sting her eyes. "I grew up not knowing my family at all. Here I am, grown, and I find out I have two brothers and a father. It has been a very interesting summer."

Lena's eyes grew haunted as she nodded, but before Tabitha could comment, she bid her good night and slipped from the room.

The evening air filtered through the window. Tabitha stood alone, staring out at the bright stars twinkling in the deep velvet sky. Were they the same stars as in her world? Were they in a different dimension but around the same planet? Was everything else the same except for that one difference? Was this what her world could have been? Should have been? Or vice versa? But her world lacked magic.

She tore her eyes from the window and turned again to the looking glass. She hardly recognized herself. The tall elegant woman in the long silver dress staring back at her was a stranger. Tabitha felt as though she were seeing herself as she could have been had she grown up here instead. The girl who had assisted her in getting ready had done wonders with her dark tresses, which were elegantly coiffed and spilled down over one shoulder. The dress was fitted to her frame perfectly, a long slender shimmering design that hung almost to her ankles, leaving enough room to reveal the matching silver shoes with tiny bells dangling from the ankle straps. The seamstress had certainly found a way to accent her full breasts and narrow waist. A light blush tinged her cheeks at image in the mirror of the swell of her breasts over the dress's décolletage. The dress hugged her ribs and waist down to her hips like a second skin before flaring gently out at her hips to fall in a graceful flow as she walked. Her token sparkled in the well of her cleavage. The set of dangling earrings and the matching bracelet her father had bestowed upon her completed the look of his well-dressed and elegant daughter.

There was a gentle knock on the door, and Jules entered in his finery: a well-cut waistcoat of deep brown over fawn-colored pants. His shirt was ivory cotton, the small collar, left unfastened at the top. Small epaulettes decorated the shoulders of his coat with tiny gold chains that looped down. Dark brown boots came to his knee, and a single shimmering long gold knife hung from an elegant wide leather strap at his hip; the lower edge of the slim blade's sheath was fastened just above his knee.

"You do look lovely," Jules commented with a slight bow.

She nodded and smiled. "Thank you, Jules. As do you. And the sword—are you expecting trouble?"

"No, it is simply part of our finery. You will see most people wearing them, as is our custom. In fact..." He held out a shining long-bladed silver knife sheathed in an intricate silver holder, a simple silver chain attached to it. "To complete your ensemble."

Tabitha accepted the rapier, never having worn or used a blade for anything other than cutting food. She slid it out of its case; it sparkled brightly. She gently touched the edge with a finger; it was sharply honed. This was not some trinket. It was a fine weapon. She was startled.

"I am supposed to wear this?"

Jules nodded, taking it from her hands. "May I?"

She nodded, and he proceeded to step behind her, slipping the silver chain around her slim hips. "Most women wear a slender rapier and most men a larger sword. Some women prefer to wear two of the slimmer variety. It depends on their preference and skill with either weapon."

"Skill? Are all women trained in these weapons?" She remembered the evening when the Faye had come looking for her at Luc's home. While the men had gone to meet the threat, the women had stayed behind to protect the homestead. Sybille, Peri, and Alena had all produced similar slim blades, as well as long bows, in preparation for defending their home.

"Yes, the women as well as the men are trained in using an assortment of weapons. Women generally prefer the slimmer blades. They do not necessarily have the upper body strength of a man, and their reflexes are generally quicker. I have found that with a pair of short blades most women are very deadly and very accurate. Both train with the bow. As they grow older, they tend to identify a weapon of choice to hone their skills on." He finished hanging the silver blade. The chain hung loosely on her hips; the end of it hung almost to her knees. She stared down at this addition to her ensemble curiously. She had never imagined herself wearing any kind of weapon before. The weight of the blade at her hip reminded her of the difference between the worlds and the very real danger surrounding her in this new one.

"You are ready? I believe your father is waiting for you to make your entrance."

Tabitha nodded. "Let's get this night over with."

CHAPTER TEN

JULES ESCORTED TABITHA DOWN TO THE GRAND BALLROOM on one of the lower floors of the estate. She clung to his arm on the stairs, willing her feet to not tangle on the edge of the dress or trip in her fancy shoes. As elegant as she felt, she knew she was better off not moving, as every step in her newly acquired finery could easily send her tumbling.

Her stress over her attire disappeared as they slowly made their way down the last steps of the grand staircase into a large round ceramic-floored foyer. People milled about in small groups. The large glass doors leading into the grand ballroom were flung wide. Tabitha caught her breath at the transformation of the simple large seating area into a warm and beautifully decorated ballroom.

For just a moment, they stood at the doorway. Tabitha had to remember to shut her mouth to keep from gaping at the splendor. The room's usual furnishings had all been removed, and the deep wood flooring was polished to a brilliant shine that caught the light from the hundreds of candles placed about the room. The room had a domed ceiling with cut-glass panels that let the beautiful late summer moonlight stream in and illuminate the room in a silvery haze.

Guests were wandering the room in their fine clothes holding elegant glasses filled with assorted colored beverages. She could not help but stare as people wandered by her, some hand in hand, gently bowing to one another, greeting old friends and shaking hands. Women pressed cheeks and men extended hands in greeting. Many of the women were in floor-length gowns; Tabitha could not get over the various weapon accessories adorning their ensembles. Many had cut jewels placed within the sheaths or highly decorated and jewel encrusted belts. Some wore matching blades resting on theirs hips, the belts and sashes constructed into their beautiful gowns.

The men, in their various-colored waistcoats and vests, tall boots polished to a shine, were equally as elegant. Most also wore slim blades along their legs like Jules, but many also carried long swords in an assortment of sheaths, from highly decorated to simple leather with fine-tooled etchings.

It took her a few moments to realize that as she stood staring at the room of people, many were also turning to stare at her. Men gazed openly with appreciation and the women with curiosity as Jules began to slowly escort her into the room.

"Why is everyone staring at me?" Tabitha asked quietly.

As he bowed his head in acknowledgement to various people as they made their way through the room, Jules's response was low. "Many are wondering if you are the mysterious daughter they have been hearing of. Your sudden appearance has caused quite a stir. Your father is a high official in our society. To find out he has a grown daughter none of them knew about has caused some uproar. No one knows from where you have come, so please use discretion when responding to that question. Simply tell people you have been living with your mother. Do not elaborate."

Tabitha's further questions were cut short as they approached her father. Antoine looked regal in his dark jacket, burgundy vest, brilliant white shirt, and white pants. Black boots completed his attire, and a long broadsword hung below his knee. His long dark hair was pulled back and tied at his nape.

He eyed Tabitha appreciatively and held out his arm to her. "You look magnificent, my dear. I am proud to have you on my arm this evening. I have no doubt that you will cause a commotion among the single males of our community this night."

Tabitha smiled and responded, barely knowing what she said under the weight of the eyes watching them closely. She felt herself tremble slightly at the attention. She was not accustomed to being the center of such observation, and it was unnerving.

Antoine squeezed her hand slightly and began introducing her around the room. She walked slowly along with him, trying desperately to remember names. People gathered around them in a throng, craning their necks to try and catch a glimpse of Antoine's mysterious daughter. Word traveled through the room, and more people joined in the swell of people surrounding them. Tabitha clung to her father's arm. Outwardly her mannerisms were cool and refined, but inside she was terrified. She thanked Jules under her breath often for helping her hone her shields so well. Had she been exposed to this before learning to protect herself, she had no doubt she would have fled by now in panic.

It seemed that the line of single men awaiting an introduction would never dissipate. Tabitha finally had to beg

Antoine for a few minutes and a drink. He chuckled warmly and excused them, signaling for a drink to be brought over. She sipped at a tall cool glass of a honey-colored beverage with assorted colorful bits floating in it. The press of people seemed to have relented slightly. Antoine held her close by him as he spoke to a small group of his advisors and the emissaries of the various regions.

She wondered briefly when Luc would be arriving, but pain and loneliness engulfed her when she thought of him, so she banished him from her mind. It seemed like a lifetime since she had spoken to him, and her uncertainties flared every time he came into her thoughts. The conversation she had overheard between Antoine and Dylan had solidified her resolve to get over him. He was, obviously, over her if he was already being considered as a potential suitor for Dylan's sister.

Of course, the other doubt that nagged at her was concern that he might be her older brother. It would certainly explain why, of all the people in this world, he was the one she was linked to. But if that were the case, why not Cole as well?

Her musings were interrupted when one of her father's guests asked her a question and she was tugged her back into the conversation. Her father kept them moving, and the groups kept changing. He seemed a master at maintaining a steady pace through the room, meeting and greeting everyone and keeping the conversation flowing until he was prepared to move onto the next group.

Tabitha shook hands and was kissed as she was introduced to countless faces and names. Antoine deflected any detailed questions about her and kept the conversations general in nature, effectively keeping her from answering.

The guests seemed even more intrigued because details about this enigmatic daughter of his seemed elusive. Antoine let slip some small detail about her to one group and another tidbit to another until the entire room was buzzing and trading what little knowledge they had gleaned.

Her nerves were irritated under the constant focus. When dinner was served, she picked at her food. The flow of conversation and the genial atmosphere were pleasant enough, but Tabitha was tired of being on display.

After dinner, Antoine was pulled away for a few moments. Tabitha glanced over and noticed Dylan across the room, his eyes intent upon her. A chill swept her body, and she looked for an escape route, but he was threading his way through the crowd, his gaze fastened upon her.

She tried to slip around a small knot of people, but as people realized she was alone, she found herself being grasped at and dragged over to chat. Alarm spread through her as Dylan drew closer. Tabitha could not help but wonder if he had detected her presence in Katie's room.

Noting that Dylan had been drawn into a small knot of people, Tabitha quickly excused herself. With his back to her, she quickly darted for the nearest door and escaped onto the veranda. A low stone railing rimmed a wide white stone patio. Moonlight lit the grounds extending out from the house. She had not intended to slip outside, but the air calmed her raging nerves. She stepped to the railing and rested her hands along the cool stone, letting the calm of the night seep through her.

Hey, Beautiful.

Warmth flooded through her when that familiar voice echoed through the vaults of her mind. Tabitha spun around, and there he stood, tall and more handsome than her memory did him justice. His jacket was black with gold-threaded trim; his black pants and tall polished black boots accented his muscular frame. A long sword hung at his side within a finely tooled scabbard of intricate design. Her breath left her and every sane thought fled her head. All she could do was gape at him, drinking in his presence. For the first time in many weeks, pain did not fill her chest. Instead her heart fluttered with excitement.

"Luc!" she breathed. She tried desperately to find a witty comment, a sultry line of welcome, but her tongue had grown heavy and all her wit had slid from her addled brain.

His smile was slow and seductive. As he slowly walked toward her, she saw the twinkle in those amazing blue eyes and she melted.

"You look amazing!" His scrutiny was slow, not missing one detail. She felt her breath leave her lungs with a thump. "I've missed you."

Tabitha felt her mouth curve into a pleased smile. Her brain slowly began to click into rhythm as she reined in her wildly cascading emotions. "Have you? I would have thought you were too busy to think of me."

He grinned and stopped next to her, facing her, one hip leaning against the wall. "You were never far from my thoughts." He lifted her hand gently and leaned down to place a warm kiss on its back. "I wanted to reach out to you a thousand times."

She tugged her tingling fingers from his grip and stepped back slowly, taking a moment to tear her eyes from him to try and salvage some dignity. She was quite sure he realized the effect he was having on her. She responded in a soft whisper. "Why didn't you? The silence has been deafening."

"If you recall, it was your suggestion that we not communicate. You thought it best that no one be able to detect our link." He tilted his head, watching her closely for her reaction.

She lowered her gaze, unable to dive into his eyes again without losing herself. *For once someone actually listened to me?*

"It was probably for the best. It has been a very busy couple of weeks," she commented.

"I am sure. How are you finding your father?" he asked.

She shrugged. "Well, I have had some time to get to know him, and I have enjoyed that. It has been a very interesting experience."

"And your mother? Any update on her whereabouts?"

She shook her head. "Only that she was here. I met the woman she visited. She came and went without leaving word of where she was going." She closed her eyes. "I have so much to tell you—I am not sure where to start."

"I have only just arrived. Why not start at the beginning and tell me everything?" he suggested, slipping up behind her. He placed his warm hands gently on her bare shoulders, tugging her back against him, setting her body on fire with his simple touch.

She let her head drop back and leaned into his arms, feeling for all the world as though she were finally relaxed and right where she needed to be. His arms tightened about her and his mouth dropped gently down to one bare shoulder, sending shivers of delight through her body, as though his kiss set her blood ablaze.

When his fingers tightened on her waist, Tabitha started to turn in his arms, mesmerized by the closeness of his body. His head dipped toward her mouth. Suddenly doubts rang through her head like a warning bell, and she slipped out of his arms and danced a step or two away from him.

She laughed nervously at his startled expression and took another step away from him. She tried to keep her voice playful when she glanced back at him over her shoulder. "Aren't you getting a bit too familiar? After all—"

"What is wrong?" He stepped toward her and she took a step back.

"I just think that under the circumstances, we should perhaps keep things a bit more casual, don't you?" She continued to step along the wall, trailing her hands casually along the smooth stone as though their meeting were nothing more than a chance encounter between friends. But her heart yearned to slip into his arms and slide her fingers through his silky hair. She wanted to bury her soul deep within him and emerge only when her need for his nearness had finally been quenched.

"Tabitha—" he began as he stalked her, his eyes fastened upon her, trying to mentally break down the barrier she had raised between them.

She lifted a hand, his assault battering her weakened defenses. "Luc! Please! I am trying to hold onto some semblance of dignity here."

He stopped. "Dignity? I was trying to kiss you. How did this become about your dignity? Did I insult you?"

"No! It's just that…I mean…Dammit, Luc!" She slid away from him, burying her hands in her hair as though to block out his words.

"What? Tell me!" he demanded, his frustration rising when she tried to hide her face from him.

"How can you do this to me? Do you think that because you know I must leave that you can play with me?" she snapped.

He looked genuinely perplexed. He stopped. "Play with you? What am I missing?"

She shook her head, not wanting to go into any more detail. Why couldn't he just admit that she was only someone he planned to play with until she left, and then he would get down to the more serious business of wedding Dylan's sister. "Luc, listen. I will be returning home. I have some things to tie up here and then I am leaving. I will not be back. You have your life to get on with. Quite frankly, I have been an unnecessary distraction. Had I not arrived, you could have gone on with your plans and I would not have interfered. But as it is...now I have to think about myself and just do what I have to do to—"

"Well, imagine finding the two of you out here!" Dylan strode onto the patio, his smile calculating as he observed the pair of them, several feet apart and obviously in a serious discussion.

"Dylan," Luc greeted him, his smile slow to reach his eyes as he extended a hand. "Perfect timing, as ever."

"Well, I should not be surprised to have caught you out here after barely having arrived. Already you are entertaining the most beautiful woman in the room," Dylan commented smoothly, his eyes gleaming with humor when he turned to Tabitha. "I must admit that I have spent the better part of the night working my way over to meet you, but it seems every time I find myself free, your attention is being drawn away."

"I have been kept more than occupied tonight," Tabitha commented smoothly, hoping for a way to extricate herself from the two old friends.

"Yes. You have been very much an enigma this night. Your sudden appearance and your mysterious background have given the masses a month's worth of gossip to chew. People are wondering where you have been and why Antoine never alluded to your existence. Such an interesting turn of events," Dylan commented, leaning back against the wall with an inscrutable smile.

Tabitha inhaled, not prepared to spar with him so soon after her emotion over Luc's sudden appearance.

"Well, I am sure that my father will be able to put the stories to rest in his own time. If there is one thing I have learned from him, it is that he has a reason for everything he does. In the meantime, I wish to keep to myself, enjoy my visit with my father, and then just get back to my life. He can deal with people's curiosity." Her statement was a simple closing of the subject. She hoped Dylan would be able to leave well enough alone.

He grinned at her sardonic response. "Do you know who I am?"

Luc interrupted. "Dylan, this is not the time for introductions. Tabitha and I were just discussing something. If you don't mind, this is a conversation we need to finish."

Dylan ignored his request. "Well, now that you have finally arrived, I would imagine the two of you will have plenty of time to get back to your drama. It won't take all that long for Tabitha to meet me, and then I will leave the two of you to your discussion."

Tabitha exhaled loudly and turned to Luc. "He is not going to leave." She turned to Dylan. "I am not trying to be rude, but I know who you are and I know what you are doing here."

Dylan cocked a brow at her. "Do you? Well, I am surprised. I would have thought that knowing who I was, you would have been more apt to make an attempt to meet me."

For just a moment, the chill in his voice sent a shiver down Tabitha's spine, and she wondered at the wisdom of choosing this more direct approach. She paused in indecision, concerned that if he had been able to detect her presence when he left Katie's room, she could be digging herself a hole. "Well—I know of you by reputation. There has been plenty of gossip about you in the halls. Apparently you are a favorite of my father's, the son of Polan, the Southern ambassador and, rumor has it, potentially a favorite to be chosen as a possible successor to my father."

Dylan nodded, the slightest of grins twisting his mouth. "So that is what you know of me? Of my ambitions? You have proven that you are learning your way around these halls, after all. Anyone who knows Antoine knows to keep their ear to the ground, for that shaking you hear is the tremor of change."

She shrugged. "Anyone can pick up gossip. This place is festering with it. So tell me, why have you been so interested in meeting me?"

He snorted lightly. "I see. So you have heard my name bandied about in connection with your father's and you have heard the rumors about my aspirations. I thought you had figured it all out, but I see that you have not."

"Dylan, where is this going? Do we have to have this conversation right now?" Luc asked, exasperated. "Can't you find another time to be obtuse? I have not seen Tabitha in a number of weeks, and I really would like a few minutes to catch up with her. What the hell is all the rush about you meeting her right now?"

"He is here to keep us from our conversation," Tabitha said quietly.

Both men turned to her, Dylan with interest and Luc in surprise. "Why should he care if we have a discussion? You two have not even met yet."

Tabitha stepped back from the two of them in irritation. The last thing she had wanted was to bring this up, but it seemed that Luc was going to intentionally avoid the subject, so it was up to her to bring it to light. "He is trying to keep us apart because there has been talk about you as a potential—" she struggled with the word "—mate for his sister."

"What?" Luc looked stunned.

Dylan exploded with laughter. "Wo ho! What I would not give to know your sources! Wherever did you hear that? I don't deny it, but that is fairly private knowledge! You will have to share where you are hearing this from!"

Luc shook his head. "Dylan doesn't have a sister."

"Really?" Tabitha challenged. "He just said he didn't deny it."

"I have known him for years, and I even spent time with his family. He is a single child," Luc retorted.

"Well, how can that be if you are a potential suitor for his sister?" Tabitha spat, frustration and jealousy rearing their heads. "What were your intentions? To lead me on? Get me into bed and then see me off to go back home and return to dating his sister?" She flung up an arm to point at the grinning Dylan. She wanted to slap that grin from his face. "Tell him!"

Luc stared from one to the other. "What sister? I have no involvements or—" He turned to Dylan. "What sister?"

Dylan threw back his head and laughed, "Oh, this is great! I must say, my old friend, I cannot recall ever seeing you at a loss." He pointed at Luc with his chin as he addressed Tabitha. "We went to school together as children, right up to college. Luc here was always the eloquent orator. He could argue any point articulately and with skill. It is truly a great moment to see him at a loss for words."

He turned back to Luc and shook his head. "You are right. I am Polan and Matir's only child." He sent Tabitha a sidelong glance as he continued. "What you do not know is that I am not the only child of my biological mother."

Both Tabitha and Luc turned to him. Tabitha still felt the jealous clench in her gut, but as he continued speaking, a slow seed of dread began to blossom in her belly.

"Polan adopted me as a baby. My adoptive parents remained in contact with the people who put me up for adoption. For a few years, they lived quite close, so contact was made fairly often. It was not until several years after my birth when my birth mother disappeared. Polan's father grew ill down in Fallomar so we moved down south. That is where she pursued her career in government. Having been taken under the wing of Antoine's father, a master politician, her rise through the political world was quick and sure."

"She knew my grandfather?" Tabitha's mouth was dry.

He nodded. "She did, as well as your father. She was an advisor here. When she opted to move back to Fallomar, he was able to assist her in her political career. So to conclude my story, my birth mother gave birth to my younger sister just a few years after I was born and subsequently disappeared with her for many years…"

Tabitha stepped back from him. *"You?"*

Dylan nodded and grinned at her, a wide predatory smile. "Yes, sweet sister. I am Mother's first son."

She turned to Luc. "So that means that you could not be…"

Luc's eyes were wide, his expression amazed. "You thought *I* was your *brother*?"

Dylan's howl of laughter was like the shattering of a huge pane of glass in a quiet space. Tabitha cringed at the sound, wanting to put her hands to her ears and just hide from his annoying glee.

"I knew my mother had a son two years before I was born, and that would explain—" She stopped, horrified with what she had almost let slip. The last thing she wanted was for Dylan to know of her link with Luc.

"But my mother died when I was young. I have pictures of her. She had black hair and blue eyes. Her name was Yolanda. She was not your mother. How could you have thought I was your brother? Is that why you wouldn't kiss me?" Luc demanded.

This brought fresh peals of laughter from Dylan. Suddenly Luc was turning to him, fury spitting from his eyes. "Dylan, it is time you left us. Don't make me ask you again."

Dylan lifted his hands at his friend's rage and backed a step. "I apologize for my humor. But this whole debacle is more entertaining than I had anticipated. I would have been more gentle about breaking the news to my sweet little sister, but she seems to have taken a dislike to me for some reason."

Tabitha turned to him. "I cannot believe you just blurted it out like that. And even when I told you what I had heard about 'your sister' and this ridiculous notion of finding her a husband, you still toyed with us."

He shrugged. "This was really too enjoyable! I will leave the two of you to your 'discussion', although I assume that the subject has shifted!"

As he turned to leave, he glanced back at Tabitha, and his smile dimmed. "You are right, though. We do have other things to discuss, but they can wait until later."

With that, he turned on his heel and departed, leaving Tabitha staring after him in shock and bewilderment.

"What the hell just happened?" she whispered.

CHAPTER ELEVEN

LUC TURNED SLOWLY BACK TO TABITHA AS DYLAN sauntered back to the party. He leaned against the wall and lifted his eyes slowly to her. "You want to start at the beginning? You not only thought I was your brother but you also thought I was to be promised to Dylan's sister? Who, incidentally, ends up being you."

Tabitha felt her face burn with embarrassment. Confronting Luc about the apparent plan to promise him to Dylan's sister had not turned out as she had anticipated. "Oh, God, I am not sure where to even start."

Luc nodded slowly, his arms crossed in front of him. "This should be interesting."

A loud scream and commotion inside caught their attention before the sound of Antoine's shout sent both Tabitha and Luc running for the door. They entered to see a man, dressed in a servant's clothing, brandishing a sword at Antoine. His face was contorted in rage, and he snarled at anyone who attempted to get too close.

"Luc, what is going on?" Tabitha whispered when Luc stopped beside her, a protective arm thrown about her waist. He shook his head.

Jules was suddenly beside her. "I think it's time we get you away from this predicament."

Tabitha shook her head. "What is it? Why is he trying to kill my father?"

The man screamed, "Where is my son? What did you do with him?"

Antoine's voice was low as he tried to calm the man. The man howled in rage and edged nearer, the sword inching ever closer to Antoine's throat.

Jules explained, "The man is a human from town. His wife recently died after giving birth. Their son was taken away for adoption to pay their debt." Jules tried to move Tabitha away from the crowd.

"They *took* his son?" Tabitha gasped in horror.

"It is not entirely uncommon," Jules said sadly. "People become so deeply indebted."

"*Quiet!*" the man shrieked. He spun around, pointing the sword toward the crowd. One of Antoine's personal guards was moving up behind the man, and in a deft effort to avoid being taken, the man jumped behind Antoine and grabbed him. They tumbled, and Antoine wrestled free.

More of Antoine's personal guards dove into the fracas. Jules and Luc each grabbed an arm to pull Tabitha away from the fight as the distraught man dragged Antoine down, shouting that he needed to know where his son was before he killed him. Tabitha was led away from the fight; she glanced back, trying to see what had happened to her father as they hustled her past the pair of struggling men. As he was dragged to the floor, the man clutched Antoine's shirt with his fist. Tabitha saw twin scar marks revealed on the side of her father's throat before she was quickly drawn out of the room.

"Wait!" she screamed. The sight of those marks was like a lightning strike.

Luc was beside her, his arms around her, lifting her through the door. "Later! Tabitha, you have to get out of here," he growled as he and Jules pushed her toward the foyer.

"Luc, but…wait! My God…"

"Later, Tabitha! That man may not be working alone. You are Antoine's daughter, and we have to get you out of here!" Luc's voice was near her ear as he hastened her to the door.

Jules was waiting by the door. "Quickly."

Luc handed Tabitha to Jules. "Wait for me. I will be right back."

Jules nodded. As Luc turned to fight his way through the panicking crowd racing from the hall, Jules took her hand and swept Tabitha toward the stairway.

"But he told me to wait…"

"He will be right behind you, I guarantee it," Jules reassured her as he shuffled her toward the stairs down to the front entrance. A servant stood several steps down, and Jules gestured toward the man. "Follow him. Luc will be right behind you. It is imperative that we get you to safety."

She began to argue, but the servant stepped from the shadows and clasped her hand. The shock of blond hair was familiar, and Tabitha gasped. "Cole? What are you doing here?"

"Taking advantage of the situation to get you out of here. This could not have gone better had I planned it myself." He grinned.

Cole and Jules hustled down the stairs rapidly, but Tabitha slowed. Jules cast an inquiring eye back at her, and she lifted a brow and pointed at the slender shoes on her feet. "These were not made for a jog."

She continued her descent as fast as the shoes would allow, one hand clinging to the railing while the other held her dress away from her feet.

"But where are we going? I have to wait for Luc."

Cole smiled and slowed his steps slightly, continuing herding her toward the exit. "Quickly. We only have a minute to get you out of here. We can't use magic until we are outside."

"What do you mean? Why not? And where are we going?"

Cole glanced back and, with a groan, dragged her across the foyer floor to the waiting doors. Jules ran ahead and spread his arms over the threshold. "Hurry!"

"Tabitha! Wait!"

Tabitha turned. Behind her, Luc was taking the stairs two at a time. Cole's arm tightened around her waist, and as they stepped outdoors, she felt her world shift. The estate vanished.

"Where are we?"

Cole released her. "I am sorry for dragging you away from him, but we need to get Luc away from the estate so he will listen to what we have to say."

"We? Where are we, Cole?" A tremor of fear snaked through her belly as she stared at the cottage before them. "What is going on?"

"I promise you, Tabitha, everything will make sense. Just come inside. He will be right behind us. I left a trail that even an—*whoof*."

As Luc tackled him at a dead run, Cole went down hard, and the two crashed to the ground.

Tabitha skipped back out of the way. Before she could react, the door to the cottage before them suddenly swung open, and three men rushed out. They were familiar, but it took a moment to identify where she had seen them before.

Luc and Cole were still wrestling. Luc suddenly gained the upper hand, and he held Cole to the ground, straddling him. His sword was sheathed, but he had slid a long dagger from his boot and held it to Cole's throat. When the hiss of steel got Luc's attention, he turned to see three men surrounding him, swords drawn.

"Do not come closer or his throat is slit," Luc commanded. "Tabitha, are you all right?"

"Luc, let him go!" Tabitha tried to push her way through but a man grabbed her arms and held her snug against his iron chest, his sword firmly across her body.

Luc watched warily but did not release his dagger from Cole's neck. "Release her."

"Monsieur, if you would release your hold, we will release the lady. Then we can speak."

Luc's eyes narrowed but his hand stayed firm. Before he could comment, the cottage door again swung open. A tall, elderly man stood in the doorway, perusing the scene before him.

Tabitha's memory clicked. "You. I remember you. I met you on my first day at my father's estate. You approached me. You are the lord regent of the Plains."

The elderly man nodded and gestured to the guards. "Release them. We respectfully request some time with them—they are not our prisoners."

The man holding Tabitha released her arms, and she slid away from him, folding her arms around her chest. Luc had not yet released Cole, but his grip loosened.

"Lord Regent Viho?"

"Yes, Monsieur DesChamps. Please, I had no intention of causing you undue distress. We need to speak to you. Your prisoner assured us that you would follow the young lady." The lord regent stepped forward and offered Luc a hand.

Luc inhaled and slowly leaned back. He slipped his dagger back into his boot and accepted the hand, rising to his feet. He was not, however, ready to let Cole off the hook so easily. He slid a booted foot onto his chest and kept him pinned to the ground. He growled, "Next time ask me. Do not put Tabitha in jeopardy."

He extended a hand to Tabitha and drew her to his side before he released Cole. "This plan to get me to listen to you used a lot of energy. What is so important that you could not simply approach me?" he asked the elderly lord regent.

"Will you join us inside? I can offer you refreshments, and we can speak. I promise you that once I have had my say, you will be free to leave."

Luc eyed the guards warily. Each had sheathed his sword. Without a word, they wandered back into the cottage, leaving the lord regent alone outside with Cole, Luc, and Tabitha. "All right, I will give you the consideration due to your title."

As they entered the cottage, Luc asked, "Did you plan the attack on Antoine?"

The lord regent shook his head. "It was but an opportunity."

Luc nodded and glanced at Tabitha as they entered the cottage. "You are all right?"

Preceding him into the cottage, she assured him, "I am fine."

The interior was warm and rustic, with chairs set in a circle around a low table that had a cheery fire dancing in a bowl set in its center.

Luc gestured Tabitha toward a seat and took the one next to her. As the others settled, he leaned over and murmured. "Next time we are threatened, it may help if you pull that shiny dagger you carry."

Tabitha glanced down in surprise at the blade swinging at her hip. A giggle escaped. "I forgot I had it."

Luc grinned and shook his head. He turned to the lord regent. "I am unaccustomed to being accosted and then sharing javé with the lord regent of a tribe. Forgive me if I seem confused."

The lord regent's face wrinkled in a smile. "No apologies are necessary. We did take undue chances to get you here. The unfortunate incident at the estate was simply a means to an end."

"Why me? There are more senior representatives of St. Mikel at Antoine's holding. Why not one of them?" Luc took the offered cup of javé and leaned forward.

"Your representatives are there, but Antoine has kept them from me. I find I am being slowly culled from the negotiations that were designed to assist my people," the elder responded.

"But I am here as a representative of my region only, one of four. There are four other groups coming. I understand that the Southern clans are also sending representation to Windrift in order to discuss what is happening in the West. Chandolyn alone will send more than twenty representatives. Antoine has requested the assistance of all of the tribes. Why would you be kept from any of this?" Luc took a long swallow of the hot liquid and watched the elder intently.

"You are Marcus's nephew. You will speak on his behalf as his family. Hear me out. My people are in grave danger."

Luc nodded. "The drought. Yes. Have you been getting the supplies Marcus has sent?"

"We are not experiencing a drought. You have been misled. Antoine does not wish people to know the truth. He fears a panic." The elder sipped from his mug. "We face the resurgence of the black elves. It is that we fight. And once they have eradicated us, they will come east."

"Black elves? They are real?" Luc was astonished.

"I have seen them myself. They destroy all in their path."

Tabitha glanced between them and cleared her throat. "What are black elves?"

"I apologize, Mistress Montfort. I take it you have not heard the legends?"

"It is Devins, not Montfort," Tabitha corrected him. "I have heard the legends, but I thought there were just that. Legends. They are some kind of being from another world?"

"Ah. Well, black elves are no more black than they are elves. It is simply the label assigned to the creature. They are not of this world.

"Many generations ago, a portal opened from another world. Through this portal entered a mist, a simple gray mist that floated across the ground, as any morning mist would do. This one, however, was different. Wherever it touched the grass, the life energy that all living entities hold was sucked from it. The grass simply withered as the mist took the life force from it. The same would happen with small insects. The gray of the mist solidified as it claimed the life force and began to assimilate to this world. After the insects, it absorbed the life from small animals and reptiles. None were safe. It drank life force as we drink water from a well. It neither cared nor noticed that it killed. It simply absorbed the life energy it feasted on. It became more solid and took on the shape of the animals it absorbed and adopted their ways. It would absorb the life and the memories of those it came across, leaving a dried and empty carcass. The same was true of the land as well."

Cole leaned forward. "Very similar to a drought."

The lord regent slowly shook his head. "It means the death of any living thing that these entities come across. If we happen across one when it is feeding on insects or foliage, it is fairly safe, but its appetite grows rapidly and its need for larger sustenance is voracious."

"So those people in the villages that were killed? The ones found lifeless...?" Tabitha asked.

"The black elves," he answered. "They leave the victim unharmed but lifeless. There are also instances of more gruesome attacks, where the people are found with holes right through their bodies, like a burn. Those attacks were not from the black elves or a sword or arrow."

"But why certain villages and not others? Are they being targeted?"

"That I do not know. Your father, though, refuses to share with the other governances that the devastation comes from the black elves, not a drought," Viho explained.

Tabitha sighed gently, her recent discussion with Katie coming to mind. Dylan was working with a gang called the Black Elves? How was Dylan tied to these attacks? She glanced up to find the men's eyes upon her.

"Why would he not want people to know what is decimating your land?"

The lord regent shrugged. "He wants to find a way to deal with them without causing a panic. He refuses to let the general populace know about the threat. He feels we can address it without general alarm."

"But the villages that are being attacked? Is that Antoine's doing or that of the black elves?" Luc asked.

Viho shrugged and leaned back in his seat. "I cannot tell you that. I suspect they are being orchestrated, but I cannot point a finger at Antoine. Would he be capable of such atrocities to further his own political aspirations? I do not know."

Luc cast his eyes down; his thoughts were his own as he considered this information. The pop and crackle of the fire before them was the only sound as the moments stretched out. Finally he lifted his gaze to the elder. "What would you have me do? I am here to represent Calais in these negotiations. You come and tell me that they are bogus? Do you intend on sharing this information among the other clan representatives?"

Viho pursed his lips and considered his answer. "I know your uncle well, and your father. I think highly of them both. I selected you from the others because I have hopes that you are of their ilk. I will head north in the morning and meet your uncle. I will solicit his aid in helping my people, and I will also ask him to help me discover the truth behind what is transpiring. If Antoine is capable of what I believe, he is a far greater threat to the land than the black elves alone."

"You know I will remain here as my uncle's appointed representative," Luc commented.

"I understand. I wish you to know the truth so you can gauge what you hear in the upcoming weeks and use this information to assess what you can. I cannot ask for your blind faith, but I request that you consider carefully what I have told you and balance it against what you will hear." The elder rose.

Luc stood as well and nodded. "Who will represent the Plains tribes once you have departed?"

"Another regent is arriving. He knows not yet that I head north, but he will discover that shortly. I am afraid he is the type to be more easily swayed toward what Antoine tells him." Viho grabbed Luc's hand and, with a wave at his three escorts, he turned to leave.

Tabitha stood also, assuming it was time for them to depart. Viho paused in front of her.

"It was a pleasure to make your acquaintance once again, Mistress Devins. I was concerned about the reception I would receive from Monsieur DesChamps knowing he was keeping company with Antoine's daughter. I fell better having met you." He bowed his head respectfully. "Be safe, mistress. These are troubled times."

Luc walked him to the door and verified that he intended to head north in the morning. Viho nodded, and the two spoke quietly. Viho sent a startled look in Tabitha's direction but nodded and departed.

When the door shut behind them, Cole slipped behind a chair and watched Luc warily. Luc stood with his hands on the back of another chair and stared thoughtfully into the flames. He exhaled explosively and raised his eyes to Cole and Tabitha.

"I would have met with him without you abducting Tabitha." His voice was low and had a dangerous edge.

"You don't know me except a servant you saw in the hall. I could not have convinced you to follow me without more of an explanation," Cole retorted. "They seemed to think they could trust you, but I was not convinced. By meeting away from the estate, we could have killed you had you proven to be strictly loyal to Antoine."

Tabitha gasped, but Luc nodded in understanding. He turned to Tabitha. "We need to get you back before they realize you are away from the estate. They must realize that you are gone by now."

Cole shook his head. "No, Jules was able to sneak her out the door. So she won't be missed, but you will be."

Luc nodded.

Tabitha held up a hand. "Wait. What does that mean? Why don't they know I am gone but Luc is?"

"The house is magic enforced," Luc explained. "No one cannot leave or enter without Antoine's knowledge."

"What? So you are telling me every time I have left the house, he has known?"

Cole nodded. "It is not like he is monitoring everyone going in and out all day, but with just a thought, he can discern people's presence."

Tabitha groaned. "Well, so much for me thinking I was taking some time to myself. No wonder he was able to have me followed on my morning walks—he knew when I left and when I got back."

"It's true," Cole said. "Can you come to Gwyn's tonight? There is someone there I think you should talk to."

Luc shook his head and moved closer. "She can't leave again tonight. That place is going to be locked down after what happened to Antoine. We are going to have a tough enough time getting back in."

Cole snapped back, "She doesn't have to get back in. They think she is already there. You are the only one with a problem."

Luc's jaw tensed, and his hand moved to the pommel of his sword, but Tabitha grabbed his hand and stayed it. "Luc, wait. Calm down." She turned to Cole. "Who is it?"

"I didn't want to tell you before, but Grandfather is at Gwyn's. He is old and crippled. Gwyn cares for him. Can you make it there to talk to him? I am afraid your opportunities are growing limited now all this is breaking apart."

"Wait! Grandfather? Your grandfather? Your father's father?" Luc demanded.

Tabitha put a hand to her mouth. "Grandfather? I have a grandfather?"

Luc eyed Cole with suspicion. "How do you know so much about her family?"

Tabitha let out a laugh. "I haven't had time to fill you in on everything! Cole is my brother, Luc. He is my twin, the one the Faye mentioned to me."

Luc, shocked, stared from one to the other. "Your twin? Another brother?"

It was Cole's turn to look startled. "Another? You met Dylan, I take it?"

Tabitha nodded and spat at Cole, "Why didn't you tell me he was our brother?"

"If you remember correctly, it was enough for you to find out your mother was Faye and that I was your twin," Cole responded.

"Wait a minute." Luc held up a hand and turned to Tabitha. "Faye? Your mother? I guess both of you are Faye?"

Tabitha nodded. "I just found out myself. I went to meet Gwyn, the mysterious Dedrel Alena found out about. She introduced me to Cole and told me my mother was Faye and from this world."

Luc stared at her. She understood the questions churning through him were best left unsaid. She knew he dared not ask about her healing ability.

"Luc, I have to get out to meet my grandfather. Cole is right. Time is running out, and with this impending trouble brewing, I think I need to start thinking about getting out of here before this gets any crazier." Tabitha rested her hands on his. "Will you help me?"

"Will you leave once this is done?"

"Yes. I promise."

"I will strike a deal with you. Get away from your father's home tonight. Go to Gwyn's, and then I will take you to meet Viho. Viho will take you to my father. He will get you to the portal or keep you safe until I can get up there to take you. Will you go?" Luc's gaze was intent, and she saw his concern.

"Luc, I have to go back to the house. I need to get the stone to the portal. I don't have it on me." She gestured to the silver dress that hugged her. "No place to put it, really."

Luc grinned and ran an appreciative eye over her attire. The mood lightened for just a moment. "No, I don't imagine you had much room for anything else in there."

"We will get what I need and go to Gwyn's. Then I will leave, I promise you."

Luc shook his head. "I don't like it. I would rather you just left. I will collect your stone and meet you up there after Antoine is convinced I am not his enemy."

Tabitha shook her head. "I can't have come all this way and not meet my Grandfather. He may be able to tell me where my mother is."" Her voice shook slightly, and she cast her eyes away from Luc. "Once I leave, I cannot come back, at least until this unrest is solved."

Luc sighed and nodded. "I will take you back and we will get the stone."

"I will meet you at Gwyn's," Cole confirmed.

CHAPTER TWELVE

THEY LEFT TO HEAD BACK TO ANTOINE'S ESTATE AND Cole left for Gwyn's. Tabitha clasped Luc's hand and let him guide her back. Her mind swirled with what they had learned. She was just as glad to let Luc direct them. With a step, they appeared in front of the estate.

"Let's try to get you up to your room with a minimum of people seeing us," Luc murmured. He slid his hand to the small of her back and nudged her toward the entrance.

Luc tread silently as he took the steps, but Tabitha's heels clattered as she hurried to keep pace with him. He paused and looked pointedly at her feet.

"Fine," she growled. She used his arm for support and leaned over to slip the straps from her ankles and snatched the shoes free, holding them in one hand. She lifted the hem of her dress and noticed he was looking intently at the front entrance, where a myriad of sounds drifted from the ballroom.

His expression became tense, and he slid his hand against her back. "Let's get you upstairs. Quickly."

"Why? What is happening?" Tabitha asked as she padded barefoot up the stairs behind him.

He didn't answer but tugged her up the remaining stairs to the foyer landing. She craned her neck to see into the ballroom. A crowd had gathered outside the doors. As they took the first steps, Tabitha caught sight of her father in the middle of the room, a ring of guards around him, a man in servant garb on his knees in front of him, head bowed.

"Luc? What is gong on? Is that the guy who attacked my father? What are they doing?"

"Just keep moving."

"But what is he doing?"

Luc sighed as he tugged her up another flight of stairs. "I imagine an execution."

"What? Wait!"

Luc continued up the stairs. "Why? Do you think you can save him?"

"But…"

"But what? Tabitha, your father will not allow the man to live."

"Will he lock him away? Can we…"

Luc slowly shook his head as he stopped at the third floor. "Which way?"

"Luc? They took his son. Isn't there anything we can do?"

Faint cries and a low moan from the crowd drifted up from the first floor. Luc's voice was a hoarse whisper. "I imagine that it is done."

"Oh, God no."

Luc gestured again. "Which way? Our time is very limited."

Tabitha led him down the hall toward her father's private apartments to her suite. Tabitha's stomach churned as she imagined what had just transpired.

"I have to get out of here," she whispered.

"Let's get you back to your rooms and collect what you need. Your father will be notified you are here. He needs to know you are safely in your room and believe that is where you are remaining. If Jules can sneak you out past the bindings, Antoine will not think to look for you until tomorrow morning. That should give us enough time to get you to your grandfather and then back to Viho. He will bring you to my father, who will escort you to the portal. I need to return."

Inside, Tabitha shut the door quietly and walked into her inner bedroom to change.

"Luc?" she called as she slid behind the changing screen and stepped out of her shimmering dress. She felt a slight twinge of regret over losing the sense of that elegant woman she had seen in the mirror. However, a part of her feared that the reflection was simply the enticement for trading herself for what her father would offer.

"Luc, when that man was wrestling with my father, right before the guards pulled him off..."

"Yeah?"

She peeked from behind the screen. "I saw twin scars on Antoine's neck."

"Scars?" Luc entered the room and lowered himself onto the bed.

She tugged a dark sweater over her head and settled it over her hips. She sighed. "Like yours. Like the ones I gave you when I healed Cyra."

He was silent. She wondered what he was thinking, and she tugged her lip with her teeth as she shimmied into dark pants.

"Tabitha, what are you saying?" Luc finally asked quietly.

She grabbed her boots. Tugging one on, she hopped over to the bed where he sat. She rested on the edge, the other boot in her hand. "I think that my mother may have given him those scars. I think that she was a healer and that was why he was trying to keep her prisoner here."

They were both silent for a moment. When she glanced up, she found him staring at her, an intense expression on his face. Finally, he commented, "That is quite a leap."

She shook her head and curled her legs under her on the bed beside him, the forgotten boot slipping off the bed, hitting the floor with a soft thud. "Listen, I know that by all accounts they had a very passionate and volatile relationship. But the stories do not exactly coincide. My father tells me that he did everything to try and entice her to stay and marry him. Gwyn said that my mother wanted to return home, but then his cousin found out something about my mother and she became more of a prisoner. What if what she found out was that my mother was a healer?"

Luc shrugged. "It is possible. I understand that the healing gene is passed from one generation to the next. It does not always mean the carrier is a healer, but the healing trait can pass to the children."

One boot on, Tabitha stood and absently tugged on the second boot. Her mind was racing. "My mother's note said that my father's father was dying or dead, I don't remember. But Luc, he was her father. She could not tell me because as far as I knew, her parents were my human grandparents. At least, the people I thought were my grandparents."

A knock on the outer door of the sitting room interrupted them. Tabitha ran to the doorway. "Who is it?"

"It is captain of the home guard. I wanted to make sure that you were safely in your room. Would you open the door, please?"

Tabitha paused, wondering if that was the wisest move. Luc emerged and, a finger to his lips, pushed her back into the inner bedroom.

Come out with your robe on, he directed.

She heard Luc open the door and voices quietly speaking as she grabbed a long robe. She slid it over her clothes and tied it at her waist. She clasped the collar and emerged from her bedroom to find Luc standing talking to the guard, his shirt unbuttoned and open to his waist.

The captain's eyes shifted from Luc's open shirt to her long robe, and a slow grin engulfed the man's face. "Good evening, Mistress. I apologize for the interruption, but your father was concerned for your welfare. I needed to verify that you are safe."

"Captain, I will be here to ensure Tabitha's safety. Trust me when I tell you, no harm will come to her under my care."

The guard nodded. "I will post a guard outside the door for the night. He insists. Your safety is his utmost concern."

Tabitha felt heat engulf her face when Luc slipped his arms around her waist and thanked the guard. As he shut the door, Tabitha moved out of his grip. "Was that necessary? I mean, really?"

He began buttoning his shirt. Her eyes caught a twinkling gold token lying against his bronze chest. She reached up to peer more closely at the disc, a wolf howling and a hawk soaring overhead cut into the gold.

Luc chuckled as he tugged the token from her fingers, buttoned his shirt, and tucked it back into this dark pants. "That will give us some latitude. If your father thinks you otherwise occupied, he will be less apt to be concerned about you departing from the house."

"My father will be thinking that you are I are in bed together!"

Luc nodded. "That he will."

"He will be down here banging the door down!"

"He will not—because he will think we are doing exactly what he instructed me to do. He wants me to entice or seduce you into staying," Luc told her. He stepped over to the fireplace and stirred the coals under the pot of javé hanging on the hook.

Tabitha's mouth dropped. "He told you to *seduce* me to get me to stay?"

"More like he encouraged me. He told me he is desperate to have you stay so he can keep his daughter here with him. He is aware that I know you are from another world, and he is asking that I encourage you to stay here with me," Luc responded, pouring a cup of the steaming liquid.

"And you said you would?" she demanded, ignoring the offered cup.

"I told him I was falling in love with you and that it was my wish that you stay with me." He kept the mug and took a tentative sip. "You are not the only one here on less than honest terms."

"What do you mean?" she whispered. Was he talking about his feelings for her? Had he been truthful when he told her father about falling in love with her?

Luc hesitated. He released a long breath and let his gaze drop to the fire blazing at his feet. A hot coal popped from the wood, and he used a booted toe to push it back in. "Marcus has long suspected that your father's peace efforts are greatly self-serving. Your father has been enlisting and gaining support from different factions and states at an alarming rate. It seems any village or governance that questions the need for a peace treaty or your father's motives suddenly faces a violent attack. Word has reached us through an underground movement that the tribes of the Plains live in terror of our attacks. They have been attacked with weapons that they do not understand and have been told that it is our way of keeping them from our land."

"Weapons? Like what Viho mentioned?" Tabitha asked.

"People are found with wounds that seem to impale them, long burn marks through their bodies that erupt through the back of them or leave gaping holes. They are not arrow or sword wounds. Because each of the attacks involves such marks, they insist they are something that the coastal clans are using to keep their numbers down."

"Holes, huh? You know what they are?"

Luc nodded. "I do. We suspect he has been smuggling weapons in from your world."

Tabitha moaned. "Oh my God. So you are here as a spy? For Marcus?"

Luc nodded.

"And Dylan...How well do you know him?"

"He and I went to school together when we were boys. I have known him for more than twelve years. We spent holidays together," Luc answered.

"You are friends?" Tabitha let the word drop from her mouth.

Luc lifted one shoulder. "We were friends but grew distant as we grew older. He tired of school and came here to apprentice with your father for politics. I never had such an interest."

"Luc, what if I told you that Dylan is somehow involved with these attacks, at least some of them." She hesitated.

"I would not be surprised. Dylan can be a cruel and cold person. I kept up our friendship in later years at Marcus's request, to try and keep an eye on him. He is a very aggressive and ambitious man," Luc admitted. "But how do you know he is behind them?"

Tabitha reached out and took the mug from his hands. She sipped from the mug. "Where do I start?"

"Go on."

"My father has been enticing women from our world who wish to give their children up for adoption. He's using those babies as political leverage." She took another sip from the mug before handing it back to him. "In fact, there is one here now. She is about to give birth."

"You know this for a fact?"

She nodded. "I met her. Her name is Katie, and I heard my father and Dylan speaking about her. I think they are going to kill her after she has the baby. Luc, we have to get her out of here."

He arched a dark brow at her. "You have been busy."

"Katie is carrying Dylan's child. He has the same genes I have. If my mother was a healer, Dylan could have passed that gene to this child."

He blew out a deep breath. "That child could be a healer."

"Yes. She may have already given birth."

"This complicates things," he admitted.

"I have to get to my grandfather and speak to him. If my mother was a healer, it would explain my father's fixation on keeping her under his thumb, and it would explain why she avoids him. If he gets his hands on her again, he will not let her go," Tabitha whispered.

Luc nodded. "If he even suspects you are a healer, he will not let you go either."

He handed her the cup, and as she took another sip from it. As the warm liquid touched her lips she imagined that Luc's lips had just been on that same edge. He was watching her intently, and she slowly lowered the mug.

Their eyes met. Everything seemed to freeze for a moment as their proximity, their mutual gaze, and their feelings began to stoke the emotions brewing between them. She could not have torn her eyes from his gaze if her life depended on it. As he lowered his head, she met his kiss, her lips warm and inviting. The gentle pressure of his mouth became a slow and thorough exploration, and she responded eagerly. As the kiss intensified to a fever pitch, she wrapped her arms his neck and tangled her fingers in his thick, silky hair. His arms tightened about her, and his hands slid down her waist and over her bottom. She pressed herself against him, molding her body to his. Their bodies fused together in an attempt to replicate the passion searing between their lips. Her body began a slow burn that seemed to ignite into a full-fledged blaze as his mouth drove all sane thought of the night and their danger from her head.

She needed him; she wanted him more than she had ever wanted anything in her life. His body would not be enough; she needed to feel him, body and soul.

He dragged his mouth from her lips and traced a burning path along her jaw line and neck. She tilted back her head, moaning at the feel of him against her.

"We have to get you the hell out of here tonight, but all I want to do is drag you back into that blasted bedroom."

She buried her face against his neck.

He sighed against her throat. "Well, that will have to wait until a more opportune time."

She looked up and their eyes met. As she rested her forehead against his, she could see the smile touch his eyes as he looked down into her silver gaze.

She swallowed hard, trying to dissipate the flames that licked through her bloodstream. After a long moment and a shaky sigh, she asked, "How do we get out of a house with a guard at our door and a magic perimeter that will alert my father to our leaving?"

He laughed softly. "It might be easier to just go back to the idea of me hauling you into bed and tearing off your clothes."

"Easier—and more tempting," she agreed with a grin. "So what is our plan?"

He stepped back, kissing her lightly once more on the mouth as he did. "For starters, I need to get the blood back into my head."

"Have some more javé, that will help."

"Yeah, good idea. Hot liquid…" he said with a wry smile as he refilled his mug.

"So…any suggestions?"

He exhaled deeply and stared down into the mug of steaming javé. "Well, I can get out of here, but I am afraid I can't sneak you out with me."

"Can you teach me?"

"Not in the span of an hour or two. It takes months to master."

"We need to find Jules," she commented.

"Yes. And get you away from here before morning."

"And Katie? Luc, I don't know if she is alive or dead. I don't know if she was faking labor pains to get me out of that room, but she risked a lot to let me escape." A fearful sob escaped her as she turned away. "And I still don't know if Dylan knows. If he even suspects that she helped me get out or even that I was in that room, he may have already killed her."

Luc nodded. "Let's get you out of here. I will return and get her out and take her someplace safe."

Tabitha shook her head. "No, Luc. We will get her out. I won't leave you to try and—"

He smiled slowly. "Stop. I know—I know what you are saying, but please, Tabitha, you have to listen to me. This is the time for you to be smart and get the hell away from your father. You know too much, and if he even suspects, you will never get away. He will use you as leverage to try and get your mother back. You are much too valuable for us to lose. My people need a healer, and we cannot allow one man to control the only one that we know of who has been born in generations. And maybe, if we can get you safely away, just maybe someday we can figure out what it is that makes you a healer and how we can save ourselves."

She listened to his plea and paused. She was so unaccustomed to anyone's help. She was used to being the one in control, the one in the driver's seat, and here he was, begging her to be selfish and run. She was not sure she could relinquish that much control. She was not ready to ask for help.

Slowly she nodded. "Okay, let's get out of here."

A soft knock on the door interrupted. Luc's hand went to his sword. She put a hand down to still his hand as she walked to the door.

"Yes?"

"Open the door." It was Jules's voice, urgent and rushed.

She did so, and he glanced in at her. "I have sent the guard away, you must get out of here."

"Jules, what is wrong?"

Jules entered the room and glanced at where Luc stood, tense and ready to strike, by the fire. "Your father will soon be putting the house on a lockdown. No one leaves or enters. You need to get out of here tonight."

"We were just talking about that. Does he suspect something is wrong?" Tabitha asked in hushed voice.

Jules nodded and glanced at Luc. "Your life is in serious jeopardy. He knows you are here with Tabitha, which is probably the only thing that has saved your life thus far. There was an attack in southern St. Mikel."

"What?" Luc roared. "When?"

"The news is just flowing in now. What we are hearing is that the village was not caught unaware. The attackers were captured, and it seems that they have informed Marcus that they attacked on Dylan's orders," Jules explained hurriedly.

"Was anyone hurt?" Luc demanded.

"There were minimal casualties. It is imperative that Antoine keeps the news that it happened under his directive a secret. You will be either killed or taken hostage if you even hint that you are aware that Marcus may have been ready for the attack." Jules eyed Luc carefully, "Have you contacted your father?"

"No. The distance is a challenge, but I will contact him later tonight when I have a few moments." Luc's jaw clenched but his words were soft. "The war begins."

Jules nodded softly. "The end of peace."

Luc nodded, and Tabitha had the sinking feeling that it was no surprise to them. "You knew this was coming?"

They exchanged a glance before both nodded. "It has been forthcoming for some time."

Luc agreed. "I had thought we might have a few more months at best. I hoped for a few weeks of negotiations and planning before this erupted."

"But does this have to happen? I mean—"

Luc nodded. "Your father's empire has been carefully built. It will require a long time to topple it. But Marcus's hand has been apparently forced. He will not allow his people to be attacked. We had word that this might be coming. Your father had concerns about Marcus's fealty. We had hoped to be able to gather more evidence and offer more opportunity to prove what was happening to the other governances."

"If we do not, it will be a very short clash," Jules commented quietly.

Luc nodded. "We have to get out of here."

Jules nodded. "You do. You are safe for the night, but Antoine will demand fealty from you come morning. Should you not convince him, all will be lost."

Luc shrugged. "I have been positioning myself as an ally for some time. I walk a very thin line. Should they even suspect that I am anything but ignorant of Marcus' actions, my position here will be in peril."

Tabitha shook her head. "Luc, you have to leave. I cannot have you put yourself in danger on my behalf. Tell them that I snuck out on you while you were sleeping. It does not matter if he knows I have left the house. As long as I have enough of a head start, I can get away and head to a portal before they catch me."

Luc laughed softly. "You do not know your way back. I will get you safely to Viho. I promised you that much."

"Which brings us back to getting you two out of here. We need to get you out without tripping the bindings," Jules stated briskly.

Tabitha nodded. "How do we do that?"

"Luc will have to fly. I will get you out. I can sneak you through an exit. But we must move quickly. I sent the guard away for a few moments, but he will be back. Luc, use the window. I will take her down. We do not have much time. I have to get back before your father suspects I have anything to do with this." Jules led Tabitha toward the door. "Meet her up on the hill, where the trail forks. I will leave the balcony doors to her bedroom open. You must return before dawn, or they will know you were gone."

Luc nodded and moved off toward the balcony as Jules tugged Tabitha toward the door. She broke from Jules and followed Luc into her room. He turned as she entered. She grabbed her mother's ring off the shelf.

"I can't leave this, it was my mother's," she murmured.

He nodded. As she moved to pass him, his arm snaked out and caught her waist; her drew her against him. "I will be waiting for you—be careful. Don't make me come back in here to find you."

She smiled. Her mouth met his in a hasty kiss, and she turned to leave. He shoved the doors open and without breaking stride jumped onto the railing. Her breath caught as in one fluid motion he stepped off, his arms spread out on either side as he transformed instantaneously. In an instant, the hawk was beating powerful wings, soaring skyward.

She ran out and saw Jules checking the hall. He tugged her behind him, and they sped down the empty hallway.

"I sent the guard on a short errand and told him I would wait for his return. I should be able to get back before his return," he explained.

"Won't they realize I left when he was gone?"

Jules shook his head. "Not if I do this right."

"I don't understand. If they do not know I left now, how will—"

He glanced back, a strained and irritated look crossing his face and pinching his features. "Trust me, will you?"

She nodded and quietly followed him down the back stairs. "How will we get Katie out?"

Jules shook his head. "One at a time, please."

"Should I wait for her with Luc before going to Gwyn's?"

Jules shook his head and propelled her down the stairs. "Just go. Once you are out, get away from this house and go to Gwyn's. Let me worry about Katie."

They reached the ground level, and Tabitha had a sinking feeling. She was about to confront him when he stopped and turned quickly to her. "All right now, listen carefully. Remember what I told you about shielding?"

Tabitha nodded.

"Okay. This is what you must do. Shield to everything around you except me. Open yourself completely to me."

Tabitha hesitated. She was not sure she liked this idea. Jules, however much he professed to be helping them, worked for her father and had for many years. What if his true allegiance was to her father and he was helping them in an effort to control the situation?

"You told me to trust no one," she said softly.

"And I meant it," he responded. "Use your instincts."

"If I open myself up to you..."

He nodded slowly. "Do as I say. Open yourself. I will leave myself open. Trust me and let your mind go blank. Let me take control. Once we are outside, I will release you. You are to run up the path and meet Monsieur DesChamps. He will be waiting on the trail to the left." Jules lifted his hands to her temples. "Trust me, let your mind go blank. Your father will know I stepped outside and then walked right back in. He will not think that unusual."

"And what of Luc? Will you promise me that when he returns, no harm will come to him?" Tabitha begged, stepping back from his hands.

Jules shook his head slowly. "I cannot. But I do assure you that I will do everything in my power to protect him. We cannot afford to lose him either."

"And Katie...?"

"By all that is holy, Tabitha. Are you going to do this all night?"

"I promised her I would get her out of here," Tabitha insisted.

"She may very well already be dead," Jules snarled.

"She may not be dead. I cannot leave her behind!" Tabitha snapped back.

"All right—I will get to her, I will try to get her out. Just *go!*" Jules insisted, his voice tense and his actions furtive.

As Jules slid his fingers along her temples Tabitha took a deep breath and tried to calm herself and let her mind go blank. She let her mind drift lazily and followed Jules gentle guidance. In what seemed only a few seconds, she was standing outside, blinking.

Jules gave her a shove. She turned to look back at him, "Jules—"

He shook his head sharply. "Go!"

She nodded and took off at a quick trot up the path toward where Luc stood waiting.

CHAPTER THIRTEEN

TABITHA AND LUC HEADED THROUGH THE WOODS under the silvery light cast by the full moon. As she trotted up a hill, trying to keep pace with Luc, she wondered at the strange turn of events and her transformation from a willowy and elegant woman in a long ball gown to racing through the woods at night wearing dark clothes. The sight of Luc, all in black, racing with surefooted ability before her boosted her mood.

"Wouldn't this be easier for you in another shape?"

He cast an eye back at her as they crested a small knoll. "Another shape?"

"Well, running as a wolf or something?"

He chuckled. "Are you trying to goad me into changing shape again?"

She shrugged. "It amazes me. I think it is incredible. If I could do it, I would do it all the time." She caught up to him and then started down the hill. He fell in step behind her. She glanced over her shoulder at him. "Besides, I've never seen you as a wolf."

"All right, but let's not make a habit out of trying to get me to do tricks for you."

He slid into his wolf shape. His fur was thick and deep black, but his eyes remained his intense blue.

Tabitha stopped to stare at him in wonder. "Luc?"

Of course, he snorted in her mind.

"You make a beautiful wolf. Did you know your eyes stay blue?"

He tossed his magnificent head. Tabitha had to giggle at what appeared to be the wolf equivalent of a highly disgusted glare.

"I take it you do not take compliments well," she commented. He glanced back over his shoulder as he started trotting down toward the village. Tabitha broke into a trot to keep up with his pace. "Too bad you are not a horse. Then I could ride you."

Don't go there. Luc's voice in her mind was amused. *You turned me down in your bedroom.*

Tabitha laughed lightly at his flirting. "The house is along this road, down at the end. It is the last one before the road curves."

Luc nodded. He slipped under a fence and leaped up over a stonewall.

Tabitha was still climbing over the first fence. "Showoff," she grumbled.

Hey, you're the one who wanted to have a tame pet to entertain you. I would have stayed in my form.

"Yeah, whatever. I would prefer it if you could teach me to change shape too."

She came around the last house and found him leaning against the portico railing, waiting for her. "I can teach you."

"Well, apparently not in time for me to use it to get down here quicker," she snapped with a saucy flip of her hair.

He grabbed her arm as she moved to pass him toward the door. The humor had fled his face, and his eyes caught hers with an intense stare. "I can teach you anything you want to know, but we are both kidding ourselves. When we leave this house, we have to get you back to the portal, and you have to leave."

Tabitha nodded. "I know. I wish it were different."

He released her arm as though surprised that he was still holding it. He was about to speak, but she lifted a finger to his lips. She shook her head. "Don't. This will be hard enough when the time comes, but if we torture one another until I get to the portal, we will be miserable."

He nodded, and she turned to the house to knock lightly on the door. She waited a few moments. There was no answer to her second and third knocks. She tried the handle, and the door slowly opened to her touch. She glanced back at Luc. He shrugged and nodded, and she slowly entered the house. The lights were dim, and there was no sign of anyone in the lower floor.

Tabitha made a quick tour through the first floor, tentatively knocking on any door that was shut, but the place was deserted. She remembered that Cole had taken a tray of food upstairs when she was here last. She glanced up the dark stairwell and quietly made her way up the creaking wooden steps.

At the top, a simple hallway with one small window illuminated three closed wooden doors. She slowly tapped on the first and was greeted with a quiet cough and the soft rasp of a voice bidding her to enter. She eased the door open and slowly peeked around it into the gloomy interior.

"Come in, come in," a thin voice called from a bed against the far wall. Slowly, Tabitha entered the room. It was comfortably decorated; a warm throw rug lay on the dark wood floors. A small dresser, a commode, and a single wooden chair were the only other furniture in the room. Moonlight spilled in through a large window and bathed the bed and its frail inhabitant in a soft white glow.

"I don't mean to interrupt," Tabitha said softly. The small orange glow from a light over the bed doused the small elderly man sitting up against the headboard. His head was bare of most hair save a few strands that stuck out in random disarray around his skull. His face was wrinkled and pinched, and his dark eyes had sunk within long cheek-bones. He lifted a bony hand and patted the bed next to him.

Tabitha hesitated but walked in and perched on the side of the bed. "Do you know who I am?"

His old head bobbed, and a smile creased his lined face. "I have long wanted to meet you. Your mother has told me tales of your growing. She has even brought me photo-graphs so that I might see you as you grew," the old man said softly. "My name is Roane. Roane Marks. Gwyn told me you were here, but I thought you would be gone before we could tell you of my presence. I think your mother hoped you would have been home by now."

Tabitha slowly nodded, and a single tear crept down her cheek as she stared at her grandfather. He lifted a frail hand and wiped the tear away with one thumb.

"Was my mother here?"

The old man nodded. "Yes, yes, but she left so quickly."

"Did she know I was here?"

He pursed his lips and shook his head. "No, she would have told me if she had known you were here. She only stopped to make sure I was well."

"And she left you here?"

"I am old." He gestured to his thin legs hidden under the worn blanket. "It is not easy for me to get around. I am best left here."

"I take it Gwyn cares for you?"

"She does, yes. And Cole. It is good that I have some family with me." His voice was a slow rasp.

"Do you know where my mother went?"

"I do not. It is best I know little about where she goes." His eyes watched her with a deep intensity. "I understand you are preparing to leave?"

Tabitha nodded. "I needed to meet you. I needed to speak to you and find out anything you can tell me about my mother. Every time I discover something, it just confuses me more.'

'I have been trying to figure this all out and piece together a life that she could have simply told me about at any time. I mean, I do not even know what to believe any longer! My father tells me she simply began to withdraw from him and that he only wanted her to stay and marry him. But Gwyn and Jules tell me a different story. According to them, theirs was a volatile and crazy relationship that was borderline obsessive and in the end she was his prisoner."

Roane nodded. "And what have you concluded from your findings?"

"I wish my mother would just tell me her side of the story."

"I believe that she never wanted you to know any of this. I think she hoped you could grow up and live a normal and human life in your world," he stated.

Tabitha rose again. "How can I have a normal life with the insanity that I grew up with? The people on my island thought my mother was abducted and I was a bastard child of some kind of rapist. I grew up with that stigma. Then I started being able to do things with this magic. No one else in my world has such abilities. And she told me nothing. I had no idea where she had been and who my father was." She sighed and turned back to him in frustration. "I found out when I got here that I have a father, two brothers, and now apparently a grandfather."

"Your mother and I have long disagreed about your up-bringing, but she believes that she was doing her best to protect you. Tell me, Tabitha, what you have discovered about your father?"

Tabitha sat again and exhaled a long breath. "Well. That is an interesting story. I have found out quite a bit. Let me tell you."

She began to piece together the long, drawn-out tale of her arrival and what she had discovered. As she pulled the pieces together in her tale, the sordid details began to paint an ugly picture of her father's ambitious and long-term plans for pitting the east against the west and controlling the land through a calculated strategy of fear. He had used every fear tactic, especially the fear over their procreation abilities, to sway people to his cause. He had inflated himself as a peace negotiator in a war that he waged against his own people. He had used the desire for a child and a family to develop alliances through obligation after supplying them with a child. He had put together a village for people struggling to have a home and then made the debt so easy to accumulate that many ended up having their children taken to satisfy their obligation. And he had lured young women over from her world with the promise of medical care and opportunity for the price of letting him find families for their children. A noble enough cause, except the young women were then tricked into a second pregnancy or more and then disappeared.

Roane stared at her, and his sharp eyes did not move. A small noise at the door caused them both to jump. Luc entered.

"Tabitha, I got worried when you did not come down."

She waved him in and stood to introduce the men. "Luc, this is my grandfather, Roane. This is Luc DesChamps. He is the first person I met when I came here looking for my mother."

Roane smiled and gestured for Luc to approach. "Tabitha has just finished telling me what she has discovered about our land in her short time with us."

Luc's smile was wry. He responded, "Yes, she has been busy."

The old man studied them closely and gestured for Luc to bring the wooden chair by the window closer. "Sit. Sit."

Luc dragged the chair over and Tabitha took her place back on the bed. Roane slipped his frail fingers in her hand

and studied her. "So what will you do with this information?"

She sighed. "I don't know what to do. I am afraid. This young girl being kept prisoner in his home is in grave danger, and I have promised to get her out. I suspect that my older brother, Dylan, the man who impregnated her and then subsequently dumped her, although he was trying to win over her affections again, might possibly know that I was in that room with her. I am afraid as soon as she has the baby, they will kill her.'

'I want to find my mother, but the plans that my father has for me may leave me as much a prisoner as she became." She glanced over to where Luc sat but could not meet his gaze as she finished. "I don't want to leave, but I am afraid to stay."

The old man nodded. "What would you do if you found your mother?"

"I would ask her what the hell happened to her. How did a Faye infant end up in my world and why, and how did she come back? Why did she take me back but leave Cole? I just do not understand her at all!" Tabitha exclaimed. Frustration stung her eyes, and she quickly wiped the tears away, but she knew that Roane had seen them. She inhaled deeply, trying to get her raging emotions under control. "May I ask you a question?"

"Of course."

"Is my mother a healer?"

Surprise flickered in the old man's astute eyes, and his lips pursed as he contemplated his response. After a moment, he slowly nodded. "She is."

"And he knew?"

"That he did," Roane responded quietly.

"And that was why she was a prisoner here?"

Again he nodded. "And it is why he keeps me prisoner here."

Tabitha's head snapped up. "You? You are a prisoner here?"

He nodded slowly. "Gwyn has long worked for your father. She was allowed to bring me here and care for me, but I am Antoine's prisoner. I am unable to leave. Should I try, he has made the consequences quite clear. I am as much a prisoner here as your mother was when she was here."

"And he keeps you prisoner here to try and capture her back?"

The old man laughed a slow and bitter cackle. "No, he well knows she is gone. He would like nothing more than to get his hands on her again, but he keeps me prisoner here for the same reason he kept her prisoner."

It took a moment or two, but understanding slowly began to dawn on her. "You? You are a healer as well?"

He nodded. "Your father can gain support when people's loved ones are ill or dying. People will pledge nearly anything to save a loved one's life."

"So he uses you to heal those people that he then gains support from?" She was incredulous.

The old man nodded again. "I grow weak. I am old, and my strength and abilities are dwindling. Each healing drains me and leaves me more incapacitated."

"How could she leave here, knowing her father was his prisoner?" Tabitha demanded. "Why didn't she try to help you?"

"I was not always his prisoner." The old man coughed gently, and Luc rose and poured him a glass of water from a nearby pitcher. The old man gratefully took the glass and sipped at it. His eyes found Luc. "So she has found her mate? I am pleased. I knew your uncle and your father well. They are men of strong moral strength. I have a great deal of respect for them."

Luc nodded, a slight blush crossing his bronze cheek as he shrugged his collar closer to his neck. The old man chuckled. "The one God willing, you will one day wear that mark with pride, but for now, keep that hidden. Few know what it means, but your life will be in jeopardy should someone who understands those twin marks see them."

"Obviously my father would know, but I don't think he could have seen them last night," Tabitha commented, a slight flush on her cheeks as well when she realized Roane had seen her mark on Luc's neck.

Roane turned back and continued his story. "I lived my life with the Faye. They knew of my talent, and what to do with me caused a great deal of strain for my people. I was the son of a healer and the grandson of a healer. Mine was the last surviving line. My family had lived among the people many generations before. Did you know only the Faye have the healing talent?" Tabitha shook her head, and he grinned at her and continued. "It is true. The healing talent only runs in a single generation, from Faye-born to Faye-born. My great-grandparents had lived among the people when the first of the humans started to appear, and we spent our time as revered and holy people among them. They were the original Caskans, the first tribes that came over to our world. They came as many others had. A portal would open, and one or two or sometimes entire tribes would be swallowed into our world. They settled here. The Faye married among them, and a new people were born. But even so, to keep the ability strong healing families were only allowed to mate with and marry Faye.

"When the white men began to come into our world we adopted your God, which overtook the teachings of the Great Spirit. There was a time when the portals were swallowing people in enormous numbers, beginning a new settling of human, Caskan, and the Faye."

Tabitha lifted a hand. "Were the Caskans all separated by their talents? Luc told me that his clan has the ability to shapeshift, but others, like water sprites or tree dryads, have other abilities."

"Yes, the Caskans were separated by the East and West. The East is separated into the three major areas. The Northern clans can shapeshift, the Bay region in the middle are the tree dryad descendants, and the Southern clans are the water sprites. The healers were integrated into their society, but it was the requirement to replenish with blood that drove the humans to consider them agents of the devil."

"The replenishing with blood," Tabitha interrupted. "Is that necessary? I mean, what is that?"

He smiled. "When you heal, your body heats up to an enormous temperature. If you do it in small doses, you do not need to replenish. Your body will naturally replenish in time. Brief healing does weaken you, but the need to replenish from another is not required. When you overextend your abilities and deplete your strength, your body will require it. Should you let yourself become exhausted, you may not even be aware of your actions."

Tabitha ducked her head, and Roane slowly lifted her chin with a bony finger. "Ah, so that is how your man was marked, is it?"

She nodded, embarrassed. "I was trying to heal a child and did not understand." Her voice dropped to a whisper. "I was not aware of marking him. I don't know how I did that."

He smiled and reached out to squeeze her hand. "We do not mark everyone who replenishes us, only the ones we consider our mate. Gwyn replenished me quite often, yet I have never marked her."

Tabitha felt heat rise in her face, and she wished that Luc were still downstairs. "But he is not my mate. We barely knew each other when that happened. I had no idea—"

The old man smiled. "Apparently your heart did. You do not have to be aware of it; it is what is meant to be."

Luc stood and walked over to the window, his back rigid as he stared out into the night sky.

Roane glanced at Tabitha curiously, and she dropped her voice. "I will be returning home. I have marked him, but our being together is impossible."

He nodded slowly. "I see. If you are destined to be mated and are truly for one another, whether you are together or not does not change the fact that you consider him your man."

Tabitha blushed again and refused to look up to see Luc's expression. Humiliation ran through her, and she felt as though her heart and soul were laid bare by those last statements. Luc had turned around, but he was little more than a dark silhouette against the moonlit window.

Tabitha cleared her throat. "So what happened next? To the healers?"

"They were eradicated. There is nothing quite like the chaos caused when people are stirred into a frenzy of fear. The healers' blood requirement became twisted into a masochistic and dark need, and in the heat of religious demand they were slowly slaughtered. Sometimes one or two dragged were from their homes, but then the destructive waves took over sanity, and anyone accused of being a healer was murdered. No trials, or perhaps a farce trial."

"The witch trials all over again," Tabitha murmured.

"The remaining few were spirited away to hide in monasteries and with friends. Many just simply disappeared with the Faye. But the same illness that took our women and children also affected the healers. We lost a great many to that. Few were born, and slowly they died out."

Luc walked back over and sat in the chair. He took up the story when Roane stopped to take a drink. "We believed the healers to be gone. No one had stopped to consider what the healers were actually healing when women were being attended to during pregnancy and childbirth. The healers were the physicians and midwives of our villages. After their numbers were depleted, the truth of what they were doing for us became apparent." He glanced up, and the old man nodded for him to continue. "By that time healing had been outlawed, and the few remaining healers were hiding out in monasteries and convents, under the protection of the same church that had ordered their execution. It seems that the few religious zealots who had called for their eradication did not represent the masses, so many of them went into hiding within the cloistered walls."

The old man continued when Luc stopped. "Of course, many of them joined the religious order and consequently did not beget heirs. The line continued to die out, and our race began to slowly dwindle as fewer and fewer babies were born. There is a tale, a story from our past—"

Luc chuckled softly. "A legend used to keep people from losing hope."

"Yes, it is," Roane agreed. "It is a tale of a young healer hidden away by her family in a convent to hide her ability. The tale says that she fell in love with a prince who came to the convent after a fierce battle. He gave up his lineage and they married, hiding away for a lifetime to keep her safe. She was the last of the healers that we knew of. But according to my ancestors, we are her descendants."

"So, tell me, why me? Do you know if either Dylan or Cole has this ability?" Tabitha asked.

"No, neither does. Dylan was brought to me as an infant. He was quite sick, and I healed him. I had the opportunity to check him then. He does not have the talent. I have known Cole since he was a child, and I know he does not have the ability. It is common for only one sibling, if that, to have the ability. It also can skip a generation."

Tabitha slowly nodded. For once, she was feeling a twinge of peace, a slight sense of completion. She finally had some answers that she needed. The information Roane had given her was enough for her to have gained at least some comprehension of her mother's motives. They may not have been the best reasons, but at least they were reasons Tabitha could live with.

"So how did you come to be here as a prisoner?" Tabitha finally asked.

"When your mother finally decided to break free from Antoine, he had no idea it was coming. She had played the game well, and she had fooled him enough to be able to sneak away with her two babies. I lived in the village. Your mother, along with friends of hers, Gwyn to name one, took Cole and me and hid us far from here. I never let anyone know I was a healer, and I spent many happy years living down in the Bay area with the family that raised Cole, among friends.

"I don't know how, but one of the times when your mother came to see us, Antoine must have had her followed. God help us for not being more careful. She barely escaped with her life. I was severely injured. She brought me and Cole back to Gwyn. Gwyn nursed me back to health, and they once again hid me with another family. Cole, a grown man at that time, stayed with Gwyn and apprenticed in midwifery and nursing the sick. My health was declining, and my injuries from the battle with Antoine's men never healed properly. Your father found me once again and let Gwyn put me here, but I am his prisoner. He sent word to your mother to entice her back here.'

'She knows I am here and was able to see me, and she got away, to the Faye I assume, before he could capture her. I did not want her life to return to his hell over me. It is just not worth it to me."

"So she went back to the Faye?"

He shrugged.

Before he could respond, a voice from downstairs called her name. "Tabitha?"

"Cole! Yes, I am here. Coming!"

"Tabitha, wait!" Luc stood and tried to stop her with a warning.

She waved him back to his seat, missing the alarm in his voice as she sped out of the room to meet Cole.

Tabitha! Stop—it may be a trap!

Oh, stop! It's only Cole. Just wait. I'll be—Oh God!

She stopped abruptly at the bottom of the stairs, face to face with Cole, his hair lank and dirty and his face swollen and bruised. Blood was running down from a multitude of cuts. His arms were bound behind his back, his expression full of abject misery.

CHAPTER FOURTEEN

TABITHA STOOD FROZEN TO THE SPOT.

Don't come down, she whispered to Luc.

He did not respond.

She slowly let out a breath and turned to see her father lounging against the back of the couch. Seven or eight of his men filled the room, one holding the bindings on Cole's hands.

"Make no mistake, those bindings will keep him from doing any magic. They are not simply cuffs, as in your world," Antoine said quietly. "Your behavior holds the key to this young man's life. I suggest you consider that before doing anything hasty."

Tabitha slowly nodded.

Antoine walked toward her. "Will you sit and talk with me? We have much to discuss."

Tabitha dragged her eyes from Cole's bloody face to her father's. With a concentrated effort, she nodded once and made her way to the couch.

He stood across from her, his arms akimbo, looking down his nose at her as if she were an errant child. "What am I to do with you?"

She shrugged, unable to summon more will than a teen-ager caught in mischief. She knew that all their lives were in a precarious balance right now, and she had no idea how much her father knew.

"What possessed you to leave the house? I was so sure you were there being methodically deflowered by Monsieur DesChamps, only to discover you had disappeared. How did you get yourself out of the house? What would have pos-sessed you to leave your lover to seek out this man?" Antoine seemed perplexed.

Tabitha kept her eyes lowered; the more rational side of her held her emotions tightly in check as she tried to decide how to respond. It seemed that he did not know that Luc had also departed, and from his disgusted tone in referring to Cole, she assumed he did not know he was her brother.

She lifted her eyes. "I was frightened and came to speak to Gwyn."

"Frightened?"

She nodded, his apparent belief in her tale giving her a small flicker of courage. "Luc was so emphatic about our relationship that I got scared. I am not sure I am ready to stay here. I just needed some air and a walk. I wanted to speak to Gwyn."

"Truly? And I take it you did not get that opportunity?"

"She's not here."

"Ahh, no, she is not. Finally, some truth."

Tabitha's eyes snapped up. She watched him warily as he stood over her. "She is not here. She is assisting your friend during birth. You recall Katie. I believe you remember meeting her?"

Her heart began to sink. She knew it was pointless to lie; she had to learn how much he knew. "And it seems that our Monsieur DesChamps has also disappeared. Do you know where he might be?"

Tabitha shook her head. Antoine lifted a hand, and before she knew what he intended, the back of his hand cracked across her cheek, spinning her off the seat.

"Now, let's try again. My patience is at its limit. Where is Monsieur DesChamps, and why are you here?"

She held a hand to her lip, tears of pain stinging her eyes, which snapped with fury. "I told you, we spoke in my room. I asked him for some time to think. He had frightened me, it was all happening too fast. I came here to speak to Gwyn. She was not here, and I was just—"

"Go ahead, continue—just about to what? Leave? No one home?" he asked in a silky voice. "And what were you doing upstairs?"

She hesitated.

"Please continue. I am interested to hear what you will tell me next. Did you meet anyone?" Tabitha opened her mouth, but before she could speak, he leaned forward, shaking a single finger in her face. "Choose your words carefully."

"I met my grandfather," she said quietly.

"And what did he tell you?"

"He told me my mother had been here to visit but left. He told me that he could no longer walk and that Gwyn cared for him."

"And?"

She shrugged. "We talked about me and my trip here and what I would do next."

"And you told him?"

"I admitted that I want to go home to my old life, but I also want to stay here. Luc has me very confused. I care for him, but I am not sure that I am ready to commit myself to him forever yet." Her words were halting and nervous as she stared at her father. The kind expressions and pleasant demeanor had evaporated.

"I see. And this young man, who is he to you?"

Tabitha glanced to where Cole stood quietly, tense and waiting.

"I met him when I was searching for Gwyn. He is a friend only."

Antoine lowered himself back into a chair and fixed her with a long gaze. "You understand that you are within my home and that I expect you, as my daughter, to live by the rules of my house. You were told we were under a lockdown and to stay in your room, yet you disobeyed me."

Tabitha nodded. "I am not accustomed to being dictated to. I understood that you had a guard outside to protect me, but I needed to get out of the house. I needed some time to think."

He gestured to the guard closest to the stairs. "Go up and check on the old man."

The man took to the stairs, and Tabitha held her breath. Fear that Luc would be discovered blossomed in her chest.

Antoine fixed his eyes on Cole. With a curt nod, he gestured toward him. "Take him out and kill him."

Tabitha leaped to her feet with a cry. "No!"

Antoine fixed her with a cold stare. "You will learn to obey me. I have been more than lenient with you, but the time has come for you to understand what I require from you." He gestured toward Cole with a dismissive wave of his hand. "He will be your first lesson of maintaining order in our world. You are my daughter and as such will only associate with people within your distinct social level. I understand the draw of speaking with Gwyn, but I will not run the risk of you falling in love with a man outside of your social rank. I understand you to be fond of Monsieur DesChamps, but it seems that he was unable to sway you to wed or promise yourself to him. In light of the evening's events, it seems justifiable that I step in and find you a worthy mate."

Tabitha gaped at him, unable to believe, even under the circumstances, what he was saying. "You will have him killed because you are afraid I will want to marry him?"

Antoine nodded. "No man will want a wife who is pining for a commoner."

He gestured to the guard once again, who seized Cole.

Tabitha spun back toward her father. "I am not falling in love with him…" Cole shook his head but she ignored him. "He is my brother."

Antoine's brows shot up in surprise. "Truly?" He stood and approached Cole. He looked closely at the man's face; Cole averted his eyes, his bloody lip swollen to an enormous level, his eye almost swollen shut. "Huh, I do not think he looks like your twin."

Tabitha could have shrieked in frustration. "Of course not! You have had him beaten!"

"He would not let us into the house. I had to have him beaten." Antoine seemed surprised at her rage.

Her response was cut off when the guard who had gone upstairs came down the steps in a rush. "No one up there, sir."

"What?"

"The upstairs is empty, Milord. No one is up there, and no sign of anyone."

He turned back to Tabitha. "Where is he?"

She shrugged. "He was up there when I was up there."

Antoine's eyes narrowed as he turned to Cole. Cole's answer was thick through swollen lips. "You know where I've been, so you know I didn't move him."

"Were you alone?" He turned back to glare at Tabitha.

She nodded.

"Goddammit." He gestured to the guards. "You, you, you, get outside and look for any trace of the old man. He has to be here somewhere."

The guards left in a snap. Two of the remaining guards moved closer to where Cole stood and another stayed behind Tabitha's back.

Antoine shook his head. He glanced at Tabitha. "We had best find him. And we had best find your Monsieur DesChamps at the house or you will answer my questions one way or another."

A chill slipped down Tabitha's spine, but she held her head up and refused to let him see her fear.

His back was still to her when he quietly asked, "How did you get out of the house?"

"I—I just walked out. The same door I always do," she responded. "You told me that your men seemed to lose me when I go off alone. I have to assume I must slip under your mental radar when I am deep in thought, and I was when I left."

He grunted and strolled over closer to the window, looking for a sign of any life outside the house. "You will be kept under very close watch for the near future. It seems that you keep popping up where you should not be. How is it you came to be in Katie's room?"

Slightly taken back by the question, Tabitha's mind raced. "I was looking for a quiet place to get away from people right before the party, and I found a sitting area with a beautiful view. I was sitting by the window when a servant came out of the room. After she left, I went over and tried the door."

He nodded and turned his attention back to the window, waiting and watching. Tabitha turned to Cole and found his eyes intent upon her. She wished desperately that they could talk, but the guards were too close. He dropped his gaze and sent a questioning look up the stairs.

Luc must have snuck their grandfather out of the house. She wanted to reach out to him but was not confident that her father would remain unaware of her intention. She lowered her head into her hands and released a long breath, waiting for something to happen.

Seconds ticked by in the silent room. Tabitha felt as though the tension in the room was almost a palpable and living thing, pressing down and threatening to suffocate her. She tried to draw one breath after another, willing herself to be calm as she searched for an avenue of escape.

Antoine's patience snapped. With a snarl, he demanded the guards bind Tabitha's hands. Her arms were yanked forward and her wrists lashed together with a solid cord. As the cord was tightened around her wrists, Tabitha could feel it sap her power, like a switch being shut off in her mind.

"Must you?" she spat out at her father as the guard shoved her toward the door. She stopped in front of Antoine, her eyes snapping in fury. "What more can I possibly do?"

He disregarded her plea and shouldered past her, out the door into the dark night. He snapped a command to the men. Tabitha was swept out among the guards while Cole was restrained a good distance away from her. The other guards returned to report no sign of Roane in the vicinity. Antoine cursed and ordered the two to remain at the house in case anyone else showed up. With a barked command, Tabitha was shoved forward with a sickening lurch. They stepped forward into a clearing just beyond the woods outside of Antoine's estate. The roof of the house was a dark and ominous line against the night sky.

"Bring them to the cellar. I wish to continue this discussion inside. Make sure none of my guests see them," Antoine snapped. He spun on his heel toward the house and disappeared into the night.

The guards prodded and pushed Cole and Tabitha down the dark lane toward the back entrance of the house. Tabitha dragged her feet, stumbling and stalling in an awkward effort to buy a few precious minutes, hoping against hope that Luc would leap from the woods and set them free. Maybe he had found help and they were racing even now to assist her and Cole. Her hopes began to shrink as they emerged from the wooded lane at the back of the house.

She paused, and the guard who had been dragging her grew impatient. He stopped long enough to heft her up. She let out a startled *oof* as she was tossed over his shoulder. His counterparts laughed and bellowed encouragement as the guard strutted forward, his prize slung over his shoulder. The awkward position was mortifying; the other guards hooted and hollered as the one carrying her strode forward as though she were a trophy.

She snarled to be released, but that only drew louder laughter and more bawdy jokes. The guard carrying her turned with his prize and, to the delight of his comrades, ran an appreciative hand along her legs and up and over her round bottom. She felt her face redden at the humiliation but bit back a response. Every reaction from her only seemed to heighten their amusement. With every struggle and kick, her captor held her tighter, his comments to his companions growing more suggestive.

Her legs began to go numb under the man's tight grip. As she struggled, she twisted her head and caught a glimpse of Cole. His eyes remained averted, but she could see his jaw tighten. Fear for him kept her silent and stilled her struggles. If he were to try to come to her defense, that would be all they would need to bestow another beating. Antoine had told the guards to keep them alive but had not mentioned that they were not to be harmed.

They were hustled into the house and quietly spirited down dark corridors into the underground depths. With the twists and turns in the dark halls, Tabitha quickly lost track of where they were. She tried to glimpse around to find a familiar sight, but the attempts only drew a gloved fist to her jaw. Her head was spinning and her stomach queasy by the time they stopped moving. She was dumped unceremoniously onto a carpeted floor.

She rolled and tried to stand, but her hips were grabbed by a guard, who dragged her across the room to a seat by a large stone hearth. Lights were lit, and soon a fire was sparking and spitting as it chewed the small packets of kindling a guard tossed into its yawning mouth.

The room was large and windowless; a settee and two matching seats were grouped around the large hearth. The dark walls reflected the glow from the growing fire, and the few lights that they had lit struggled to illuminate the corners of the spacious chamber. The hallway outside of the single doorway was dark. The gloom seemed to further emphasize the depths of the hopelessness of their captivity, and Tabitha felt the cold chill of fear.

Where is Luc?

Cole was dragged to a seat to her right. He grunted, and Tabitha could see the lines of pain around his mouth as he struggled for a breath.

"Are you all right?" she whispered.

He glanced over at her. One eye was painfully shut, and the other crinkled in a semblance of a smile. "Yeah, nothing a few weeks on a beach wouldn't cure."

Any further comments vanished when Antoine strode into the room, taking in his children's bound hands. His smile was slight and enigmatic as he gestured toward the door. "Come in, come in. Let's have a family reunion."

Dylan strode into the room at Antoine's beckoning. A cold smile spread across his face as he regarded his siblings, bound and beaten, before him. "What a pleasant sight. If only Mother could be here as well."

Antoine chuckled and nodded. "Well, we can only hope that your fair mother will wish to join her family. To think it has taken me eighteen years to finally bring all three of my children together." He sat in the center of the settee and stretched his arms out along the back, regarding the pair huddled in chairs before him. "My only wish is that one day we will all be able to truly enjoy each other's company, perhaps even looking back at this time with humor."

Tabitha felt growing ire, but she swallowed her anger. Her voice was steady as she met her father's gaze. "I would like to know why we are being bound. What have we done that you feel the need to have us tied? Are we such a threat?"

"Threat?" Antoine laughed. "You two have barely realized your abilities. Had you placed your trust in me, my dear, I would have helped you achieve your full potential. Why, with your pedigree, you can have anything. You have your choice of futures, any man you choose, whatever you would want. As my daughter, I can offer you a life that you would have never even dreamed of in your world."

He leaned forward, placing his elbows on his knees as he stared at her. "I know of your life in your world. An aging and eccentric aunt—that woman is the laughingstock of the island with her tarot cards and foolishness. She has not an iota of ability. Your mother, when she was there with you, was disinterested. You kept a mate at bay." He clucked his tongue and grinned at her. "He found elsewhere what you would not give him."

Tabitha's cheeks flushed as Antoine's last comment hit home.

"How do you know this? How do you know so much about me?" she hissed, humiliation rushing through her.

"Oh, I had people watching. I received reports fairly often about your whereabouts and doings," he responded lightly.

"So that was just another lie? The one you told me about not knowing where I was and wishing you could find me?" she spat.

"Well, you could look at it that way, but I prefer to believe that I waited for you to find me. I knew if I was patient enough, at some point you would find your way here. If you did not, I had plans in place to entice you here," he admitted. "What I have not quite figured out, however, is how you and Monsieur DesChamps found one another. That little tidbit of information is missing, and I was hoping you would supply it."

Tabitha shook her head, her eyes on the floor. Her privacy had been sold; she had been spied upon. Her movements and personal trials and tribulations had been boiled down to a weekly report, a summary on a desk. To make it worse, her father had also been given information about Greg cheating on her. The thought of his infidelity as a paragraph in a weekly summary drove the air from her lungs. She caught her breath in a quick sob as she tried to drag herself back to the present. She could not let her father's gloating destroy her.

"It seems you have more information about me than I would have thought possible. If you want to know anything more, you will have to figure it out for yourself." The fight had momentarily left her, and her response was little more than a whisper.

Antoine shrugged. "I will ask your lover. He will tell me."

"You are well aware that he is not my lover," Tabitha snarled.

Antoine chuckled, as did Dylan, his eyes shining with interest as he watched the exchange. He propped himself on one corner of the back of the couch, his arms crossed on his upraised knee.

"Little sister, it is only a matter of time. I have known Luc for many years, and he is a patient hunter." Dylan's voice was silky and low. When Tabitha glanced at him, the leering sparkle in his eye set her on edge. She felt her skin shiver all over under his intent gaze but chose to ignore the comment.

Antoine cocked his head to the side and turned to Cole. "And you are a very pleasant surprise tonight. To think I almost had you killed. In one evening, I finally have my two missing children with me. It has taken me more time than I would have liked, but I knew in the end I would bring you both back to me."

He glanced at each of the twin siblings, and a short laugh escaped him. "When I thought that Tabitha was running to you, I had you watched. I was sure she had come to care for you. I actually had planned on showing Tabitha your infidelity to her, thinking of course that she had romantic designs on you. I had no idea that my missing twins had found each other."

Cole lifted his face, and a look of pure dread crossed his face. Tabitha looked at them, confusion on her face. Before anyone could comment, a brief knock on the door interrupted them.

All eyes turned to the door when one of the guards swung it open. A slight woman entered hesitantly.

"I was sent here to…" As she took several steps into the darkened room and stopped in horror, her voice dropped off. Her eyes were wide as she stared at Cole, his badly beaten face a mask of misery. Dylan rose with a casual stretch and walked over to shut the door behind her.

Antoine turned to glance at the girl. "Ah, yes. Please join us." Antoine waved her in.

As she took a hesitant step forward, Dylan slid behind her, his hands locked on her waist. The girl gasped in shock as he pushed her toward the center of the room. "Does everyone know Lena?"

Cole dropped his eyes, and Tabitha gasped as she recognized the young woman who had so recently introduced herself.

Antoine grinned, again leaning back in the center of the couch, his arms spread over the back, one ankle resting on his knee. He looked the picture of a contented father surrounded by his children. Tabitha fought the urge to leap to her feet and claw his smirk away. "Well, we are only missing…"

After a brief knock, the door again opened, and Luc strode in. Tabitha felt her jubilation at the sight of him safe dissipate as Luc shut the door behind him and walked confidently into the center of the room.

"Excellent timing, Monsieur DesChamps, excellent. You are all we needed to complete our little party. Of course, Doni's presence would truly round out the evening. We must all wish her here with us in spirit, eh?" He turned to Luc, "Is our friend resting comfortably?"

Luc nodded, avoiding Tabitha's shocked stare. "He is. Gwyn is with him. He is none the worse for being moved."

Antoine nodded, and his gaze turned to Tabitha and Cole. "No need to fear. Your grandfather is well and comfortably ensconced in a suite upstairs. I will allow you to see for yourselves, once we have completed our business."

His words were like tiny daggers spearing through Tabitha's gut. Luc, her trusted confidante, had taken her grandfather and then brought him here? To Antoine? He stood quietly beside Dylan, and Tabitha felt the blood drain from her face. *Luc?* He was not here to rescue her. He had not been stalking them through the woods, preparing some fantastic and elaborate rescue. She had imagined him swooping in and saving the day, carrying her out and...and what? Saving her? He had betrayed her. She swallowed the bitter moan that threatened to engulf her.

Antoine spoke again to Luc, his eyes fastened on Tabitha's tortured expression. "And the other? What of her? Has she had the child?"

Luc nodded, "I regret to be the one to tell you that the child did not make it."

Antoine's fist clenched, but otherwise his expression remained the same. Dylan slammed his open palms down on the table next to the couch with a snarl. Antoine glanced at him and opened his fist, extending an open palm in Dylan's direction. "It can't be helped. We will find another. And the girl?"

Luc lifted one shoulder in a shrug. "I understood you to have no further use for her. Gwyn did say that the loss of blood in childbirth is often fatal. Would have probably happened in time anyway."

Tabitha could not control the pain that sliced through her at his cold words. She dropped her face, blocking out the sight of him as tears coursed down her cheeks. She had led him to Katie. She had begged him to help her save Katie, but he had been the one to kill her. A sob escaped her lips, but she quickly gulped it back. Never in her life had she felt such pain. Greg's betrayal had been humiliating but this...Luc's betrayal had sliced a hole in her soul. She fought to regain some semblance of control over her emotions.

Antoine nodded. "We will speak of this further. I would still like to hear your thoughts on your uncle's apparent defection. His actions could incite civil war."

Luc's eyes were steady as he met Antoine's. "I agree. But in the meantime, there seems to be little reason to keep these two bound and imprisoned. They were trying to protect their grandfather; it would seem to me that now they know he is safe, they pose no further threat to you."

Antoine nodded and gestured for Luc and Lena to approach him. "There is one simple thing left to determine." He stood and approached the two who stood warily before him. Lena's face reflected her fear. Luc watched with steady curiosity, calm but tense.

Antoine waved a hand toward Tabitha and Cole. "Unbind them."

He approached Lena first. With a polite nod to her, he lifted a hand to the neckline of her blouse. "If you will allow me, my dear, I mean only to glance at your throat."

Lena nodded, her eyes wide in apprehension. Antoine gently slid a finger into the collar of her blouse and with his thumb lifted her chin in both directions, revealing her throat on either side. With a grunt, he turned to Luc and did the same. Tabitha held her breath, but when Antoine checked his throat, no scars were visible. Confused, she glanced at Luc. When his eyes met hers, the betrayal of his actions quickly swept her glance away.

Antoine harrumphed and turned back to Tabitha and Cole. "You are both no doubt aware that your grandfather and your mother have the healing talent. As Dylan does not have it, I suspect one of you carries it."

When neither spoke, Antoine stood between them and Luc and Lena. "I give you one opportunity to tell me which of you is the healer. If you fail to step forward, I will be forced to test you on my own."

Tabitha and Cole stared at him; neither spoke. Luc pointed to Tabitha. When Antoine lifted a brow in her direction, Tabitha's mouth dropped in shock. Why she would be surprised after Luc's previous traitorous behavior, she did not know, but this final deceit stunned her.

"Truly?" Antoine asked.

Luc nodded. "I have witnessed it myself."

"And did you replenish her?" Antoine asked him.

Luc appeared confused. "Replenish?"

"How did she behave after the healing? Was there any indication that her…uh, energy levels were low? That she needed something?" Antoine persisted.

Luc shook his head, looking perplexed. "No, she was fine, maybe a little tired."

Antoine nodded slowly. "It was a small healing? Something insignificant?"

"A scratch only. My cousin's daughter had fallen."

Tabitha stared in shocked silence. Why had he told Antoine of her healing ability but hid his scars? Her anger was reaching epic heights. How could she possibly contain herself from simply blowing his handsome head off his shoulders? And how had he hidden the scars?

Antoine nodded to Dylan and stepped back. Dylan tugged a revolver from the back waistband of his pants. In a flash of light and an explosive boom, a shot rang out.

Tabitha screamed, covered her ears, and fell to her knees, unsure what had happened. As though in slow motion, she raised her eyes. To her horror, Luc was collapsing to the floor, blood spurting from his chest.

CHAPTER FIFTEEN

TABITHA ROSE IN A FLASH AND WITHOUT FURTHER thought was at his side. Her hands were on his chest, the warmth of the healing energy coursing down her fingers before her knees hit the floor beside him. Her last thoughts were a desperate plea for Luc to not die. And then the calm of the healing power overtook her. As she concentrated on repairing the damage inflicted in a split second, all thoughts and stress drained from her body.

As the tissues knit back together and the arteries and veins reconnected, Tabitha's last thought before withdrawing was to direct the energy toward his throat, attempting to heal the twin scars she had given him the last time she had expended the healing. It was bittersweet to see that the scars remained. She withdrew, her eyes heavy and her breathing raspy. A deep hunger gnawed at her, and every fiber screamed out for nourishment.

She sat back on her heels, her face tilted up toward the ceiling, as she tried to gather enough strength to crawl away from him. His shirt lay open across his chest, the muscle and skin intact, not a trace of the wound remaining. Tabitha became aware of the long fangs in her mouth, and she hated them.

Luc's eyes were open, watching her, when she glanced down at him. His voice was soft. "Take from me what you need."

For a moment, her energy levels were so low she wanted to collapse into his arms and feel their strength envelop her. She wanted to drink from him and feel his blood return her strength. But with every breath, her energy trickled back, and anger slowly seeped into her consciousness. Through her hands, still on his chest, she felt the warmth of his skin and the soft thudding of his heart just below her fingertips. She shoved away the warmth, reminded herself of every betrayal. She listed his offenses in her mind to rid herself of anything but hatred. She swallowed the last of the gentle feelings and let fury bubble up.

She leaned down, her eyes fairly snapping with rage as she hissed, "I will *never* touch you again. You should be thankful that I am not the type of person who can easily watch a person die. If I were, I would just as happily let your life pour out on the floor in front of me. As it is, I hope you rot in hell when you finally get what you deserve."

She tried to get up and walk away with her dignity intact, but she had not yet recovered enough. Antoine snapped for Dylan to assist her. Tabitha felt herself lifted in his arms. She growled for him to release her, but Dylan strode from the room, taking her with him. She let her head drop back. The darkness she had been fighting swept her away from the pain and shock of the evening.

Luc slowly lifted himself onto his elbows, his body still reeling from the shock of being shot and the healing that had returned him to almost normal. Blood soaked the front of his shirt, and his head pounded with the effort of lifting it. Soft sobs were the only sound. He let his eyes focus on the orange flames hissing and popping in the hearth beyond his feet.

He glanced up and saw Antoine quietly sipping a drink, watching Cole holding the sobbing Lena. Antoine lifted his eyes to Luc's hard gaze.

"You want to warn me next time you plan something like that?" Luc growled as he slowly sat up.

Antoine lifted a shoulder in a negligent shrug. "I am thinking you would not have been quick to agree. I needed Tabitha to simply react. I do, however, wish she had not thought you had betrayed her. I was concerned she would not be as apt to assist."

Luc released a short, brittle laugh. "Yeah, that thought crossed my mind as well when she told me she wished me dead after she had healed me."

Antoine's glance swept back to Cole, huddled on the floor, holding Lena, whose crying had subsided into short hiccups. He gestured to the guards. "Take them from here. Lock him below. Do with her what you will."

Luc glanced at the couple on the floor, absorbing their expressions of stark terror. Luc saw Cole's jaw harden and said, "If I may suggest that you let this all pass…"

Antoine shot him a glance. "Why would I do that? I have a healer. I do not require him."

Luc slowly rose from the floor and lifted himself into the chair, his limbs shaking. He was determined not to let Antoine see him struggle. "Yes, you do. You have a very headstrong and angry healer who right now will not be apt to do anything for you. She has recently found her twin brother, and I would hazard a guess he is the only one in this world she trusts. If you lock him away and throw his girlfriend to your guards, you will never win her over. At some point, you will need her to do as you wish if it will ever be to your benefit to have a healer to do your bidding."

Antoine grunted and appeared to be listening. "And you know her so well?"

"Better than anyone else you have at your disposal."

Antoine nodded briefly. "And do you think she will ever come around with any approach except threats?"

Luc shrugged. "If she does not, it would be best to keep him nearby. He is, after all, the one person you have that she cares about right now. And if you ever want him to help you, letting your guards rape and dispose of his girlfriend will not win him over to your cause."

Cole shot to his feet. "Stop speaking about us as though we are not here. I will tell you right now that I have no intention of ever helping you or even—"

A fist to his jaw from the guard behind him silenced Cole's unspoken outburst. As he crumbled to the floor, Lena released fresh sobs.

Luc watched this all impassively and gestured to the carafe at Antoine's elbow. "The least you can do after having me shot would be to offer me a drink."

Antoine smiled and poured him a drink. He passed the younger man the glass as the guards dragged the still-comatose Cole from the room. Lena stumbled after him. "Put him in a secure suite and post a guard outside. Put her in there with him for now, until I decide what to do."

He turned back toward Luc. "And when I have won her over, what then? What use will he ever be?"

Luc regarded the amber fluid in the glass and took a long drink before answering. "You have a tendency to find people either useful or not. Once you have discarded someone, you will never again be able to make use of them. Your son also carries the healing gene. He may not be a healer himself, but he may father one. You need to think in longer terms than the immediate future."

Antoine sat back and regarded the younger man with interest. "You are proving your worth. I had not considered his ability to father a healer. And his woman? She is human and as such unable to give birth to a healer."

"Are you so sure that is not possible? Simply allow him to keep her. He can marry anyone to sire a child, but if he is able to keep this woman as his own, what harm does it do?" Luc swished the fluid around the crystal glass with a nonchalant ease that he wished he felt as the words emerged from his lips.

Antoine chuckled. "I must admit, I had not thought you were quite so calculating. But we still have the obvious issue of your uncle's actions. Which side of this do you fall on? I would know now to name you friend or foe."

Luc glanced up. "What makes you think anyone is choosing sides? Are you telling me that you consider yourself against Marcus?"

Antoine nodded. "He attacked my forces. Marcus's people attacked a simple, peaceful platoon of men. I take that as an act of war."

"The reports stated that the villagers thought themselves under attack and were only defending themselves," Luc countered.

"Defending themselves? Villagers?" Antoine scoffed. "There were hundreds of Marcus's men awaiting my legion. They were simply passing through, and they were attacked," Antoine argued.

"Why would a legion of your men be traveling through Marcus's territory? Was Marcus aware of your intent or their destination?" Luc persisted.

"I can allow my legions to go wherever I please. Marcus may be the governing chancellor of St. Mikel, but we are all one large territory. I need not ask Marcus's permission to send a peacekeeping legion through his lands."

Luc held up a hand and leaned forward. "We have all heard the reports of attacks on random villages. Reports of attacks and whole villages being decimated by unknown forces were prominent at the last village council. Prudence would suggest that it is in your best interest to alert villages of your legions' intentions rather than send them into St. Mikel territory without warning. These are dangerous times, and if we wish to avoid future missteps, we should all communicate thoroughly and effectively. Had those people waited to learn your legion's intent, and it had been hostile, they would have paid for that with their lives and the lives of their families."

"You are saying that Marcus's act of open aggression and hostility was simply the result of miscommunication on my part?" Antoine was incredulous.

"I am saying that I do not have enough information to judge Marcus's intent, and, frankly, neither do you. I do not claim allegiance to you anymore than I will defend Marcus's actions until I know what happened and what transpired between my people and your legions." With the statement, Luc intended to let the matter lie. He dared not allow Antoine believe he was entirely in his corner. A little uncertainty was more believable than his blind trust.

Antoine nodded and sat quietly for a moment, digesting the information. He was certain he could spin it in a way to work in his favor. Luc was giving him the ammunition to salvage the situation. It was far too early to lose the entire Northeastern territory. He glanced up at the younger man, quietly sipping the drink in front of him, his gaze clear and steady.

"You may be right. Perhaps between us, we can make sure that the situation is rectified," Antoine said slowly. "But tell me, what are your feelings for my daughter? At this moment, I believe she thinks you have betrayed her. Why would you allow that if you care for her?"

"Tabitha is frightened and in a strange world. She is out of her element but desperately wants to find answers to questions that have nagged her for years. She is unfolding eighteen years of mystery in a matter of weeks. She is asking the wrong questions. She does not need to know the whys but the hows. *Why* is a futile question that demands nothing but an emotional and open response. Yet she asks it again and again. She need only question the how, and that is more of a factual timeline. If she continues to delve into who said and who did, she will never get to the truth, because the truth is hidden behind a veil of emotion and perception," Luc replied.

Antoine's eyes narrowed slightly. "Are you saying I lied to her or intentionally managed her perception?"

Luc shook his head. "I am saying you gave her your perception of what transpired. If she finds her mother, that perception will be her mother's own. Each of you has different perceptions. You would have to in order for your relationship to have eroded. Tabitha wants to know what happened and how things became what they did. She is slowly finding out that the answers are not that simple. She is receiving a conglomeration of multiple insights, and the truth is nothing more than each person's individual beliefs."

"You have effectively avoided my question. Why did you betray her? What are your feelings for her?" Antoine persisted.

"I did not betray her. I did what I thought was right. I brought Roane here because I felt he would get the best care here and be safest. I do not know what Cole's intention was regarding his grandfather, but a healer is too important to our people to lose. Tabitha will see that in time. He can help her if she will just get over the belief that you have some sinister plan for him. You have had ample time if you intended the man harm. He has been in the village for years under Gwyn's care.'

'She thinks that telling you about her healing ability was a breach of trust. You have a right to know—her ability is something we all need. Our people are dying. You are well aware that either Cole or Tabitha had the ability. Why hide it when the truth is easy enough to uncover? We need her to help us save our people and our children. My father told her as much when she was in Calais," Luc explained.

"And Katie?" Antoine asked quietly.

"She may never forgive me for Katie. Katie was beyond help when I found her. She was already dying." Luc lifted his intent gaze to Antoine. "I hope to have a lifetime to win her back."

Antoine could not help but laugh. "You are quite a speaker. What a politician you would make if you have that desire."

Luc shrugged and grinned at the compliment. "Perhaps. But right now, I think it is time I try to realign our territories and bring some sense to the outstanding issue of Marcus's apparent defensive attack."

Antoine stood and extended a hand to him. "My daughter is in her chambers. She is yours for your loyalty."

Luc hesitated. "I have not yet pledged any fealty or allegiance. I have only promised to review the facts and pass judgment on what transpired."

"I have no doubt that when you have done your diligence, you will find that you are ready to offer me fealty. In the meantime, my daughter is yours. When we can ascertain what transpired and you can give me your allegiance without reservation, we will plan the wedding." Antoine clapped the younger man on the back.

Antoine called to the guards outside the door to find Jules. He and Luc then spoke briefly of their intentions and a potential plan until Jules arrived.

"Jules, have Monsieur DesChamps's things moved into my daughter's chamber. He has a lot on his agenda, and I would like him to be able to enjoy his free time." Antoine laughed at his own wit. With a final shake of Luc's hand, the older man strode off, his voice booming down the hall as he headed toward his offices.

Jules was stunned when Luc sagged back against the wall, his face pale. "What happened?"

Luc smiled wanly. The energy it took to spar with Antoine and keep himself upright had drained what little strength he had. "I will tell you on the way, but I need to lie down soon."

"I would imagine you do," Jules observed, gesturing to the blood on Luc's shirt. "Whose blood?"

Luc groaned and ran a hand through his hair. "Mine. If I miss one step in this game, it won't be the last I am going to shed before I get her out of here."

Jules slipped his arm around the younger man's waist. "Let me help you. You can tell me what happened on the way."

Luc nodded. "I am juggling so many fiery balls in the air right now that I am bound to get burned."

They made their way through the dark hallway, and Luc slowly revealed what had transpired in the past couple of hours.

CHAPTER SIXTEEN

TABITHA WOKE WITH A START AND FOUND HERSELF lying atop her bed in her dark and quiet room. A quick check with her tongue assured her that, at the very least, the dreaded fangs had receded. She rolled off her bed and kicked off her boots before padding barefoot into the bathroom to brush her teeth. Her teeth clean, she wandered over to the windows; it had to be only an hour or so before dawn. Fatigue tugged at her body, but the thought of climbing back into bed was less than appealing. Dreams and nightmares waited at the edge of her conscious mind to drag her back into the last hours of the previous night. The memory of being again called upon to use her healing ability and consequently display her canines filled her with shame.

Bertòn had warned her, as had the Faye, but she had insisted that she could handle it all. She had been so sure that she could just take care of everything. And Luc...

The memory of watching him tumble backward, the bullet wound gaping on his chest, played itself over and over in her mind. Rage at his betrayal circulated through her nerves and the pain tore at her heart, forcing her to swallow her tears over and over. Anger and pain vied for top billing in her ragged thoughts. When she tried to push them aside, the vision of Katie, lying in a pool of blood, Luc standing over, her threatened to push her over the edge into useless blubbering.

How had he killed her? Had he strangled her? Stabbed her? The images played themselves over again. Finally, she could bear it no longer, and she slowly sank to the floor, her head against the cool window, and let the tears flow. Agony welled up in chest. She could not even begin to think about what she would do tomorrow. Right now, she simply wanted to crawl into a hole and never come out.

Luc stood outside of the door, his forehead resting against the wood. He heard her crying on the other side and could not bring himself to intrude. He needed her rage; he needed her determined to escape. He could not afford to allow her to forgive him until she was safely away, but the knowledge of the pain he was causing her played heavily upon his heart. He rested his palm against the door, his thoughts and his heart heavy as he listened to her sob.

Jules entered the outer sitting area room just after dawn and found Luc sitting on the couch, still wearing his bloody shirt, his head leaning against the back of the couch. A cup of javé was in his hand, forgotten, his long legs stretched out in front of him, ankles crossed.

"You did not get far," Jules commented.

Luc grunted and rose. "I am going to get dressed and bathe. It is time I started my day. I have a farce to keep up. Were you able to find anything?"

Jules nodded. "I will bring it by later today. When would you like your things moved?"

"Tonight. Just make sure someone keeps an eye on her today until I can get back. I don't want her alone. I don't want her doing anything crazy." Luc rose and headed for the door.

"Crazy? Tabitha?" Jules quipped.

Luc let out a low laugh. "Yeah, if she simmers too long and feels backed into a corner, I am afraid of what she may do."

"She will be well watched."

Tabitha slept the morning away. Tears helped, and once they were spent she had finally crawled back into bed and tried to hide from the world. Midday, Jules knocked on the door and left a plate of food for her, but it remained untouched. She got up, showered, and finally opened the balcony doors to the late afternoon sunshine. Shadows were slowly creeping along the lawn, and she felt the warm summer air begin to slowly cool. She drew in a deep breath and tried to find some peaceful thought, any semblance of calm that she could cling to, but it escaped her.

A knock on the door brought her out of her reverie. She considered ignoring it but knew that whoever had been sent would eventually come in, regardless of her welcome. The guard who waited on the other side of the door then informed her that her father had sent for her. Her refusal was met with an apologetic explanation that he was to deliver her, one way or the other.

Tabitha took her time dressing, letting the man and her father wait until she was good and ready to leave. She knew her delay was pointless and nothing more than irritating, but her sense of helplessness at her captivity was slightly eased by the slight act of defiance. She brushed out her hair and slipped into shoes, her stomach still quaking. It was not her safety that she worried about but rather the safety of anyone her father thought she cared about. She was not sure what he was capable of and to what extent he would demand her acquiescence. She did not feel prepared to find out how far she could push him.

She followed the faceless and nameless guard; one of many at her father's beckoning. She could not tell one from another and frankly had little interest in even trying. Upon coming to the estate, she had been eager to learn of the people there: the servants, the people who worked there and assisted her father. It had come as a difficult lesson that those who served her father would not interact with her. They placed her in a category of people they considered to be the elite, for lack of a better description. Tabitha found the arrangement uncomfortable and unnatural. She had no idea how to deal with such social inequity, especially being considered on the upper rung of this odd societal ranking.

Now, after the events of the past few days, she could not care less. There was no one in the large estate that she cared to speak to or even know other than Cole, Gwyn, and her grandfather. She did not know whom to trust or believe, let alone how to even begin to reconcile herself to the possibility that if she did not come up with some plan, she might become a permanent prisoner here.

The guard rapped on her father's study door, opened it, and stepped aside to allow her to enter. She could have spat a curse at him for so being quick to abandon her to her fate in that room but it would have been pointless.

"Well, you took your time," Antoine said as she entered.

"Maybe you can have me beaten for that," Tabitha snapped before she could stop herself.

He stood and slowly approached her. With one hand he gently lifted her chin, turning her face from side to side to view the blossoming bruises from his hands the night before.

"Perhaps I will," he replied, releasing her chin and stepping back. "It got your attention, did it not?"

"Is that what you wanted? My attention? There are less violent ways of getting my attention," she responded.

"Yes, I saw that. By asking you to remain in your room… Hmm, if I recall, that did not work. By asking that you refrain from speaking to anyone…Well, that was ignored as well. Asking you to not get into additional mischief? No, I do not recall that worked." He lifted a hand sharply before her face and smiled maliciously when she flinched. "Ah, but I think you may have finally learned something."

She clenched her jaws in fury and balled her hands into fists. Her reaction to his raised fist fueled her anger even more. She forced herself to remain standing before him, defiant and furious, willing herself with every fiber to quell the fear.

"Where is Cole?" she demanded.

"Resting comfortably," Antoine responded as he stepped over to the sideboard and poured himself a drink. He lifted the decanter over an empty glass and looked at her with a question, but she angrily shook her head. "Well then, to your own ends."

"May I see him?"

"Eventually," he replied as he sipped his drink.

"May I see my grandfather?"

"Yes, I will have you taken to him when we have finished speaking," Antoine responded.

She had to admit to being slightly startled. "And Gwyn?"

"She is with your grandfather. I have asked her to move here temporarily to care for him until such time that all quiets down. He may find himself more comfortable here anyway. I understand he enjoys having an easterly facing window and the breeze it affords him," Antoine said conversationally.

"And what of me? Why don't we get to that? Am I a prisoner here?"

He nodded. "You are. And you will be watched and followed until you have proven to me that I can trust you. If that time ever comes. Be thankful that I am not having you locked up in a cell. You will have comfortable rooms and be able to move around—limited access at first, but that may change in time."

"Thankful? I may as well be in a cell if I am locked in those rooms!"

"Your rooms are not too unpleasant, I think. You have plenty of space, and they are quite comfortable." He seemed to consider for a moment. "Although you are right. Because you will be detained here for the foreseeable future, you may find a larger suite more accommodating to the two of you."

"Two?" Tabitha could only repeat the word.

"Yes, you and Monsieur DesChamps. I have rewarded him for his loyalty and solicitous behavior. I was impressed that he acted with logic and foresight rather than following your emotional responses. He is proving himself to be of some value to me, unlike your older brother who shares your temper and gift for emotional react—"

"Wait…wait! What do you mean, for me and Monsieur DesChamps? Exactly what are you saying? You rewarded him?" She could barely spit out the words as she tried to make sense of what he was telling her.

"Monsieur DesChamps. He is quite taken with you, and I approve of the match," Antoine said simply. He took another long drink from his glass.

"You approve of the match? *Approve of the match?* I want nothing more than to tear that lying son of a bitch's face off! There is no match!" Tabitha's voice became more intense as a blind rage roiled through her.

"Oh, but there is. You see, you lost all ability to make your own decisions when you chose to disobey me. Had I not intervened, what exactly would you and your brother have done? You were trying to get to your grandfather, and you were going to leave. You cannot deny that!" Antoine snarled in return, slamming his glass down.

"So you have decided that I am supposed to what? Marry him? You are seriously saying that you expect me to be his 'reward'? He lied to me! He betrayed me! I would sooner slit my throat than marry him or have anything—"

Antoine rose to his full height, his finger pointing at her face. "And that is exactly why you will be watched and guarded closely. You are too valuable to me to leave unguarded. So during the days, a guard will remain posted. If you cannot be trusted, a guard will physically be with you every moment. At night, Monsieur DesChamps will have the duty of keeping you out of trouble." His finger dropped and a slow grin spread over his face. "And I did not say marry. I only said I have given you to him. We will discuss marriage if and when he opts to swear fealty to me."

Shear amazement diminished her anger. For several moments, as his words slowly sank in, she could not even speak. "Are…you…telling me that you expect me to—" She held up a hand and slowly shook her head, unable to grasp what she was about to say. "Are you thinking I am going to *sleep* with him? Are you seriously telling me that as a *reward* for betraying me, you have given me, a person, who is not you, who you have *no* right to even begin to have any say about…You are telling me that you are saying…" She stopped. *No way.* It could not be what she was thinking. "Okay. Tell me again what you gave him?"

Antoine smile was cold and cruel. "I have given him… you."

"Me? You think I am going to go back to my room and just hop into bed with that lying, deceitful, scumbag of a—"

His hand rose again, and this time he did not stop it. Tabitha spun away with the force of the blow, her hand to her jaw; she doubled over, gasping as pain seared through her brain. All rational thought fled her mind as she bent over, her hands protectively covering her face.

"You will. You will do this because you are my daughter and it is what I demand of you. You are part of something bigger than your own little ego. You are a piece of a very intricate puzzle, and your behavior and your actions not only rule your future but the futures of those around you and those you love. Those lives are in a very slim balance, and your actions will determine what will happen to them. You think long and hard about that when you decide your actions tonight. You will lie beneath him and you will accept him as your lover, and if he does not decide to swear fealty to me, you will be my negotiating tool with another ambitious young man who would like to gain the status that marrying you will bring him." Antoine's voice was a cold whisper behind her.

"I won't," she sobbed through her hands, wondering if she even cared what he did. All dignity was being stripped from her. She was slowly edging down a dark chasm of despair.

"Then I will kill your brother's woman," he responded.

She slowly lifted her head to him, tears coursing down her cheeks. He simply stared back, his face impassive.

"And he will watch, as will you. And then I will kill Gwyn and then your brother and then your grandfather. You, I keep. You are my healer and the key to my gaining the support I need to render this one large territory and stop the fighting. I will not lose you. And I will not hesitate to do what I feel is necessary to ensure your obedience. Don't forget that I have access to those you love in your own world as well."

Tabitha's heart was pierced by those words, and her legs began to buckle.

He continued. "Your two cousins would, no doubt, be excellent candidates for child-bearing, and of course, your aunts and uncle are always within my grasp."

He wandered back and lifted his glass again.

"You will obey me. You are mine, and you will obey me. I want Monsieur DesChamps because he can command the respect of the Northern territory. With you married to him, Marcus will be apt to listen to me. I can sway them, with his help. If you succumb to him, bed him and win his heart, he will swear fealty to me to keep you. If you do not, if you fight him and wound him further with that dammed sharp tongue of yours—if I lose him, I will find another man for you, possibly one who will not be as gentle. I need your ability to heal. I need you able to bear children—I do not need you happy."

Antoine waved her off and carried his drink over to a chair by the window. Tabitha choked back a sob as she flew to the door. She yanked it open and raced from the room. She heard the guard's footsteps trying to keep up with her, but she ran as fast as she could to get away from her father.

In her room, she slammed the door behind her and sank to the floor. Sobs filled the air as a complete sense of helplessness overtook her. She could hear the guard's movements outside the door, further fueling her anger and sense of vulnerability.

How had this happened? How had a simple mission to find her mother turned into such a chaotic misadventure? How would she break free of her father, and if she did, what would happen to those she left behind? Would Cole, Gwyn, and others she loved bear the brunt of Antoine's fury should she find some way to escape and try to get home? Would she ever be able to find her way north to that particular glade where the portal had been? In her own world, it would mean hundreds of miles along the coast, but here it would be a coast that she would not recognize. She could wander for days trying to pick out that spot, which was so similar to Porta Negra but different enough that she could easily miss it.

She scrambled to her feet and tore through her meager belongings to locate the black stone that held the key to her return home. It lay tucked in among the jewelry her father had given to her. She had left with Luc that night to race to Gwyn's without it. What if they had made good on their escape? Of course, Luc no doubt knew that she would not make it—he apparently had his own agenda. But how stupid had she been to race from the room, still giddy from his kiss, with only her mother's ring?

Damn him! Had he kissed her to put her off balance? She slid her fingers along her lips; the memory of that kiss still sent tickles of warmth through her. But her new realization that he had kissed her only to keep her from thinking sanely fueled her rage even further. She stared down at the stone in her hand and the little chain attached to it with a tiny silver ring. She removed her necklace, tugged the stone from the little chain, and placed it on the necklace along with her mother's ring. Wherever she went, they would go with her. And she would take whatever risk she had to get out of here and away from her father. Cole would have to take care of himself. She could not bear a life of being her father's prisoner.

Suddenly, a sliver of truth appeared to her. She saw for the first time the life that her mother had run from. She envisioned Doni as a young woman, a prisoner of Antoine, a man she had apparently loved but maybe learned to hate as he used her to further escalate his ambitions, turning everything that he had promised with his loving words into a question or a lie. She would have been forced to lay with him night after night, a bittersweet experience—a man she had once loved who she came to hate, night after night.

Had she witlessly put herself in the same position? Would she follow her mother's footsteps so closely? She had prided herself on being different. The woman she had lived with who she knew as her mother had been little more than a shell of a human, barely existing.

Human? The thought prompted a bitter laugh. Of course she wasn't human. Her mother was Faye, and in a strange world. And she had left two children over here. Had she spirited Tabitha away because she was a healer? Had her mother been able to see that in her?

Her head dropped down, and she stared at the tiny black rock on her necklace. Could she give into Luc, become his lover and convince him and her father that she had surrendered to them? The thought of Luc touching her, in her bed and in her body, sent shivers and bitter shame coursing through her. How could she possibly think that way after what he had done? How could she possibly ever lay with him and wonder day after day if she were little more than a pawn to his ambitions?

But, she had to admit, he had not known who she was when he met her. He had not known she was Antoine's daughter...or had he? She would now question his motives for every move. She would wonder at everything he ever said or did. She would never trust him.

Shame eroded her physical feelings for him. A warm rush of humiliation washed over her at the thought that their first kiss had been little more than a tactic. A strategic move. He had played her and used her. And with a grain of humility, she had to admit that Luc had won this round.

CHAPTER SEVENTEEN

COULD SHE DO THE SAME? COULD SHE ALSO PLAY THAT game and win her freedom? And what if in the midst of the subterfuge she became pregnant? They would never let her out of their sight if they thought she carried a child, doubly so because of the possibility that the child might be a healer.

She had to see Gwyn. Gwyn could help her. Gwyn may be able to give her something that would keep her from getting pregnant. They had to have something like that here, right? She had heard a number of times that people opted not to try for a child because of the risks to the mother; they had to know of some option. Gwyn would know. Tabitha felt a slight sense of hope sparking deep within the dark cavern that the past day had locked her in.

Not an hour later, her face washed and her feelings deeply hidden, Tabitha sat at her grandfather's bedside, holding his aged hand as they spoke quietly.

"He did not give me to Antoine, my dear," Roane was saying, his voice a raspy whisper. "I was already in Antoine's control, under his thumb. Your man just brought me here to get me away from the house in which, from what I understand, a dark drama was unfolding."

"He is not my man," Tabitha growled.

"Well, he was at one point. You marked him," Roane pointed out.

"I didn't know what I was doing, for Chrissakes. I was barely conscious, and when I came to, I was...Oh, forget about it!" she snapped. The image of her fangs lodged into Luc's throat was too unsettling.

Roane laughed quietly, prompting a small attack of coughing. Tabitha rose and got him a glass of water, supporting him while he drank.

She sat back down, her eyes worried as she watched the old man's pale face. He lay back against the mound of pillows behind him as the later afternoon summer breeze floated through the open windows. He closed his eyes for a moment and simply enjoyed the sensation. "I must say, I do enjoy this room. It is so bright and cheery, and I am woken in the morning by the sunrise. Even if I wake during the night, I ask them to leave the shades open so that I may watch the stars do their ancient dance across the sky."

Tabitha glanced out the window, wishing she could take a moment to simply enjoy something again. A sunrise, the breeze...it felt like many years had passed since she had taken a few minutes to simply be. Just be. Quiet. Existing. For a simpler moment, exist as a tiny part of a changing landscape shaped by winds and water and rain and storms. The thought evaporated as she realized that even that simple fantasy begged the question: which world? She was part of both now. She had been born here; she had history here and family here—as slightly lunatic as part of it was—and she had roots. But in her own world was the familiar and the everyday life she had built out of fragments and shards of existence.

"What are you thinking?" Roane asked, squeezing her hand.

"When I get home, I will find that the life I built was all built on lies." She snorted softly as the sad truth tolled through her. "I learned that I do not have family there. I do not have a life. I am not part of their species. I am not even human. I cannot stay here, and I do not belong there."

He nodded sadly. "Your mother felt the same."

Tabitha glanced up at him and looked into those dark eyes. "I wish she had told me. I wish she had explained all of this to me. I would not have come. I would have known what danger awaited me."

He lifted a frail hand to her cheek. "If you had a daughter, a precious little girl that you gave up everything to protect, would you try to explain this to her? Would you instill the fear of a dangerous father from another world who would try to keep her and control her should she ever go there? What would you do? How would you speak to her? How would she react?" He watched Tabitha and turned her face back to him when she would have turned away. "And tell me, what would you have thought? A wonderful and exciting other world—every time something in your life went wrong, you would be tempted to run here, as she did. You would see all of the good, and your own world would never match up. Every offense and trial in your world would not have happened had you only been here."

Tabitha opened her mouth to argue, but he placed a gentle finger on her lips. "You would not have made a life for yourself there. You would have watched that world, growing to hate it there, and looked for reasons to come here. This would have been your utopia. You would imagine life here as idyllic, and you would never have been able to know a true and committed life there."

"But to have left me in the dark, telling me nothing! She should have told me something."

"She could not. She spent every ounce of energy every day trying to protect you. You lived with a net of power around you that she maintained day and night. Your father's people may have been able to watch you, but they could not approach. It weakened her. Every time she left your world to come here, she would weave such a powerful web around you that no one from our world would have been able to find you," he explained.

Tabitha was thunderstruck. Was that why her mother had been so distant? Had every day of Tabitha's life meant a constant drain of energy as her mother tried to hold off the enemy? Had the reason for her mother's wan and listless face been because of a constant energy drain from maintaining protection around her daughter? Tabitha felt a wave of guilt over her mother's sacrifice and her own inability to recognize it.

Gwyn slid in through the door, and her face lit up with delight at seeing Tabitha. "You are safe!"

Tabitha rose and embraced the older woman warmly. "For now, I am here. My safety remains to be seen."

Gwyn shook her head slowly as she went over to check Roane. "Oh, you are safe. Make no mistake about that. It is not his intent for anything to happen to you. You are much too valuable to him to risk any harm to you."

Tabitha lowered herself on the end of the bed. "Except an occasional right hook should I speak up."

Gwyn turned to her and gently took her face in her hands, observing the dark bruises on her cheek and jaw. "He is none too gentle with you."

Tabitha shook her head free of Gwyn's grasp. "I need to speak to you. Please."

Gwyn nodded. "Of course! What can I do for you?"

Tabitha gestured toward the door. "Outside, please. In private." She hesitated at her grandfather's gaze and blushed. "It is about a female issue."

Gwyn nodded in understanding and tucked the blankets around Roane. "I'll be back after your dinner to settle you for the night."

She and Tabitha walked to the door. Tabitha blew a kiss to the old man. He waved warmly and smiled as they left the room. Tabitha's guard was waiting outside, and she groaned in frustration. Gwyn gestured toward a warm and sunny seating area tucked into the corner at the top of a large set of stairs. The two women sat by the window, and the guard positioned himself close enough to maintain his watch but far enough to afford them some privacy.

"Tabitha, how are you? Are you all right? I have been worried sick about you. If your face is any indication…"

Tabitha shook her head slowly. "That is all that is hurt, other than my dignity, my sense of independence, and my sense of self."

"Who hit you?"

"My father," Tabitha said slowly, her pain resurfacing as Gwyn leaned forward, gripping her hands in her own. "Please. Don't. I need to keep myself together."

"Tell me what I can do to help."

Tabitha felt a blush warm her face as she prepared to actually tell someone that her father had given her to a man for his personal use, as a reward. The thought was so ludicrous that she had trouble believing it, let alone voicing it to another. She stuttered and spat out the explanation, the words sticking in her throat as she tried to explain.

Gwyn nodded, not seeming surprised. "It sounds like something your father would do. And Luc, what does he say about all of this?"

"What the hell do I care what he says? I haven't seen him since, and quite frankly, I am struggling with the thought of seeing him. I want to rip his head off every time I even imagine him coming near me, the bastard. That lying, stinking—" Tabitha tried to keep her voice low, but the thought of his deceit sent her spiraling again and again into a blinding rage.

Gwyn lifted a hand. "You have not seen him?"

"No. My father only told me this afternoon that I was to be given to Luc as his *belonging* for his good behavior," Tabitha spat, her face reddening again at the thought.

"Tabitha, I am sure it is not simply that he is giving you—"

"It is." Tabitha cut her off bluntly. "He made that perfectly clear, as well as letting me know that if I did not make sure that Luc swore fealty so we would wed, then I would be given to any other ambitious little prick my father needed to kiss his ass."

Gwyn's eyes reflected her shock at Tabitha's outburst, and Tabitha mumbled an apology. "I am upset and beside myself about this. Even I hate the way I am speaking. I have never been much for cursing, but this seemed like a great time to start."

Gwyn squeezed her hands. "Tabitha, at least Luc is someone you care about. I mean, you and Luc—"

Tabitha snapped, "Luc and I are nothing. He betrayed me, and I will never trust him again. I have trouble even trying to imagine being civil to him, let alone being intimate with him. It sickens me."

Gwyn nodded slowly. "Well, I believe that Luc cares—"

"Gwyn! Stop! I don't want to talk about him or any possible reconciliation. I have two options here: either I make the best of having to be intimate with Luc *or* I get stuck with God only knows what other yahoo my father will shackle me to. This is a matter of the devil I know being better than the devil I don't," Tabitha barked. She had to stop herself and take a breath. "I am sorry. But what I need from you is some kind of birth control."

Gwyn's eyes widened. "Birth control?"

"Yes." For a moment Tabitha wondered if she was right to trust Gwyn. Her gut told her that Gwyn would not betray her trust, but her sense of caution raised a flag, suggesting she limit how much she told her. "Gwyn, until I can wrap my arms around what is happening and find some sense of stability, I cannot risk getting pregnant. If I get pregnant, I will never have any freedom. I need an opportunity to come to grips with my father keeping me here as a prisoner. I need to find some peace before I can take that risk."

Gwyn nodded, and her eyes settled on the younger woman with concern. "Tabitha, will you listen to me? Luc will never force you. If you are not prepared to give yourself to him, he will never do that to you. Take your time and promise me you won't do anything rash."

"Luc is not my concern, my father is. If he thinks I am holding back, he may well give me to some other little minion. I just have to be prepared." Tabitha sighed.

Gwyn nodded. "Just give yourself time to think things through."

Tabitha shrugged as she stood. "Think things through? I am not suicidal, if that is what you are concerned about. And I am not going to do anything crazy or rash, but I cannot promise not to put my own needs first. Quite frankly, whatever else happens, I have no intention of getting pregnant right now. I have too much to think about. I may be on the same path as my mother, but I can at least try and learn from her mistakes."

With that, she turned and followed the guard back down the hallway toward her rooms.

She had not paid much mind to their direction, but as they climbed the stairs to another floor, Tabitha hesitated.

"We are we going? My rooms are that way, over there… and down a floor." Tabitha stopped, her bearings confused because she had not been paying any mind to where he was leading her.

Her guard kept walking and indicated with a wave of his hand the long hallway ahead of them. "You've been moved. Your father said that he wanted you in another suite."

Her heart sank. "Oh, right. That."

He continued to the end of the hall and opened a doorway on the right. He stepped back to allow her to enter. "Your things are already here."

"Of course they are," she snarled as she walked past the ever-so-helpful guard.

The corner suite before her was similar to her last suite but larger, with a large set of windows facing east. An inviting window seat below the windows offered a multitude of fluffy pillows along the comfortable seat. The hearth was along the wall in front of her and had a cheerful fire snapping within; an ever-present glass pot hung over the flames. The couch and matching chair were large and looked comfortable, each loaded with a multitude of assorted pillows.

"What is it with these people and the goddamn pillows?" she snarled to herself as she made her way to the double doors of the bedroom.

She stepped through the elegant glass doors into a large and spacious bedroom. The windows and balcony faced south. Heavy drapes had been tugged over the windows, but the balcony door was open to let in the warm breeze. The usual multitude of cabinets and closets were tucked around the room, their inconspicuous drawers flush with the walls. A large chaise sat in the corner, facing the hearth. The crackling fire sent a warm glow through the room. She noticed the doorway into the bathroom. With a heavy sigh, she turned to her left, facing the enormous bed jutting from the wall. A soft comforter had been smoothed over the mattress, the ever-present multitude of pillows propped against the headboard. In her other suite, the wide bed with its hanging curtains to ward off the evening chill was built into the wall, but it occurred to her with a start that that would not be practical for more than one person.

She opened one closet and saw unfamiliar clothing hanging from the hooks: a dark jacket and men's pants. She swallowed the lump in her throat. Well, that answered that question. Apparently he had been moved in at the same time.

A soft noise, a shuffling, and a quiet caw caught her attention. She turned and noticed a tall cage standing by the balcony doors. A gloomy corner had hidden it from view. Tabitha slowly approached it. The cage was quite large, obviously meant for a large animal. It hung from a heavy iron hook that sprouted from an enormous base on the floor. She approached slowly and saw a crow with glossy black wings and a pair of deep ebony eyes that watched her warily. It cawed again questioningly as she approached. Tabitha stood back to watch the beautiful bird.

"Hmm. Well, I guess I should feel better, huh? At least I have not been put in a cage to hang on display," she murmured to the bird. "Not yet anyway."

"His name is D'Noir."

The voice behind her startled her, and she spun, alarmed.

Luc strode into the room, his face impassive but his eyes alert. Tabitha felt her anger stir at the sight of him. What would once have been a shiver of pleasure was transferred into a simmering boil. She wanted to lash out immediately, scream at him and claw at him, rail at him for his betrayal and her predicament. But her rage silenced her and tied her tongue against the multitude of epithets she wished to hurl at that handsome face.

She tossed her head and walked away from the bird; the fact that it was obviously his pet had spoiled her interest in it.

"You have spoken to your father." It was a statement, not a question. He stopped in the middle of the room, his hands resting on his hips as he watched her.

She had barely had time to formulate the words before she spat them at him. "Oh, yes, I spoke to my father, or should I say he spoke at me and gave me my instructions. You must be so very pleased with yourself. I have never met anyone else who was given a person as a reward, to do with as they pleased. In my world, rewards are normally some cash or maybe a gift certificate to a restaurant, a bottle of wine…you know, the usual. I wish you had mentioned to me that as a woman in your world, I ran the risk of becoming a gift." He started to speak but she was still bubbling over with anger. "A gift? Should I be wearing a bow? Is that how this works? Or maybe some lingerie as I simply wait for you in bed—how about that? Would that satisfy your male ego? Please, instruct me further on the rules here. Am I supposed to rub your back and ask you how your day was? Pour you a drink and serve you?"

Luc held a hand up, weariness catching up with him after an exhausting day. Dylan had spent the better part of the day taunting him with constant references to bedding Tabitha later that night. Luc had tried to stay one step ahead of Antoine, who seemed to be testing him and trying to gain a foothold in Luc's family relationship in the North. Luc had been less than thrilled when Jules had informed him that, per Antoine's instructions, his things had already been moved to a joint suite with Tabitha, who had, apparently, just found out herself.

"I don't want anything more from you than to just maybe share some dinner with me and leave me be. I have no intention of taking anything more from you than that." Luc groaned, dragging his hands over his face.

"I have no intention of giving anything to you. I have no wish to share dinner with you or to spend any more time with you than needed," she snapped.

"Fine. But you will have to stay here with me or be accompanied by a guard to wherever else you wish to go," he growled back as he shrugged out of his coat and kicked off his shoes.

"And where am I going to go? I cannot move in this house without a guard on my heels every step." She pointed to the caged bird. "I am as much a prisoner as he is!"

"It is your own doing," he snapped back. "And you have more freedom than that, but I warn you, if you attempt any other foolishness, your freedom will be the first thing to go."

"Really?" Her voice dripped sarcasm. "If I attempt any other foolishness? You were right there with me, telling me I had to leave. You encouraged me to get away, and you promised to take me to a portal! Obviously this is your doing. You were the one who told me I had run out of time and had to leave! Why would you have bothered with that? Entice me to leave and then turn me in? What was that? An attempt to prove your loyalty to him? I *trusted you*! I thought you were on my side! I trusted you, and I have lost everything because of you!"

"Tabitha, you have no idea what has transpired and what a fine line you walk. Every day, the game changes and the rules shift. No action of mine was designed to trap you.

Whether you believe it or not, that is not the case," he snarled between clenched teeth.

"And what of your family? You have betrayed them as well. Is he worth it? Do you honestly believe his promises?" she cried.

He spun to face her at that, unbuttoning his shirt. "I did not betray my family—they betrayed me! I was sent here on a peacekeeping endeavor. I spent a month gathering the thoughts of my people. I was to come here with three other people, at their request, to negotiate peace with the Plains tribes. We did not want a war, and we most certainly did not prepare for a war within our own territory. I was the first of the four to arrive, and on that first day, Marcus has a platoon of your father's men attacked! I could have been hung that night as a traitor, but your father was willing to believe, or at least entertain the idea, that I knew nothing about it!"

"How can you say that? Jules told us that the captured people told them they were there on Dylan's orders! They were there to attack your people," she countered.

"We don't know that! We don't know what their intent was. We attacked before we even asked the damn question." Luc tugged his shirt off his shoulder in frustration. Tabitha shivered, and she took a step back. He caught her movement and rolled his eyes. "I am changing my blasted shirt, not stripping down to toss you."

He grabbed a shirt out of the closet. "I am in as much hot water here as you are, although you fail to see that. I have had to figure out a way to negotiate with your father and Marcus before my entire territory erupts into civil war. All the while, we have a fragile attempt at peace with the people of the Plains. We cannot battle each other and hope to stave them off our land. What an opportunity for people who are starving and possibly considering an invasion—we'll decimate ourselves first in a bloody civil war."

She crossed her arms in front of her and demanded, "How could you have been so quick to tell him I am a healer but hide your scars? Why would you do that? He could have killed Cole!"

"Your father knew it was you or Cole, and I fully expected that he would want proof. Why the hell do you think he had Lena there? Had I not told him it was you, he had every intention of shooting her. Probably the two of us at once...and then whomever was the healer would have run to their...Well, I guess from your father's point of view you could say, to the one that each of you cared for. Had Cole been the healer and if Dylan shot me and Lena, you can rest assured that he would have saved Lena before he saved me," Luc countered.

"Well, you cannot imagine that this makes anything right. You betrayed me, and you let him take me. You promised to help me get away, and now, here I am, your little bed bitch," she whispered accusingly.

Luc turned to stare at her, his gaze cold and hard as he observed her defiant stance. "Let me tell you, I have no intention of forcing myself on you."

"And then what? When my father sees me and senses my apparent condition...my everlasting virginity, which apparently grates on his nerves, then what?" she tossed at him.

Luc stepped forward. His response seemed to die on his lips. He lifted a finger to her face and looked at the bruises there. Was she imagining things or was that a flare of anger in his eyes, a tightening of his jaw?

"I am going to get something to eat. Don't leave this room," he snapped before he turned on his heel and left.

Tabitha sighed heavily and sat back on the bed, exhaustion overtaking her. Before they separated, Gwyn had promised her something to keep her from getting pregnant, and with any luck, she would have it tomorrow. She ran her hands over the bed, imaging sharing it with him, his long body stretched out beside her. Despite every attempt at rage she mustered, she could not mistake the surge of warmth that spread through her as she pictured sharing the bed with him.

Icy fingers quelled that warmth as she remembered her father's words, his demand that she bed Luc and entice him to marry her. What would he say if he found out Gwyn was supplying her with birth control? What would his reaction to that be? And how long could she and Luc play this game? Luc had been emphatic that he would not take her unwillingly. The thought of avoiding rape was a small consolation. For that, she was grateful. But how long would her father remain patient about their relationship? She needed a plan. Her best guess was that she probably had only a matter of days, perhaps a week or two at the most, before Antoine grew weary of their game and sent in another prospective mate for her.

Tabitha was lost in thought when a small dinner tray for her was dropped off. She had to admit that after a day and a half of not eating, her hunger was returning. She had to get some strength to keep herself ready for any opportunity. She brought her food over to the chair facing the balcony and shared bits of her dinner with D'Noir, who nibbled from her fingers with a hearty appreciation for everything she shared. Her hunger was sated quickly, although she had eaten less than she'd thought she would. She absently passed bits of her remaining dinner to the hungry bird, her thoughts wandering over possible scenarios for getting out of the house undetected and traveling quickly up the coast to try to find the portal.

Lost in thought, she leaned her head back on the chair, her tray forgotten, the breeze ruffling her hair. How could she get away undetected? The third floor—she leaned forward and glanced over the balcony. Fourth floor. Her every move was observed, except when she was squirreled away, alone in this suite. Of course, even if she could get away from the guards, as soon as she stepped outside and broke through the house's magical perimeter, they would know immediately.

She could journey north, but she was still so new at that, and she did not know the land. She would exhaust herself into uselessness before one day and probably fewer than one hundred miles were covered.

D'Noir shifted in his cage, his wings flapping as he settled on his perch. She glanced over and noticed for the first time the bird's injured wing. He gingerly flapped the wounded appendage. He seemed to be able to move it, but only slightly.

"I wish I were you. I would just fly out of here," Tabitha whispered.

The night wore on, and she grew weary of devising plans and tossing them out. She finally rose and began to get ready for bed. She was determined to be in bed and at least faking sleep before Luc returned. She changed and brushed her hair and teeth quickly. She threw half the pillows onto the floor in order to find the top of the bed. The lights out, she climbed into the huge bed in the glow from the hearth.

As she settled down, she let the crackle of the fire soothe her nerves as she watched the orange tongues of the flame slowly tear their way through the remaining logs. The mesmerizing display was enough to settle her thoughts. Her eyelids drooped, and she slowly succumbed to sleep.

CHAPTER EIGHTEEN

ONLY A MOMENT HAD PASSED, OR PERHAPS AN HOUR. The pain was gone, and Tabitha drifted in sleep as though floating. The sounds of the fire crackling blended with the creak of the summer bugs singing their praise to the silvery moon floating above. A gentle breeze fluttered through the balcony window, and the lace curtains sighed and quivered over her, seeming to settle on the bed beside her.

Tabitha felt herself begin to rise. Her surroundings began to sharpen as she realized with the hazy awareness of sleep that she was up from the bed and walking toward the balcony. Her brain began to struggle against the sludge of deep sleep, but as in any dream, the tendrils holding her were tight and her consciousness could not seem to break free. She remembered a trick that Bertòn had taught her. With a slow and deliberate breath, she forced herself to relax and let her mind stop struggling.

Her feet slowly picked their way through the myriad of pillows to the balcony. The breeze lifted her hair, and she lifted her face toward its gentle caress. Salt. She could taste the tiniest bit of the sea in that cool caress. It gave her the strength she needed to fight against the mental hold. She remained calm as she followed the suggestion from the intruder. Without searching further, she flicked the offender out of her mind and woke with a jolt. Her elation turned to terror when she found herself perched on the railing of the balcony, her feet balancing precariously on the narrow ledge.

Her arms peddled wildly as she fought for equilibrium, but she was too far out. With a scream, she felt herself pitch off the balcony railing. Her stomach clenched as she dropped, and her mind cried out in shock.

"Tabitha!"

"Mom! Help me!"

Tabitha's body wrenched as she fell, and she clawed violently to stop her descent. Amazement overtook her terror when the wild flailing of her arms turned into flapping. As the cobblestone patio below her approached, she closed her eyes and felt a swoosh as she skimmed the ground and began to rise.

She cracked her eyes open and stared at the ground rushing by her as she soared above it, her body zooming barely a couple of feet above the ground.

How did this happen? Am I flying?

She glanced to her right. Instead of her extended arm, a long white wing, soft and elegant, held her aloft. She quickly swiveled her head and saw the same on the other side. The approaching ground slowed, and when she flapped her arms again, she felt herself rise ever so slightly as her speed increased. Her shadow sped along the cobblestone. In it she recognized the rounded head and deep, graceful wingspan of an owl. *I am an owl and I am flying!*

Tabitha, come to meet me.

Her mother's voice filled her brain. Tabitha could barely believe she had heard it.

Mom?

Yes. Come to me. Here, let me show you.

The world shifted, and Tabitha found herself suddenly flying through woods, greatly testing her new-found flying abilities. With a thud, she plowed into the ground face first. She slowly lifted herself and realized that she was back in her own body, with a multitude of twigs in her hair and a mouthful of moss.

She lifted her eyes and found herself staring at her mother and another woman. Her mother watched her with a cross between amusement and frustration; the other woman's face was impassive. As Tabitha slowly rose and dusted herself off, she recognized the other woman as the one she had met the night she had left Luc's home to meet the Faye.

Her mother, however, was almost unrecognizable. Her long white hair was caught in a long braid that hung over one shoulder, her clothes dark and obviously made for her body. High dark boots were elegantly crossed at the ankle as she leaned back against a rock.

Tabitha took a deep breath and turned to face the woman she had hunted, sworn at, begged for help, and cried over. She didn't even know what to say.

"You have had quite an adventure," her mother commented softly.

Tabitha let out a rough laugh. "Yes, I have. And a lot of that could have been avoided had you just been honest with me from the start."

Doni shrugged, and Tabitha saw that familiar curtain fall behind her eyes. She sighed, knowing that information would not be forthcoming, even after everything she had been through.

"I had hoped to keep you away from all of this. I wanted so badly for you to remain unaware of it. I wanted you to have a normal life," Doni sighed.

"Normal? Are you kidding? I blew up Trude's china closet!" Tabitha cried.

"You what?"

Tabitha waved her hand. "That doesn't matter. What matters is that these powers have been bursting out of me. I couldn't control them! If you had known this could happen, why wouldn't you tell me?"

"I had hoped that my control over them would keep you safe from them. It seems that they were escaping my muzzle," Doni admitted.

"Muzzle?"

Doni nodded. "I kept your powers under some semblance of control until I could figure out how to either remove them or lock them away completely. I think I might be close to finding that answer."

"Are you kidding me?" Tabitha took a step back. "I may have never wanted them, but I will be damned if I am going to let you lock them away on me now!"

"Tabitha, watch the cursing," Doni calmly admonished.

Tabitha stared at her. "Cursing? You want me to watch the cursing? You have got to be joking. Let me tell you a little about my vacation here!" Tabitha held up a hand and began ticking off on her fingers. "I have found my father, my two brothers, and a grandfather. My older brother is some kind of sociopath, and my father is a dictator who is keeping me imprisoned in his house. At least he was until you came to get me…"

"I am not here to get you out," Doni corrected her.

Tabitha stopped and stared at her mother in shock. A moment ticked by and then another. "What?"

Doni shook her head. "He has imprisoned you in there, and he has a perimeter. I cannot just take you out of there."

"But I am here now…"

"You are not here physically," Doni retorted.

Tabitha patted herself in confusion and looked down. "Yeah, I *am* here."

"Tabitha, you are not here physically. Just as you were not there when you met Larissa in the glade back in Calais," Doni explained patiently. "Your body is back in bed. I woke you and gave you the suggestion to separate, just as Larissa did back in Calais."

"But I was falling!"

"You only thought you were falling."

"And I turned into a bird…"

"I forced you into the bird shape."

"Can I shapeshift?"

"I really don't know. You should be able to, but you would need to focus and really take the time to learn it." Doni's voice was so patronizing that Tabitha almost screamed.

"Sure! Let me add that to my study list for this fall, when I am not screwing guys that my father has insisted I sleep with or face the consequences!" she shrieked. "Do you see my face? He hit me! He hit me twice! My father! You could have saved me from this with a little bit of honesty and maybe a little intervention before he goddamn gave me as a gift to a man who betrayed me! And if I don't behave myself, he will give me to yet another conniving bastard!"

Doni nodded, and her voice was a pale whisper. "Do you think I don't know how cruel he can be? We tried to warn you not to go to him."

"You could have told me yourself what he was like! You sent someone else to advise me not to come here!" Tabitha waved an arm at the other woman. "Maybe you should have mentioned he was a maniac who is trying to rule the world and will kill anyone that does not do as he says. And maybe you could have mentioned that once he found out I was a here, he would use me to buy minions for his little empire!"

"You would not have listened to me, and quite frankly, I have other things to worry about that are a little more pressing than your virginity," Doni hissed.

Tabitha stared at her mother in shock. "How about my life? Your father's life?"

"Antoine will not harm you or him as long as you do as he says," Doni argued.

"You are kidding me. You have to be kidding. You have no intention of getting me out of there?" Tabitha felt her strength wane as the truth of her mother's words sank in. "You are going to leave me to him?"

Doni inhaled deeply, and her shoulders dropped. "I want nothing more than to go in there and just remove you. I want you home safe and sound, living your own life in our world. But he has you, and I cannot go in there. But you can get out. And when you do, you must take Katie with you."

"Katie? You want me to get Katie out?" Tabitha felt a sob catch in her throat. "We are too late for that. Katie is dead, as is her child. She was murdered by the man my father has given me to."

"Luc?" Doni looked baffled. "Luc murdered Katie?"

"You know him? Yes. He did." Tabitha swallowed the lump that threatened to swell into tears.

Doni stood and pursed her lips, pacing the small clearing. Larissa's eyes followed her, although she remained silent.

"It may be for the best. Until the child was born, we could not determine if it had the ability."

Tabitha stared at her mother while a cold lump formed in her belly. "Are you seriously saying that the baby is better off dead because it may or may not have been a healer?"

Doni's head snapped up. "What did you say?"

"You heard me. Can you actually be saying that it is better that the child is dead than be born a healer into Antoine's hands?" Tabitha sneered, her rage at the callous disregard for Katie's life barely contained.

Doni waved her off. "I am being realistic. We cannot afford to have a healer in Antoine's hands. It is too dangerous."

"Ah. Well, I wish you had mentioned that a few short days ago, because not only does he have one healer, he has two!" The volume of Tabitha's voice was gaining momentum.

Doni strode forward and gripped her shoulders. "Tell me how Katie died."

"Luc killed her. He admitted it when he told Antoine that the baby didn't make it!" Tabitha shrugged out of her mother's grip and turned away. "So you were willing to risk everything to save Katie, but you will leave me to my fate."

Doni shook her head. "No, Luc was to be your savior. But it seems he has been beguiled by Antoine's promises."

Tabitha threw her hands in the air. "Yup! Boy, I hate it when your twisted plans are ruined by treacherous antics!"

"Your sarcasm is hardly appreciated," Doni murmured. She paced again, deep in thought.

Tabitha rolled her eyes and groaned. "I promise to curb that, right long with my swearing—once you get me out of there."

Doni glanced up. "You will get out because you have no choice. You must leave, as I did. Let me show you what I have been dealing with."

Before she could react, Doni grasped her wrist. Tabitha felt the world around her tilt as her surroundings shifted once again. The clearing they stepped into was dark, and Tabitha's eyes needed a moment to adjust. As she became aware of a tall figure standing next to a large metal standing cage on wheels, she gripped her mother's arm. Tabitha gasped when she recognized Dylan standing in the shadows, watching some activity behind the tall cage.

Tabitha gripped her mother's arm. "It's Dylan! What is going on?"

Doni tugged Tabitha's hand, leading her past Dylan, who seemed oblivious to their presence. Tabitha cringed, but Doni dragged her, ignoring Dylan and the two men standing beside the front of the cage. The shadows were playing tricks in the moonlight; Tabitha could almost make out a hazy gray shape standing quietly next to Dylan. She squinted into the darkness. It looked as though the smoky head had two dark holes where eyes should be, and they seemed to be following her.

"Mom?"

"Tabitha, look." Doni stopped, and Tabitha collided with her.

"But that thing next to Dylan...I mean, am I imagining things or is that...?" Tabitha's voice dropped when she turned forward, suddenly staring in horror at four bodies lying on the ground before them. "Oh, God. Is that Viho? And his...Oh my God. Are they—?"

Doni nodded. The mist that covered them slowly slid off the bodies and swirled back toward where Dylan stood. Tabitha gasped in dismay and stared at the four men lying side by side on the ground, their faces still, blank eyes staring up toward the sky.

"We have to help them!" Tabitha started to rush forward, but Doni caught her arm.

"It's too late. We are in the past."

"What? The past?"

"Yes, this has already happened. We cannot do anything for them now." Doni gestured toward Dylan. "He cannot see us because when this happened we were not here."

Tabitha's retort froze on her lips as she watched the lazy silvery mist drift over the ground at her feet and swirl back to the human-shaped shadow next to Dylan. The black eye holes still were fastened in her direction when the mist began to swirl at its feet. She could not tear her eyes away; the mist seemed to be absorbed into the apparition's body. Its vague features began to sharpen and assume a more human-oid appearance. The gray mist drifted up the being's body and the black holes finally blinked using newly formed eyelids.

Tabitha clicked her mouth shut and stumbled backward into her mother. Her voice escaped her in a short whisper. "Did you see that?"

"I did."

"Is that a black elf?"

"Yes."

The being stood quietly beside Dylan, the last of the mist absorbed. Dylan said, "Let's go."

He waved a short silver stick at the being. Tabitha watched as the gray being waved its arm in mimicry of Dylan's action. Without a sound, it drifted into the cage and turned back, still mimicking Dylan's motions as he tugged the caged door closed. As Dylan swept himself up onto a seat affixed to the wagon, he signaled to the driver to proceed.

The wagon began to creak forward, the two men in the front walking beside the horse that pulled the wagon back toward the estate. As they journeyed forward, the entire entourage disappeared from sight.

Tabitha turned back to her mother and then regarded the men on the ground. "They were going to bring me north so I could leave. I wonder if Luc betrayed them as well."

Doni shrugged. "I don't know."

"And you want me to go back to that house?"

"Did you see what it did?" Doni asked. "It sucked the life out of them. It took their life energy and left them lifeless."

"But why them and not Dylan?"

Doni lifted one shoulder and cast an eye over the four dead men on the ground. "I don't know, Tabitha. But we need to find that out."

Tabitha lifted her eyes from the dead men and stared at her mother. "We?"

"Dylan was able to keep that creature at bay. And once it had fed, it went where he directed it. Why is that?" Doni responded.

Tabitha lifted a shoulder. "I have no idea."

"What control does he have over it?"

"Why are you asking me?" Tabitha snarled in frustration, turning again with a sick stomach to the four men lying on the ground.

"Tabitha, Antoine has some kind of control over them. He is using them to incite fear into the people that will bring them to him in a panic. He is manipulating these people with fear," Doni said. "How is he doing it? The black elves are not conscious beings. They feed. They exist."

"But that thing was imitating Dylan, doing whatever he did."

"As it feeds on human consciousness, it seems to absorb their life and develop awareness of itself and its surroundings. Once it can comprehend its surroundings, it can be devastating." Doni admitted, "We know so little about them. But Antoine seems to have found a way to harness and use them. We need to know how he is doing that so we understand how to eradicate them."

Through the horror of what she had seen, a slow dawning began to filter in. Tabitha lifted her eyes from the dead men to her mother's face. "And so you need me to figure out how they are doing this?"

Doni nodded.

"Me?"

Doni released a single soft chuckle. "I wouldn't trust anyone else. I don't know anyone else quite as smart and quick-witted. You have the street smarts these people do not possess. You can think on your feet, and you can lie."

It was Tabitha's turn to laugh. "I believe that Alena explained why that can be a valuable skill to have." She eyed her mother with wry deference. "So you need me to help with this? I did not see that coming."

"Tabitha, many generations ago, the black elves all but decimated this land and destroyed almost every living creature. The Faye opened the portals to escape them. When they found the means to destroy them, they used the portals to begin to repopulate the land. The animals and the people that lived in your world were our new beginning."

"So the animals were not indigenous to this world?"

"No, very few were. Most were destroyed. So we used the people of your world to develop the Caskan people. And we took the animals that they were familiar with to repopulate the land," Doni explained.

"What people? How long ago was this?"

"Centuries. The Caskan people come from the original Native American tribes. Over the centuries, most of the portals have closed, although some remained open and a few even opened on their own. We saw an influx of French settlers in the north, English in the midcoastal area, and Spaniards in the south. Of course, the far northern territories had the Vikings. So each of our tribes are a mix of this world and ours," Doni explained. "The knowledge of how to kill the black elves was lost, and the truth of their existence. Time erased that truth and they became little more than a legend."

"If I get this information, you will help me escape?"

"Tabitha, if I could break you out of that home, I would not be asking for your help. I am working on a plan to get you out, but while you are in there, use your time to help us find a way to destroy this infestation." Doni sighed. "Remember, the portals remain open. Once this land is destroyed, they will move someplace else. Logically that would be to our world."

"And you are trying to get me out?"

Doni nodded. "I will work on that. Find out what you can about how Dylan controls them."

Tabitha nodded. "Fair enough. I want to get Cole out as well. And Grandfather."

Doni nodded. "I agree."

"Will I be able to contact you?"

Doni shook her head. "Once you are back there, no. I will try to reach out to you."

Tabitha nodded. "Before you take me back, you have to tell me one thing."

"All right."

"Whose body was it in Dark Hollow?"

Doni inhaled deeply. "They found her?"

Tabitha nodded.

Doni slowly shook her head, and pain filled her eyes. "I thought she would never be found."

"Who was it?" Tabitha asked quietly.

"A woman who tried to help me the night I escaped. She was my closest friend. She risked everything to get me home with you," Doni whispered.

"What was her name?"

"Yolanda DesChamps."

Tabitha exhaled sharply. "Luc's mother?"

Doni nodded.

"But Luc told me that she had died from a fever when he was two."

Doni's laugh was caustic and humorless. "I imagine that I am not the only parent who lied to their child to protect them from the truth."

"Does that have anything to do with why Luc and I are linked?" Tabitha asked.

"It does," Doni admitted. "After Yolanda and I smuggled you and Cole from the house, we left Cole with Gwyn. Then she and I ran for the portal. Yolanda knew that I had to get you away because you had the healing ability. Our biggest fear was that something would happen to me and then the last of the healers would be lost to the people of this world. So I linked you and Luc when he was just a child. In the event that I was unable to return, they would be able to find you."

"You formed that link between us?"

"Yes. And of course, Yolanda died the night I passed over, and I was unable to ever tell Luc or Bertòn about it," Doni explained.

Tabitha nodded, the pieces slowly starting to make sense. "How did she die?"

"We were pursued that night. Thankfully, Cole was already safe, but the men trying to stop us killed Yolanda as we approached the portal. She died in my arms as we passed over into our world. I could not bring her back. I buried her. I never imagined they would exhume her for their own ends." Doni's voice shook, and her eyes blurred with tears.

"Who? Who was trying to use her to abduct me?"

Doni lifted a shoulder and dropped it. "I am not sure but I will find out. Come, it is time to get you back."

Tabitha turned back to the bodies. "Will someone take care of them?"

Doni nodded. "Larissa knows they are here. She will return them to their families."

Tabitha extended a hand to her mother. As their hands connected, she found herself on the bed back in her father's house. She sat up with a start and stared around the room, half expecting her mother to be sitting there with her. But the room was empty. She slid from the bed and padded over to open the balcony doors.

The moon had shifted in the sky. The air chilled as clouds skidded and began forming a soft curtain over the stars. Tabitha smelled rain and shut the balcony doors. The warm glow from the fireplace illuminated the room.

Tabitha knew she would prefer to be back in bed before Luc returned, but the messages from her mother were still resonating through her. There was too much to try and absorb. Of course, now Marcus would receive no news from Viho and his men. She felt tears sting her eyes at Viho's needless death. His concern had been the welfare of his people. How would they react when his death was discovered?

Tabitha thoughts returned to the cage and the silver stick that Dylan had used to direct the misty creature. What was that? Why did the creature respond to it?

She glanced back at the bed. Luc would return eventually. She wondered if she would be able to keep from smothering him in his sleep. The fantasy made her smile. Her smile widened at the thought that she was fairly sure that image would keep him awake as well.

As fatigue began to tug her eyes closed, Tabitha climbed into bed. She knew she needed to rest. She had a lot to accomplish, and she would need her wits about her. She might be a prisoner, but her mother was right—she would only trust herself to figure a way out. If there were some way to turn the tables, she would find it.

The End

If you enjoyed Dark Legacy,
Follow Tabitha's adventure in Dark Sacrifice Book 3 in the Hidden Heritage Series